REKKE AND VARGAS INVESTIGATIONS

Dark Music

Fatal Gambit

THE MILLENNIUM SERIES BY DAVID LAGERCRANTZ

The Girl in the Spider's Web

The Girl Who Takes an Eye for an Eye

The Girl Who Lived Twice

ALSO BY DAVID LAGERCRANTZ IN ENGLISH TRANSLATION

I Am Zlatan: My Story On and Off the Field

Fall of Man in Wilmslow

POST MORTEM

POST MORTEM

David Lagercrantz

Translated from the Swedish by Ian Giles

ALFRED A. KNOPF
NEW YORK
2026

A BORZOI BOOK
FIRST U.S. HARDCOVER EDITION PUBLISHED BY ALFRED A. KNOPF 2026

Published by Alfred A. Knopf, a division of Penguin Random House LLC, 1745 Broadway, New York, NY 10019. Originally published in Sweden by Norstedts Förlag, Stockholm, in 2025. Copyright © 2025 by David Lagercrantz. This translation originally published in hardcover in Great Britain by MacLehose Press, an imprint of Quercus Editions Limited, London, in 2026. Published by agreement with Quercus Editions Limited.

Knopf, Borzoi Books, and the colophon are registered trademarks of Penguin Random House LLC.

Library of Congress Cataloging-in-Publication Data
Names: Lagercrantz, David author | Giles, Ian translator
Title: Post mortem / David Lagercrantz ; translated from the Swedish by Ian Giles.
Other titles: Post mortem. English
Description: First hardcover edition. | New York : Alfred A. Knopf, 2026.
Identifiers: LCCN 2026012000 | ISBN 9780593319253 hardcover | ISBN 9780593312940 trade paperback | ISBN 9780593319260 ebook
Subjects: LCGFT: Detective and mystery fiction | Thrillers (Fiction) | Novels
Classification: LCC PT9877.22.A44 P6713 2026
LC record available at https://lccn.loc.gov/2026012000

penguinrandomhouse.com | aaknopf.com

Printed in the United States of America
1st Printing

The authorized representative in the EU for product safety and compliance is Penguin Random House Ireland, Morrison Chambers, 32 Nassau Street, Dublin D02 YH68, Ireland, https://eu-contact.penguin.ie.

POST MORTEM

A storm blew up that night, bringing with it the strays, tortured, forsaken and malnourished. They gathered around the old oak, whose branches reached upward as if worshipping the sky with thirty arms.

When the time came, the dogs lay down to die at the foot of the tree, and the end arrived with gnawing solitude.

ONE

Professor Hans Rekke could find nothing that morning—not even a bowl and spoon for his yogurt.

"What on earth's going on?" he called out.

His lodger Micaela Vargas entered the kitchen wearing one of his dressing gowns, which was dragging along the floor like a royal mantle.

"We needed a change," she said.

Rekke gave her a sceptical look before pulling open a drawer that contained pot holders and towels instead of the expected knives.

"It's ever so cleverly organized," she said with a wry smile.

"I'm sure it is. But it's new, and I can't abide . . ." *new*, he meant to say, but it occurred to him that instead of being amusing it was merely true and rather pathetic.

"Well," he said, cutting himself short. "I daresay it'll be a good excuse for my helplessness. Did you stay up all night?"

"All night—until well after it was over. I'll make you an espresso—if you're nice."

"My kingdom for a bowl, more like. And a spoon. And the papers."

He sat down at the kitchen table. Micaela handed him the coffee, yogurt and newspapers with a quite shamelessly cheerful air, and while that secretly slightly annoyed him, he could hardly blame her. It was a big day, even if everything was in the wrong place. An unusually talented and agreeable senator from Illinois had won the race for the White House, and he longed to read about it and lose himself in his thoughts. But he barely had time to make it beyond the headline: "America's historic verdict." There was a knock at the door and he glanced hopefully at Micaela. But Micaela and her regal train disappeared into the apartment's interior regions, and he reluctantly rose to his feet and went into the hallway.

He opened the front door, and on another day—a more focused morning—he might have taken an interest in purely phenomenological terms in that second in which we are expecting anything and then note what's there, and for a moment imagination and reality merge into one. But on this occasion he noted with a blink that the caller was a man in his sixties of southern European extraction with big, deep-set brown eyes.

"Good morning," said Rekke.

"I'm sorry to bother you," the man said in heavily accented English.

"What's this about?"

"My name is Rafael Corales," the man said. "I'm a Deputy Police Commissioner in Pamplona. I've telephoned and emailed several times."

"Ah yes, indeed. Might I nevertheless ask that you come back later? I'm in the middle of . . ."

The man shifted his briefcase as if it were too onerous to turn away with such a burden.

"In that case it will be late tonight," he said. "I'm at a conference all day, and then there will be the dinner afterward."

Rekke shrugged.

"Then you must come in, Señor Corales. Perhaps I might offer you a cup of coffee?" he said, returning to the kitchen. Of course, both the utterance and the action were mistakes.

When Rekke saw the papers he became even more annoyed that his reading had been interrupted. Furthermore, he could find no cups—nor anything else for that matter.

"Is it cold outside?" he said, largely to conceal his kitchen-drawer-related helplessness.

"They say there's going to be a blizzard," Corales said, draping his ostentatious fur coat over the back of a kitchen chair. "What are you looking for?"

"A cup for my guest. Alas, it would seem this exceeds my detective skills."

Corales, who wore an austere suit and tie but had a rather daring haircut—a mullet of sorts—looked like he didn't understand, or couldn't in fact comprehend, that Rekke couldn't find anything in his own kitchen. Considering he was a master detective and so forth.

"You're reading about Obama?" the Deputy Commissioner said, glancing down at the newspapers.

"I'd like to be," Rekke said, without disguising his annoyance. "It's quite incredible," he added more warmly.

"I suppose so," Corales said.

This also annoyed Rekke.

"You suppose so?"

"I preferred McCain."

"Why on earth would you?"

"A man who endures torture and captivity like that is a man one can rely on," Corales said, and Rekke wondered whether to respond to this and embark upon a small political discussion just for the hell of it.

"But God saved us from Sarah Palin," was what he opted for. "Tell me, which conference is it that you are attending?"

"It's on digital collaboration and all that entails. But the best parts are the lunch and coffee breaks. We talk over old investigations and when I mentioned that you and I had been in touch, everyone was immediately interested."

Rekke tried to surmise what the case was about, glancing at the much-too-heavy briefcase now on the kitchen floor, and feeling concerned that this visit might drag on. He then resumed his search for the cups, and of course found them to be neatly lined up in the cupboard immediately above the espresso machine. At least that is one success, he thought.

"The mystery has been solved. What sort of coffee would you like?"

Rafael Corales looked pleased.

"Oh, that's quite a machine you have. A cappuccino—extra strong—if that can be arranged. They say you're a master at deciphering old leads, Professor."

"Well, I don't know about that," Rekke muttered as he frothed the milk, pondering whether to let the man finish his coffee before sending him on his merry way. These unexpected visits were beginning to become a nuisance.

"Will you reacquaint me with your case?" he said.

Corales leaned back and made himself alarmingly comfortable as the machine ground the beans.

"Yes, of course. I could give you a detailed account, if you wish?"

"That won't be necessary," Rekke said, handing the Spaniard his coffee.

Corales took a sip and beamed.

"Exquisite," he said. He sat up straight. "I shan't bore you with my life story."

Please, dear God, don't, Rekke thought.

"But there is one thing I will mention since it is of significance to what I have to tell you."

"Pray tell," Rekke said, beginning once again to slyly read the newspaper with his right eye.

"I'm a competitive man," Corales said.

Oh no, Rekke thought.

"I know that's what everyone says these days," the Deputy Commissioner said, as if reading the Professor's mind.

"I'm sure you're right."

"But for me it has been as much a curse as an asset. It has moved me forward but I have also become embroiled in failure and sometimes I've refused to admit I am wrong."

Rekke smiled encouragingly.

"And yet you just did."

"The good thing is that I never give up, which is why I'm here with you this morning, Professor. I made a hash of my most important investigation."

Rekke listened hopefully for signs of life from Micaela in the apartment beyond the kitchen, but there was silence. All he heard was the wind rattling the studio-loft windows, and he wondered whether he might proffer a good excuse right now and be done with this. By the by, hadn't he promised his frightful brother that he would attend some reception today?

"Remind me, how many years ago was that?" said Rekke.

"Twenty years ago."

"A cold case."

"Not for me," said Corales. "For me, the wound is still fresh."

I was referring to myself, Rekke thought. I need something hot to dispel my irritation.

"And where do we lay our scene?"

"Santander—by the Cantabrian Sea."

"Far away," Rekke murmured, but he did remember the case.

"I was in charge of the city's CID," Corales added. "We were preparing for the annual festival, the Semana Grande. I don't know whether you have any experience of our traditions in this respect, Professor?"

"I'm more familiar with the theory than the practice," Rekke said, not altogether truthfully, but this was not the right moment to confess old sins.

"The fiesta runs around the clock for seven days. People are typically intoxicated but happy," Corales said.

"But a young woman was murdered, was she not?"

"On the first night of the fiesta."

On the first night, Rekke thought, momentarily possessed by an almost dreamlike image of a girl dying on the ground while the party heated up around her; he felt himself reluctantly becoming interested at an almost existential level. It was the prospect of dying during a party, a carnival, a delirium pounding away in the distance; it awakened melancholy in him.

"Tragic," he said.

"Yes, very. Everyone said she was one of a kind. She always had her nose in a book."

"A talented girl."

"Oh yes." Corales slipped a hand into the inside pocket of his suit jacket. "You must see her."

He held out a photograph. Rekke waved it away, he wasn't quite sure why. Perhaps he didn't want to commit emotionally.

Corales looked surprised.

"Don't you want to look? Is that one of your methods?"

"My methods vary," Rekke said. "But there is *one* rule that I always apply fairly consistently. It's my preference that my colleague be present when I hear something interesting. Do excuse me for a moment."

"Naturally," said Corales.

Rekke stood up and left, passing the grand piano in the living room and making for Micaela's bedroom, which was furthest away from the kitchen. He stopped a couple of metres short, feeling the stillness of the air and thinking: *leave her alone; don't always drag her into your life.* Nevertheless, he advanced, nudged the door ajar and saw her inside, curled up with the covers halfway up to her shoulders. She looked fragile, as if she had taken off the armour she usually wore, and he contemplated her for a long time. He was tempted to move closer and stroke her hair and say a few kind words.

On the other hand, it wouldn't be at all kind to wake her, so he turned around and realized at that moment that he must have caught a glimpse of the murdered girl earlier. A purposeful yet uncertain look flickered through his eyes, but he didn't know what he'd really seen in the photograph and what merely derived from his inner vision.

"She's asleep," he said when he returned to the kitchen.

"I see," Corales said, adding with a smile: "Well, I'm glad it's Sunday for someone."

Rekke nodded, thinking he might as well listen to this story if his peaceful morning with Obama was ruined anyway.

"Proceed," he said.

TWO

Santander, 12 July 1988

After breakfast—which consisted of two eggs and half a glass of orange juice—she walked to the restaurant where she worked part-time. It was half past nine in the morning, which meant that Roberto wasn't yet in situ to scold her, so she sat down on a chair in the bar area with her back to the terrace and the sea and wrote in her diary:

The stray dogs came with the storm.

As a girl, she'd been bitten by a stray—a Galgo—not far from there. But seeing as she wanted to be an author—albeit without telling anyone—she kept on changing the story, and the latest version was that she no longer wanted to describe the dog as a monster, as a soulless, emaciated husk. She wanted to give it a personality, which was because she had read about Galgos in the *National Geographic* and come to realize what terrible lives they had.

"Well, don't just sit there."

Roberto had arrived earlier than expected. He wore black chinos and a loose-fitting white shirt, and very much looked like the asshole he was.

"Hop to it," he snapped.

She got up and began to move about behind the bar while gazing out toward the water and thinking about her stray dogs. Down in the harbour, the fishing boats had long since set sail. None of the market traders were out. She couldn't see even a single person—just birds and a lean cat limping by. It was oddly calm. Perhaps people were sleeping in before the fiesta. But there . . . down to the left by the red barrels filled with fish, she saw two young men. Beautiful boys, one blond and graceful, the other darker-haired and taller. Each carried a book in his hand, and that alone was a thing for her. No-one she knew read novels—at any rate, not like she did—and sometimes she wished that an outsider would arrive who really understood her.

"Who do those posers think they are?" Roberto said. "Tell them we're not open yet."

"Tell them yourself," she said, which earned her a kick to the leg. She noticed that the young men really were on a course toward them.

Come and save me, she thought.

THREE

Micaela sensed Rekke's presence in the doorway, but she was drifting off and didn't move. She was shattered. She'd been up all night and now she fell into a dreamless slumber. It must still have been a shallow sleep, because she came to with a start as if something threatening had woken her. But nothing seemed to have happened—nothing except that a male voice not belonging to Rekke was speaking in the kitchen.

She couldn't hear what was being said, but it sounded like English—English with a Spanish accent—and judging by the tone she guessed the topic of conversation was dramatic, and that made her smile. She realized why Rekke had been standing there in the doorway—he wanted her to listen too. As soon as he heard something enthralling, he wanted her there too, which was of course flattering. But that wasn't enough to bring her peace. She looked down at Rekke's dressing gown lying on the floor with the arms splayed like something from an old-fashioned crime scene photo.

"I'm an idiot," she muttered.

She should just tell him, just spill it: I'm moving out. No big deal. Yet she kept putting it off, and now she angrily tugged the covers over her face, annoyed by the voice she could hear. Stop talking, she wanted to scream. Stop wanting me to get out of bed. Naturally she'd pondered her relationship with Rekke a thousand times. Were they friends, colleagues, or more? They definitely weren't a couple, even if there had been moments . . . although that had been ages ago. Now she supposed they were most like brother and sister. But no—that wasn't quite true either. That was why she was lying there agonising. She always struggled to discuss affairs of the heart with Rekke precisely because she didn't want to ruin what had been simmering beneath the surface ever since their first encounter in Djursholm. And then there was Caspar; that felt like more than just a flirtation.

Caspar Amiri was an Ericsson engineer who had helped them sort out their mobile phones at work. He'd annoyed her. He was so macho and full of himself, and he'd stared at her far too greedily. He'd called that night. She assumed he was checking that everything was working, but he asked her out and she said no, no way, and that was it, or so she thought. But he didn't give in and kept calling and one night she said, "Fine, one drink."

They met at the Tudor Arms, a block away from the apartment on Grevgatan. Caspar had shown up in a grey blazer and freshly ironed shirt and wasn't playing it macho any longer; on the contrary, he was nervous. He told her he was from Iran and had hoped to become a doctor but that he couldn't stand the sight of blood, so he'd enrolled at the KTH Royal Institute of Technology instead.

"Do you get along better with machines than people?" she said.

"That's a tough one," he said with an enchanting smile, and for the first time he seemed rather handsome and genuinely interested. It turned out they had a lot in common.

Their families had both fled dictatorship, and they both had siblings who were dumb as rocks, and dads whom they'd had all the time in the world to idealize because they'd been dead for ages.

There was common ground; plus he had great-looking arms.

"How did you get under my skin?" said Micaela.

"Because I was playing the tough guy. You saying it didn't work?"

"Not for one second."

"So what should I do?"

"Telling me you don't do blood was cute. You could continue in a similar vein."

"You mean show my sensitive side?" he said.

"Yeah, but if I start bleeding and you don't take care of me I'll kill you."

Then she kissed him—quite spontaneously—and figured that this was just a temporary thing, if it was a thing at all. But Caspar continued to astonish her, and unlike Rekke, his musical tastes extended beyond classical—thank God—and she didn't have to be constantly exceptional around him. She could say more or less whatever she liked, and while he was sometimes touchy and suspicious, she was still drawn to him. The only thing was . . . she hadn't said a word about Caspar to Rekke, and the longer she held off, the more charming and attractive Rekke became. Presumably out of sheer contrariness.

But she'd tell him soon. Just not today when a black man had become President of the United States of America and a feeling of hope had awoken within her, and she could hear that the voice in the kitchen was now speaking with a sudden tremor, as if someone had met with a terrible fate.

She decided to go back to sleep instead.

FOUR

Señor Corales had kept going for three and a half hours straight but had now finally left, and Rekke breathed a sigh of relief. He settled down to read the police case files that the Deputy Commissioner had deposited in stacks on the kitchen table—but he didn't get far. Micaela entered, once again clad in his dressing gown, which was trailing along the floor.

"What was all that about?" she said, sitting opposite him.

"A twenty-year-old unsolved murder," he said.

She made a gesture as if she didn't care.

"I was more thinking about what you just said about your visitor's fingers. Sounded like classic Rekke to me," Micaela said.

He shrugged.

"Ah well," he said. "Señor Corales got worked up and was drumming his fingers so persistently that it was driving me insane."

"And you heard something in the sound?" she said.

"I couldn't help it. His fingertips sounded leathery, and given his rather unfashionable rock 'n' roll haircut I guessed that he played the guitar and loved Jimi Hendrix. Which rather flabbergasted him."

"So you were right."

"More or less. He'd played since he was a boy, until his fingers became quite hard."

Micaela laughed.

"It was elementary, really," Rekke said. "But I think this story may amuse you, and at any rate I need help with the Spanish."

He pointed to the stacks.

"Don't feel like it," she said with a sigh.

"Nor do I, really," he said. "But I can't help but find it somewhat interesting."

"I'm going out. I have to get ready," Micaela said evasively.

"No need," he said. "My dressing gown suits all social contexts."

"Very funny."

"Just take a look at this."

He pushed a photograph from the case file across the table and Micaela leaned forward to scrutinize it.

"What is this?" she snorted.

"A mighty oak on a hillside above the city of Santander in Spain, and the exact spot where . . ."

"So you're trying to tempt me with a tree?"

He smiled wryly.

"In a manner of speaking," he said. "The tree is the murder scene, and the great mystery of the investigation. You might say that there are two copies of it: one in the literary universe; the other in more physical form on this hill."

Micaela stared at him as if he weren't quite right in the head.

"But if you insist that I play to the gallery, then I might add that it's my belief we're looking for a serial killer," he said.

She glanced at the stacks of files on the table.

"That's more like it," she said. "Why do you think that?"

Rekke glanced toward the window.

"I can tell from the injuries to the body, and there's a mark on the shoulder that seems familiar," he said.

"Then shouldn't you be packing a bag for Santander right this instant?" said Micaela.

"My incurable pride tells me that I might solve it from my own quarters."

"After twenty years?"

Rekke laughed.

"Yes, as it happens. New circumstances have emerged and I just had an inkling that the killer might be a Swede and . . . very literary."

Micaela looked at him in reluctant surrender.

"Alright then, Professor. Tell me more."

FIVE

Santander, 12 July 1988

She was lousy at hiding her insecurities. She blushed much too easily and allowed her gaze to wander too much, and it was doubtless as bad as usual when the two young men entered the restaurant.

She became palpably nervous and at first she could barely tell them apart. They blurred into one, like two copies of the same thing, both urbane and elegant in their checked shirts, books in hand. But as they got closer, she could see the differences—as if they were united by being opposites.

"We're not open yet," Roberto said.

"It's alright. *Buenos días.* What can I get for you?" she said, which earned her another kick to the leg.

That didn't bother her, but she felt uneasy that the blond man didn't appear grateful for the hospitality, opting instead to glare down at the bar.

"A *doble* of beer and a Fernet," he said.

"Just coffee for me," said the dark-haired man, adding a "please" that seemed to cover both of them.

Objectively, he was the more handsome of the two, with a rounder, more harmonic face, and his gaze was as friendly as his friend's eyes were cold. But the friend's silent anger affected her.

"Of course," she said. "Take a seat and I'll bring it over."

"I'll have mine here," the blond man said.

"Lovely place," the friend said, in an obvious attempt to counter the awkwardness.

She nodded, turned around, got out a bottle of Fernet and a glass and filled a *doble*-sized glass with beer, relieved that Roberto had taken himself off to the kitchen but tense in case the blond man became even more steely. She turned nervously toward his friend. He had a gentle, rueful air, which was only reinforced by the chilliness of his companion.

"Thanks," she said. "This place'll be chaos later. As I'm sure you know, the fiesta starts today."

"Yep, we know."

She slid the two glasses across the bar to the blond guy without daring to look him in the eye. Then something strange happened. He downed their contents in the space of a couple of seconds and then a wonderful smile appeared from nowhere on his face, which really startled her. It was such a transformation.

"Hit the spot?" she said.

"That was heavenly," he said, his eyes no longer cold. "Same again, please. We'll be on the terrace. You have such a beautiful smile."

You too, she wanted to say, but all she managed to mumble was a "Yes, of course," and then she poured a fresh beer and another Fernet as the men went outside and nonchalantly dropped their books onto the table. That was all she had time to see. There was the sound of footsteps returning from the kitchen—angry footsteps—and she started, anxious she was about to be kicked again.

"Faggots," Roberto said, glowering at the men. "And stop flirting with the customers."

"I'm not flirting," she said, taking a couple of steps away from him, worried that he would make her drop the glasses or slap her on the shoulder where she had the bruise from yesterday.

Then she took a deep breath and walked past him, before remembering that she'd forgotten the other young man's coffee. Still, she didn't turn around—the coffee wasn't all that important in the context. She concentrated on keeping her head held high and not thinking too hard about her smile, because if she did the smile would only end up being stiff and strained.

As she got closer, she heard the men's voices. They were speaking what she thought might be a Scandinavian language. She didn't know which one, and she glanced discreetly at the blond guy. He had a high hairline and beautiful cheekbones. There was something elegant about his lean figure.

"Your drinks," she said. "Coffee won't be a moment."

"*Gracias*," said the darker-haired one, who hadn't yet had anything, while the blond man who had just complimented her now appeared completely self-absorbed again, and she avoided his gaze and looked instead at his book on the table.

It said *Louis-Ferdinand Céline* on the jacket, and beneath that there was a title in a language she didn't know. *Journey to the End of the Night*, she thought, her heart beginning to pound. She'd read it, and she wanted to tell them. But she didn't dare. The man gripped the shot glass and the atmosphere became tense again, and she reflected that there had to be a backstory, something unspoken that she didn't understand. So she left the men with a nod, but stayed close by wiping down the adjacent tables and straightening the chairs.

It felt reckless, and not just because it was a way of spying. She also knew it drove Roberto nuts. No matter how broken up they were, he remained hopelessly jealous. She thought about this as she watched the men.

The blond one was now speaking with a breathless vivacity, and she did her best to listen, without understanding a single word. Sometimes he would look at her a little covetously, and she ventured closer, and in that moment he posed a question in English.

"How lonely do *you* get?" he said, adding another phrase, but she didn't catch that.

She slipped away without noticing that Roberto was shaking his head indignantly. "How lonely do I get?" she muttered, thinking once again of the stray dog, the one she was writing about, and in that moment she imagined that it was the dog who had asked the question. *How lonely do you get?*

Then, at last, she poured the coffee and returned to the table, resolved to tell them she too had read Céline.

SIX

Micaela looked at Rekke. Something about him was different. It wasn't anything obvious, not at all. It was his eyes, she decided. They looked unusually restless.

"Who was the victim?" she said.

"A young woman—only a girl really, twenty years old, a literary talent," he said. "Her name was Sandra Ramirez and she was found beside the old oak with her head pulled into a hollow at the base of the trunk. She'd been badly knocked about, especially down her left side, and her face was beaten beyond recognition."

"Sounds like a fit of rage," she said.

"Undoubtedly, but it's contradictory. The fingers were broken with a degree of precision right by the carpal tunnel, and then there was the mark on the shoulder, which I shall return to. There's something gruesome about this. I believe I even detect signs of two assailants."

She raised her eyebrows.

"That would be unusual."

"Yes," Rekke said, "and I've probably been too hasty in my

conclusions." He wrapped a hand around his own long fingers. "But as I said, the interesting thing is why this girl ended up by the old oak while the fiesta was in full swing in the city."

Micaela looked at the picture again. The oak had shed most of its leaves. It looked mighty and a little ethereal.

"Why is that so strange? I daresay such a monstrosity might attract interest."

Rekke pulled a magazine from one of the many piles on the table: *London Review of Books.*

"On the very day she was murdered, this girl wrote a short story about a stray dog—a Galgo," he said. "Do you know what a Galgo is?"

Micaela shook her head.

"It's a sight hound, reminiscent of a greyhound," he said. "In Spain, they breed them in big litters and train them to run fast in races or when chasing game in the woods. But once hunting season is over, they're often dumped and abused. Torturing them in the most refined ways possible is an old custom, with the ones that did worst on the track bearing the brunt. They're thrown down wells or hung from trees and left to slowly strangle."

"And she wrote about that?"

"In a manner of speaking. But not from an external perspective. She was the Galgo. She saw the world through the dog's eyes and followed it into death," said Rekke.

"And?" said Micaela.

"The Galgo dies by the same old oak that she did. Well, not the very same one, if we are to respect literature as a domain unto itself."

"Okay," she said thoughtfully. "So the girl wrote about a dog that ends up dying by a tree, and then she gets beaten to death at the same spot."

Rekke nodded.

"And there is another respect in which this short story is

intriguing," he said. "Much later on, it was published in a prestigious magazine." He pointed to the literary journal again. "And I believe it tells us more than the police understood. *Ars revelat veritatem*."

Micaela gazed at Rekke, perceiving all the sophistication in his nervous being, and wondered whether she really was going to move out. She supposed it was inevitable.

"You mentioned a Swedish killer," she said.

He perused the heaps of files.

"Exactly," he said. "It's not the only lead, but it merits examination. In any case, I promised to take a look."

"Who is this Swede?"

"There are two of them, actually. Two young men who patronized the Cervantes restaurant in Santander on the morning of July twelfth, 1988, which was where Sandra Ramirez had a part-time job. Evidently handsome. One slender and blond. The other darker-haired and taller. Both had books with them: Hemingway, according to one witness."

"What makes them interesting?" she said.

Rekke laughed, somewhat without reason.

"Not very much," he said. "Yet they still pique my curiosity. No-one has been able to establish their names—the lead cropped up much too late in the investigation—but according to witnesses, they were trained journalists and wanted to become writers. And then there's the car."

Micaela smiled indulgently.

"Cars are good in murder investigations."

"Not this car, I'm afraid," he said. "Nevertheless, this particular detail reinforces the suspicion that the Swedes—or one of them—had something to do with the murder."

She noticed that Rekke was peering at her as if he had discovered something rather troubling.

"What was it about the car?" she said.

"A young man climbed out of it, highly intoxicated. He was staggering all over the place and holding his hand. It looked as if he'd been in quite a scuffle. His trousers were covered in stains."

"Where did this happen?"

"Laredo, which is less than fifty kilometres from Santander. But that's not the most intriguing part of the story. There's a cliff-hanger here, if we're to stick to literary idiom."

SEVEN

Santander, July 1988

She placed a jug of milk, a bowl of sugar cubes and a cup of coffee on a tray and returned to the men on the terrace. It was still morning and not yet as hot as it was going to be. A cooling breeze was wafting in off the sea. Her mouth was dry and she was nervous again, and she noted a group of backpack-wearing youths coming into the restaurant, with others waiting behind them. Yet she concentrated on the men.

The darker-haired guy looked at her almost helplessly as his friend continued to talk. As she approached, she heard the name Shakespeare.

"Sorry to keep you waiting; here's your coffee," she said.

"No problem," said the dark-haired man, smiling uncertainly.

His blond companion suppressed a grimace, and she wondered whether she should leave right away. But she wanted to say just a couple of words about the Céline.

"Sorry," she said, pointing to it. "How's Bardamu doing?"

That was the name of the book's hero.

The blond man looked up and his gaze wandered across her body.

"Oh, you know," he said. "He caught a fever in Africa and then got better. But now he thinks that life at 37 degrees Celsius is banal—and he may have a point."

His ensuing laughter was infectious, and she would have done anything to reply with her own witticism. She could think of nothing to say except that she liked the book.

"It's written with such pace," she said.

"You can almost forgive him for becoming a fascist," the man interjected, a comment she did not favour with a reply.

Fascism was so sensitive on the home front—two of her uncles had worked for the Franco regime—that it was no joking matter for her. She turned toward the dark-haired one.

"What are *you* reading?"

"Well . . ." he said, and once again it struck her what a beautiful face he had.

He radiated anxiety and a certain tenderness, even more so since she'd just caught that helpless look. Still, it took an effort to keep her eyes on him. It was his blond friend she was drawn to.

"Dag's a little ashamed," said the blond man.

"Ashamed is an overstatement. But it's a bit of a tourist cliché," Dag said as he turned over the book.

She smiled. *The Sun Also Rises*. She wasn't exactly sure it was a cliché, but she had definitely seen other tourists reading it.

"But it's good, right?" she said.

"I'm starting to get bored of Hemingway."

"Dag thinks he drinks too much and is cruel to bulls."

"Shut it," Dag said, and she resolved to change the subject and be bolder.

"I was kind of eavesdropping before," she said.

The blond man's eyes sparkled.

"Wonderful," he said. "Here I was—longing for an audience. It can't have been easy understanding our Swedish."

She played with her hair.

"No," she said. "But you also said something in English. You asked a question. *How lonely do you get?* Right?"

The man gave his friend, the one named Dag, a triumphant look that was difficult to interpret.

"Exactly," he said.

He seemed to be deliberately withholding an explanation.

"So was it a quote or what?" she said.

"More or less. And an existential ponderance, inspired by a song."

"Who by?"

"Who do you think? But you didn't answer the question. How lonely *do* you get?"

She felt her pulse quicken, not only because she was very alive to the fact that his gaze still contained that fiery spark, but also because she was thinking of the stray dogs again, and what she had begun to write.

"As lonely as you like," she said. "There's no limit. Loneliness is infinite . . ." Like the universe, she meant to say, but that seemed pretentious and she fell silent. Still, she noticed that the words had had an effect.

The blond man pouted his lips sensually.

"Wow," he said. "Probably true. Loneliness doesn't bottom out."

"Perhaps not."

"But we have to seek out comfort, right?" the man added, pointing to his glass. "Here. Or . . ." He grabbed the breast of his shirt. "Or in some embrace."

She felt self-conscious.

"Or in a temperature in excess of 37 degrees Celsius," she said, feeling proud of herself.

The men both laughed, and she thought, *good God, if only it could be like this all the time.* This brief exchange alone had made her realize how dull her usual surroundings were.

"Exactly," said the blond man, taking another sip. "One should always be drunk—with wine, with poetry, or with fever, as you please."

"Baudelaire, right?"

"Exactly; a travesty of the old syphilitic."

She drew breath before asking: "Who was it who sang about loneliness?"

The blond man's broad smile was infectious.

"Leonard Cohen," he said.

"Who?"

"Behold the barbarian! He's only a genius. It's on his new record, *I'm Your Man*. He's asking Hank Williams, but he doesn't answer."

"Okay," she said.

She didn't know who Hank Williams was either.

"Do you read poetry?" the dark-haired man said kindly, and naturally she should have been grateful for the question, but she found it boring and too staidly adult.

She wanted to cross swords with his friend.

"Yes," she said politely. "All the time."

"Lorca, perchance?" said the blond man, his tone becoming more challenging.

"I love him," she said.

"Cohen does his own take on one of Lorca's poems on the new record. 'Take This Waltz,' it's named. Check it out and maybe we can regroup later and discuss it over a drink," he said.

"Are you going to the fiesta?" she said, unsure whether it was a date that he had suggested.

"I thought I'd soldier through it," he said, grinning happily. "But I'll need another beer."

He looked at her with that same smouldering expression.

"Of course," she muttered, hoping she hadn't started blushing.

Then she made herself scarce, surprised at how many people had turned up in no time at all; luckily it was possible to greet them on autopilot.

Her only thought was that she needed to track down that Lorca take and find something interesting to say about it.

EIGHT

Rekke noted a tension around Micaela's eyebrows. She's tormenting herself, he thought, as he heard the wind rattle the windowpanes. Maybe there really was going to be a blizzard, like Señor Corales had said.

"What kind of cliff-hanger are you offering me?" she said. "I've got to go soon."

"You do place such pressure on the poor storyteller," Rekke said. "Although I daresay I laid the groundwork for that. The man who emerged from the car in Laredo was probably the same person who visited the restaurant in Santander the day before and drank Fernet-Branca. He had blond hair, was of slim build and wore a checked button-up shirt. It was two or three o'clock in the morning, and according to the witness he was limping. At any rate, he seemed to be in pain and his right shoe was in tatters. On the other hand . . ."

Rekke smiled self-consciously just to be safe.

"Yes?"

"It might be a red herring, and there's not exactly any shortage of suspects in this investigation. But it's at least mildly intriguing that the police engaged in door-to-door inquiries in Laredo, which was how they happened upon Señora Castro, or rather, her sister to be precise. Don't you think you'd be best off taking acetaminophen and going back to bed?"

Micaela gave him an annoyed look.

"Huh? No, why would I do that? When did they hear about this sighting?"

"About two years after the murder," he said, "and thus it was rather complicated. Señora Castro died from a heart attack six months before the police called, but her sister told them that the family let out the attic room in their house by the square during the summer months. No records were kept and no photocopies were made of guests' passports. But Señora Castro had mentioned two Swedish men who stayed in one of her rooms in July 1988. They were recently qualified journalists, she said. One of them was the most charming young man you could imagine. The other was very arrogant. He had a beastly gaze, apparently."

"Oh really," Micaela said impatiently.

"And it was that night—well, I'm presuming it was that night, I should say—that she was woken in the small hours by a terrible ruckus coming from the men's room. She meant to go upstairs and give them a piece of her mind, but the voices frightened her. By morning, both of them were gone and a bedside lamp and two flowerpots had been smashed. There were brown stains on the floor that she wiped up."

"There must have been other people in the city who saw them," Micaela said.

"Surprisingly few, and as far as we know, nothing seems to have been caught on film. But there's another trivial thing that occurred in Santander that evening," he said, once more contemplating Micaela and the tense expression on her face.

"Go on," she said.

"There's not much to this either," Rekke said. "But at least it came up in the early phase of the investigation, when witnesses' memories were still fresh. It pertains to observations made of an intoxicated, blond-haired man sitting on the sidewalk outside a Santander restaurant named La Mar and smoking an unfiltered cigarette. Perhaps a Gauloise. He was a little reminiscent of a young Mick Jagger, they said. Graceful body; sensual lips; sunken cheeks; fine, thinning hair."

"Dead ringer for a Jagger."

Rekke smiled.

"A girl from the town of Castro Urdiales approached the man and asked him who he was."

"Sounds promising," Micaela said.

"The man said 'Sisyphus.' "

"Sisyphus?"

"Exactly. He said that each day he rolled his boulder up the hill in the hope of a reward come evening. Then he pulled a hip flask from his pocket and took a swig as if its contents were the reward he meant. Then he added with a wry smile: 'So I suppose you'd say I'm happy.' "

"So he'd read Camus. What happened?" said Micaela.

"Nothing much. But the interesting part is that Sandra Ramirez was seen outside that same restaurant a couple of hours earlier looking for someone."

"I see."

"And while nothing is set in stone," Rekke said, picking one of the bundles of papers off the table, "and the whole investigation is an impenetrable thicket, this would seem to be the same young man who was seen both at the restaurant that morning and getting out of the car in Laredo in the small hours."

Micaela smiled derisively.

"So that's your mission: to find this literary wino twenty years later."

Rekke shrugged.

"Yes, more or less."

"And there's no facial recognition, no composite of his characteristics, no scar, no tattoos?"

He shook his head.

"It was deemed that too much time had passed for it to be worth bringing in an artist."

Micaela rose to her feet and Rekke wondered whether he should do something for her—rustle up some lunch or tuck her back into bed. But as she stood, she made a deprecatory gesture.

"So what you have," she said, "is a man who is now about forty, but who was once slim and handsome, and who might have gone to journalism college and is conversant in literary matters. He might have a booze problem, and he might not be very nice. On the other hand, his behaviour at the time may not have been typical of him. He might have grown out of it and become fat and bald."

"A very good summary," Rekke said. "And we might add that he possibly smoked Gauloises and read Camus. Admittedly, there was something of an epidemic in that respect in the eighties; there were people to be found on every street corner who wanted to become French existentialists. But it's still a start, I think, and we've got your databases at work to call upon, as well as this new marvel you occasionally venture onto . . . Facebook. I daresay you must be able to run all sorts of searches on it?"

"You're kidding?" she said.

He opened the fridge to see whether he could lay his hands on any food for her.

"Perhaps a little," he said, extracting the tzatziki from dinner the night before and then finding a half baguette in the bread box. "But I'm also serious," he added. "I want you to take a look at the pictures of the body—then you'll understand."

"I'm not hungry," she said. "Besides, I think I'd rather see the victim in life first."

Rekke asked Micaela to sit back down again and laid out the bread and tzatziki on the table in case she changed her mind.

"Sensible," he said.

Then he pulled the copy of the *London Review of Books* back to him and opened it at the photograph that had been published next to Sandra Ramirez's short story.

NINE

Santander, July 1988

When Sandra emerged from the kitchen, her nostrils detected Roberto—not his usual scent of eau de cologne and sweat, but the sharp, pungent stench that always preceded his outbursts, and she at once sensed danger.

She'd already smelled that scent on their second date, back when she'd been infatuated with Roberto and hadn't realized how dangerous he was. Nowadays, she knew all too well that the odour was an omen, a warning sign, and she quivered. A moment later, she was flung forward, her head striking the door frame.

"How dare you stand around like a cheap slut when we've got customers pouring in!" he said.

"I'm not," she stammered, thinking she would be driven insane with rage and humiliation.

But to her surprise, he unexpectly reined in his temper. The anger faded away, and at first she couldn't understand why; it was quite amazing. Then she realized—it was because of the blond guy. His promise that they would meet up was like armour, and she straightened up and went to the bathroom to smarten up with something akin to a smile on her lips, and as she looked in the mirror she realized that he wasn't the only thing that made her strong.

It was also what had been there all morning: the throbbing desire to write. Everything apart from that and the blond man seemed petty, and once she'd adjusted her hair and dried her eyes, she went back out into the bar.

The restaurant was teeming with people, and she raised her hand to her temple. She hoped it wouldn't bruise, as if that were the only problem the assault might give rise to. Then she began pulling pints and gazed at the terrace and all the new patrons, and at that moment something happened that intensified the tension in her body. She knew what to do with her story.

It was through the eyes of the dog that she had to see the city, and as that insight washed through her like a wave, the sentences followed. They came with such force that it was only with an effort that she was able to remain in place until the beer glass was full. But she had work to do.

So much suddenly needed doing in that second that it was hopeless. She would have to get to grips with it, but first she needed to take the drinks over to the Swedes, which was exciting too. But it was noticeable that something was different. The one named Dag was regarding her with shock.

"What happened?" he said. "Did he hit you?"

Sandra came to life. She hadn't realized that any of the patrons had seen the shove.

"No, it wasn't that bad," she said.

The man's eyes flashed daggers; the anxious, somewhat tormented look was gone. He looked furious.

"That's not how it looked. Who does that dick think he is?"

Sandra didn't reply. She set down the glasses and stole a glance at his blond friend. Unlike his compatriot, he didn't seem at all troubled; instead he appeared amused, and this time he drank quietly. He looked at her with a jaunty smile.

"Do you want us to kill him for you?" he said.

She took note of the light, ironic tone.

"Might be a bit much," she said.

"Then we'll save you instead. You can come with us on our road trip."

Where are we going? That was what she wanted to ask, but she considered it too bold and she also noticed that the dark-haired one wasn't participating in the schtick. He was still upset.

"Has he hit you before?" he said.

Sandra didn't want to answer; she didn't want to turn this into a serious conversation.

"No," she said.

"It didn't look that way."

"What do you mean?" she said, immediately regretting it.

She knew perfectly well that an ingrained habit could be seen in a movement.

"Your reaction," he said. "You reacted as if it had happened a thousand times."

"No, no, I just . . ." she said, wanting to tell them about what she was going to write, but she was nervous that it would sound pretentious.

"Don't listen to Dag. He can be a sanctimonious old bore."

Dag hissed a couple of words in Swedish.

"As you can see," the blond man added. "But he's the one who holds the purse strings, so we have to stay on his good side."

"I was just worried," Dag said, as if he really meant it, and in that moment Sandra wanted to say all sorts of things.

She wanted to thank them for their consideration and to ask the blond guy whether they really were going to meet up later, and to ask—even though it would probably be much too personal—why the atmosphere between them was so fraught, because in that moment she realized that their enmity was as familiar to them as the shove Roberto had given her was to her. But she was stressed, and Roberto's unsolicited gift was stinging at her temple.

"Thank you," was all she said. "Do you want more coffee?"

Dag shook his head and awkwardly moved his hand as if to pat or comfort her. When he didn't accomplish this, she nodded and left, thinking that soon, so soon, she really would need time to write her story. But it would have to wait—there was constantly more and more to do, and further to the left by the front door she caught sight of a weather-beaten man with a silver cross around his neck and a battered guitar propped up against his chair. The man was staring at her with a glassy gaze, and it left Sandra feeling irresolutely uneasy. But she ignored him and went on with her job on autopilot while she continued to craft sentences in her head.

TEN

The first thing Micaela noticed was the girl's eyes.

They were big and brown, at once inward-looking and curious, and she understood what Rekke meant. It wasn't hard to feel sympathy toward her. But as she continued to scrutinize the picture which filled the top half of a page in the newspaper, Micaela saw something more worrying.

"She's taken a blow to the collarbone," she said.

Rekke looked up.

"A waiter at her place of work—Roberto Ortega—often struck her around that area. He was jealous and unstable."

"Did they look into him?"

"Oh yes," said Rekke. "They arrested him and held him on remand. Tunnel vision meant that for a long time they were focused solely on him."

"But he was innocent?"

"Not necessarily."

"But you're inclined toward the Swede," Micaela said. "The Swedes," she said, correcting herself.

"I'd certainly like to find them."

"Why have they suddenly become relevant?"

He pushed the chunks of baguette and the tzatziki toward her.

"In part, it's to do with the short story, which has recently been published and sheds new light on the events. But above all it's because of new information about other murders where I was able to make my own small contribution."

Micaela rested a hand on her belly. It hurt so very weirdly.

"Okay," she said. "Can I see the pictures of the body?"

She was most definitely not sensitive. She'd seen enough murdered women to be able to take them in with a calm gaze. But she felt reluctant today, and when she saw the photographs she immediately grimaced.

"That's bad," she said.

And it was. There was nothing left of the pretty face she'd just seen. Not only were the lustre in her eyes and her dreamy features gone, but so was everything else. The nose had been crushed, the eyes kicked in, the lips and mouth too. There was a big, gaping hole by her temple, and the rest of her body hadn't fared much better—at least not down her left side.

Only her lower legs—covered in old, pale scars—were unharmed, while her shoulders, stomach, side, hips and thighs had been subjected to a severe beating. Initially, Micaela couldn't say anything more than that; the violence was senseless and extensive. The perpetrator must have spent a long, long time meting out punches and kicks. The body was shades of black-and-blue, the left arm was unnaturally contorted, the rib cage had caved in and two fingers were—as Rekke had said—broken and almost severed.

"Well," said Rekke. "What do you think?"

She clasped her stomach again and turned toward the window where the storm seemed to be intensifying.

"You said there might be two of them," she said.

"The killer was right-footed," he said. "Here on the left side . . ."

he added, pointing to the body, "... she only seems to have been kicked by a right foot. You can tell from the pointed, upward pattern of the bruises."

"Perhaps," she admitted.

"But then look here!" Rekke said, tapping a finger on the right side of the woman's hip. "There's a different angle of attack. That's a left shoe that has been applied to her, and these injuries aren't as marked. They seem more careful. Cautious almost."

Micaela considered this.

"You mean there were two murderers—one of them brutal and wild, and the other more reluctant and left-footed?"

He shrugged. "Perhaps."

"Is there any other evidence to support such a theory?"

Rekke shook his head.

"They recovered fibres from leather shoes, fragments of textiles from socks, splinters from a branch used as a weapon, but no DNA. Nothing that could be used with the technology of that age to tie a person or persons to the murder."

"And these fibres and fragments—were they from a pair of socks and shoes?"

"Yes."

"So perhaps it's a little far-fetched to conclude there were two killers."

Rekke smiled self-consciously.

Micaela looked at the picture again.

"But there's something really ritualistic and nasty here," she said, as if trying to agree with him nonetheless. "It's as if the attacker wanted to erase the girl's identity—her very humanity, no? You mentioned a mark."

Rekke pushed aside the full-body picture and handed over another photograph—a close-up of the victim's shoulder. The shoulder was also bruised, but the point of interest was at the top. There were two deep wounds, each some six or seven centimetres in length and so evenly cut that they must have been inflicted without resistance.

"Ugh," she said, looking at the dark crust over the wounds. "Obviously made post mortem," she said.

"Most definitely," he said. "There's no sign of blood circulation. Of course, the important question is this: what is it? Why two lines in particular?"

Micaela gave the obvious answer.

"The second victim."

"Indeed."

"And they haven't found a body with one line like that, or one with three or four?" she said.

Rekke looked rather disconcertingly dramatic and began to peer at his laptop, which was also on the table hidden behind a couple of stacks of case files.

"Not really in the obvious way," he said. He was about to turn the screen toward her when the landline rang. When Rekke made no effort to answer, Micaela stood up instead.

"Leave it," he said.

"Fine," she said, sitting down again and readying herself to see something even worse on his computer.

ELEVEN

Undersecretary Magnus Rekke needed his brother's help, which vexed him.

More than anything, he longed for Hans to crash into depression and addiction once and for all. But Hans—hopeless dolt that he was—had lately been in unusually good form, practically detoxed, and wouldn't it be just typical if he, the big brother, became the family drunkard?

He really should dial it down, although sobriety was itself a cross to bear. And there was a beeping sound in the kitchen, like there always was when he forgot to close the wine cooler. But instead of reminding him to shut the door, the beep told him to drink more. Preferably that Puligny-Montrachet he'd just opened despite the fact that it was barely past noon. But then again—damn it—it was always the same time of day for him. Time to work.

He went into the kitchen, got out a fresh wineglass and filled it to the brim before firmly shutting the wine cooler so that its beeping wouldn't lure him back again. Then he read about the presidential election in the United States and offered a silent prayer that the Republicans would nail Obama.

Magnus despised harmonies and rising popularity curves. He thrived best when there was conflict and intrigue—other people's conflicts, preferably, because there were certain types of problems he didn't want on his desk. Such as this Gina Mo woman he'd been saddled with precisely because of the liberal winds of change emanating from Washington.

"Hag," he muttered before taking a big mouthful. Well, there were hags and there were hags—she was as pretty as a picture, even when shaven-headed and in shackles. And truth be told, that was part of the problem. Anything could be big in this god-forsaken feminist era, and Gina Mo was deadly in that respect.

She had populist talents, and while she might be pals with terrorists and guerillas she was also a hero of the left, and she was bright enough to exploit that in every way she could to bring the human rights organisations and press associations onside. But she wasn't really one of them, nor was she one of the extremists. Rather, she was affiliated to herself and only herself and whatever gave her the most kicks and generated the most PR and newspaper headlines. But knowing anything for sure was hard, and he didn't blame the CIA for having given her a real going over—even if it was perhaps a little unfortunate that that picture had come out, of her in a red jumpsuit with her arms and legs in chains inside a small cage.

Oh come on, he snorted. She'd been asking for it. She'd been arrested disguised as a man in Kabul in 2002, which was why she had been sent to Guantánamo and given her own little annex—especially after she'd hinted that she knew where Osama bin Laden was. Obviously it was all a bluff conceived by an over-confident brain that thought it could cut a deal, but in reality the cost to her was her life, and it was in connection with that—and thanks to the enhanced interrogation techniques deployed on her—that a whistleblower leaked the story and she became what she loved to be: a novelty, a talking point, a scandal. Leaving him, God forbid, having to pretend to try to secure her release.

He engaged in the charade and looked concerned on television and said blah blah blah to the media, because what else was he supposed to do? After all, she was a Swede, and on paper she was a journalist—a war correspondent, or whatever it was she claimed to be. Not that she had either him or any serious media outlet duped; it was common knowledge that she stole other writers' columns and reports and made up her quotes.

But that wasn't the big problem. The concern was that she had become a personal threat and therefore he had managed to arrange a little respite before she embarked upon her series of press conferences. Gina Mo would be held in Swedish custody for a couple of days while she was debriefed by the Security Service and the Military Intelligence, and whatever those dolts failed to turn up could be left to Hans. While his loyalty did not extend to his brother, Hans had an unfortunate—and sometimes useful—ability to see through anything.

He was capable of spotting a glance, a scratch of a hand, a twitch at the corner of a mouth or a shift in complexion, and deciphering exactly what someone was up to, unless . . . Magnus sipped some more wine and pictured Gina Mo. Unless even his brother were to be bewitched by Mo. But no, a narcissistic vamp like this Mata Hari knockoff was hardly Hans's type. He preferred his women dark, dogged and from the projects, like that lodger of his, even if he was apparently so inhibited that he couldn't act on that, instead letting the chick get it on with an Iranian with a lousy security classification, which admittedly suited Magnus completely. All he had to do was ensure that projects girl and Rekke came to the reception later that day so that he could apply some pressure to them. Magnus had therefore called his secretary and asked her to remind them. It would all be fine.

He opened the wine cooler door so that it would emit its enticing beep again. He drank another couple of mouthfuls, and perhaps it was just the wine, or maybe it was the blizzard howling so dramatically outside, but suddenly life felt exciting. He might be a mere *éminence grise* as opposed to an eccentric genius like his brother, but he was the one who pulled the strings. He was the one people danced for, and who was Kleeberger but his puppet, his front man?

Magnus stood up and headed for his walk-in closet to select an extravagant suit, and found himself in such sudden good form thanks to the wine cooler that he had yet another brilliant idea. He would put the fear of God into Hans's young lodger and see to it that she too would do him a good turn.

TWELVE

Micaela was taken aback, just as she had expected to be, and in accordance with the heightened state of sensitivity that she was apparently afflicted by today of all days. A photo on Rekke's computer showed another young woman—naked and dead—lying on a steel table.

It took only a glance to see that the victim had met with a similar fate to Sandra Ramirez. Her name was Regina Lassen. She had been a Reader in Nordic languages and taught creative writing courses at the School of Media and Journalism in Aarhus, Denmark.

She was found dead on June fourth, 1994, aged thirty-three years, at a stud farm on the outskirts of the city, having been terribly beaten and kicked, and with the fingers on her left hand broken. Nevertheless, the cases hadn't been connected for a long time due to failures in communication and other unfortunate circumstances. Lassen's ex-husband had initially been convicted of the murder before being acquitted by the High Court, according to Rekke.

"But you remembered it right away?" she said.

"Not right away," he said. "But it rang a bell."

The woman hadn't just been kicked and beaten, Micaela noted. Her thighs and breasts had also been stabbed.

"There are differences," Rekke said. "But the pattern is still worryingly similar. A huge assault on the left-hand side. Only a few careful kicks to the right."

He changed the photograph on his screen to a close-up of the woman's shoulder. Micaela studied it reluctantly.

"It was different," she said.

On her shoulder, there were no lines visible—no simple markings like those on the Spanish girl. Instead, there was an E artfully carved with swirls and arcs.

"What do you think?" said Rekke.

Micaela thought that she wanted a hot bath and to be left in peace.

"It's been carved in deep, post mortem," she said.

"And?"

Stop questioning me was what she wanted to say.

"The middle line in the E is quite a lot shorter than the top and bottom ones, which makes it a little odd," she said.

"Exactly," he said. "Then we have the bows to the upper and lower lines. It's disturbingly playful, and it occurred to me at once that it was probably not a regular E."

Micaela looked at him and at his eyes that were so strangely bright.

"Then what is it?"

Rekke leaned forward.

"I believe it's a number."

She raised her eyebrows.

"If we are right," he said, "that the lines on the Spanish girl's shoulder denote the number two, then it's reasonable to search for other ways of counting, isn't it? And E—Epsilon—is more than just the fifth letter in the Greek alphabet. It also denotes the number five in Greek numerals."

Micaela glanced at him sceptically.

"So you're saying this is the fifth victim?"

"Yes, that's my working theory."

"Isn't it strange that the other women haven't turned up?"

"We haven't been searching very long," he said.

But others should have been, she thought.

"E might also mean Eva or Erik. Ericsson telecommunications. Anything," she said.

Rekke smiled.

"Indeed, but if we're to search the literary sphere—which I'm inclined to do—then I have another thought to accompany the first."

"And what's that?"

"The Aldous Huxley novel *Brave New World* came to mind."

"I know it," she said irritably.

"The book is a dystopian depiction of the future—although some might say utopian—where people can use a select drug to lose themselves in a state of bliss. But what I'm referring to is the classification of all people upon birth into five categories. Alpha and Beta are at the top, and our killer no doubt considers himself part of that. At the bottom of the hierarchy we find Epsilon—a group consisting of individuals who are predestined to obey and submit. They are classified with an E not unlike the one carved by the killer."

Micaela grimaced again and checked the time. It was half past twelve and she supposed she should eat something, but she didn't feel like it and matters had hardly been improved by this E carved into a black-and-blue shoulder. When the landline rang again, she immediately stood up.

"I'll get it," she said, going into the hall, glad to escape for a while.

THIRTEEN

Santander, July 1988

Where did all the people—and the heat—come from? The air was very still, and beyond the terrace and the harbour the sea was almost motionless, and Dag felt it with every inch of his body—he couldn't do this any longer. He wanted to leave and go home, and yet . . . life should have been smiling upon him.

He'd graduated from journalism school at Columbia University in New York and had become unexpectedly wealthy when his father sold off a chunk of his art collection and gave Dag some of the proceeds. In early May—not so long ago—he'd walked into a BMW dealership on Birger Jarlsgatan looking somewhat unshaven and dishevelled, wearing tatty jeans and a threadbare flannel shirt. Dag thought he looked bohemian, cool. But the car salesman by the door had looked at him contemptuously, and something primitive had been awoken in Dag.

"How may I help you?" said the salesman.

"I want that one," Dag said, pointing to the hottest car in the place—a red BMW 325 convertible.

The salesman's expression had become even more pointed.

"A little out of your range, perhaps," he said.

"I'll take it," Dag said, telling the salesman to telephone his bank manager, and the look the guy gave him afterward was one he would have given anything to see.

It was like a scene from a film. Instead of ordering a new car he took the very one he'd pointed at in the showroom. He would never forget it. In that moment, the car promised him a new life, and he drove away from the dealership with the feeling that it was now that everything would begin; all the incredible things that he had somehow been promised.

He took the less direct route, crossing over the Västerbron bridge. "Live is Life" was playing on the stereo and the world was his oyster. As he whistled past Norr Mälarstrand en route to Östermalm he let out a whoop, and when he reached Kungsträdgården a group of school children waved to him as if he were royalty out for a drive. On Karlavägen opposite their old school, Östra Real, he caught sight of Pompe. Pompe was talking to two girls that Dag recognized, whom he'd never even got close to because they'd never given a shit about him. He could tell right away as he pulled over that they were looking at him in a new way. It wasn't just the car, he thought. They'd doubtless heard about the legacy. When the girls had left, Pompe jumped in and they drove on toward Djurgården and Rosendals Trädgård while singing "You Can't Always Get What You Want" with such overbearing joy that it felt as if they might refute the claim itself.

"Who's going to stop us in this thing?" Pompe said, and the very word *us* was intoxicating in that moment.

Never before had Pompe been *us* with Dag. To him, Pompe had always been the epitome of cool. No-one was as quick-witted. No-one possessed such natural arrogance or looked richer or was more liberatingly cynical. No-one at all. Pompe and his tailor-made suits came as a package, and it did no harm that he was so careless with them.

He was a free spirit who got into all the bars and clubs because he behaved as if he already had access to them. But in reality, Pompe was poorer than most people Dag knew. He just acted rich, and was helped by the suits made for him with love by his father before he'd died all too soon, leaving behind a small tailor's shop on Artillerigatan that wanted for assets but had a surfeit of debts.

Perhaps for that reason, Pompe had sought out the wealthy children of Östermalm at an early stage and immediately been accepted by them. Well, more than accepted. He'd become their role model, and was often regarded as the classiest scamp of them all. That was surely also why he'd adopted that absurd nickname that smacked of throwaway upper class and become ever more careless with material possessions. Even the Wallenberg boys, Douglas and Sachs, had been impressed. They could only dream of the nonchalance he radiated.

Pompe carried it with him like a superpower. He looked like he didn't care, and he probably didn't either. He could order a wildly expensive wine without a penny in his pocket and pull it off. Someone else always turned up to cover the bill, or he'd simply walk out with such confidence that the staff assumed he'd already paid. He was a phenomenon, and when Pompe suggested that he and Dag head south in the new Beemer it felt like a party and nothing else, and for a few days in early July just after they had left Sweden it really was a party.

They bombed along the Autobahn at two hundred kilometres per hour while talking nonstop and listening to Pompe's mix tapes featuring Van Morrison, Cohen, Dylan, Cash, Nick Cave and Tom Waits. Hoarse men, all of them, and while Dag preferred lighter material like Cat Stevens and Billy Joel, he learned the songs by heart and sang loudly in the car with Pompe. Afterward, he'd often be on the receiving end of a minor lecture on the artists and their literary role models.

Pompe's cultural knowledge was nothing short of encyclopaedic, and Dag was hardly uninformed himself, given his hereditary burden on that front. But Pompe surpassed everyone and that was a party in itself, and perhaps that was why Dag ignored the warning signs, like Pompe not being bothered about sobering up before driving and always finding ways to ruin things. They were like his tics. He might walk past a park bench and topple it, or smash a window without even passing comment. And then there was the malice. At first, Dag accepted it in the way many young people accept the gibes delivered by those cooler than them, but on their journey across Europe it only got worse and he was constantly on his guard. When was the next blow coming? The next comment that he was naïve, ignorant or stupid?

Still, the booze was the most troubling aspect and the one that it took the longest to get a grip on. Alcohol was the very foundation of their friendship. They would drink and feel invincible when they did. But in the south of France, Dag stopped drinking. All of a sudden, he no longer felt like it. He blamed his stomach. "Gastritis," he said. But of course it was because of Pompe. Pompe drank until Dag lost any inclination to, and that was the last thing he'd pictured happening. Dag had always been a heavy drinker, and he loved all the boozy stories about Hemingway, Faulkner and Truman Capote, just like Pompe.

But now . . . he could wake up in the morning without having drunk a drop the day before and still be thinking he should quit for good. It was mad, although probably quite natural. Pompe went insane when he drank. It was bad before La Rochelle, but after La Rochelle things went from bad to worse. And yet Dag didn't leave. He was stuck to Pompe's side, whether in codependency or as a hostage. But soon I'll ditch Pompe, he told himself, and drive far away from him. Although that proved harder than he'd thought. It was a curse, and it got worse.

As they glided across the Spanish frontier, it was as if he were already reduced to a shell of himself. All he came out with was the stupid things that Pompe seemed to expect of him. Everything died on his tongue; his courage failed him too. Dag sat next to Pompe like a fool, a prisoner to his own paralysis, and the worst of it was that the paralysis was an invisibility suit. No-one saw him anymore. The girls only looked at Pompe, dumbstruck by his carelessness and wit, or rather dazzled, right up until Pompe got drunk and spiteful.

Dag raised his gaze from the table. Pompe was staring at the waitress. She hurried past with a stack of plates, muttering to herself, then glanced back. Dag wanted to shout at her: look at me instead. He's out of his mind. He's awful. I'm better and I can write. I'm funny when I write.

Then it hit him that this wasn't exactly true. He wasn't getting anywhere with his writing either. He was like that character in Camus's *The Plague*—Grand, wasn't it?—who was stuck on the same sentence, compulsively fixated on finding the perfect melody, the perfect touch. Well, he presumably lacked an aptitude for literature too. Otherwise he would have got further with his novel, his attempt at a novel, and maybe Pompe was right. He was a nobody, he was nothing. Now, somehow at an even lower ebb, Dag stared at the waitress who despite being shoved into the door frame was rushing around the restaurant with a secret smile on her lips as if she were immersed in her own, more beautiful world.

FOURTEEN

Perhaps Rekke was right after all, Micaela thought. She wasn't feeling herself.

"Yes?" she said into the receiver.

"Good afternoon. This is Stina Jonsdotter speaking. I'm calling from the office of the Minister of Foreign Affairs."

Micaela jumped, although not quite as much as in previous years. Nowadays, she was accustomed to the upper echelons getting in touch.

"Foreign Minister Kleeberger will be hosting a reception in his home on Tysta gatan later this afternoon. He merely wishes to be sure that you and Professor Rekke will be attending. It starts at five o'clock," Jonsdotter said.

Micaela smiled wryly.

"So I'm invited too?"

"This is Police Constable Micaela Vargas with whom I am speaking? The Minister noted that you and the Professor usually attend together."

That's not true, Micaela thought, and now even less than ever.

But she kept her counsel and wondered what she should wear in the event she did happen to accept the invitation.

"Was there anything in particular on the Minister's mind?" she said.

"He always seeks to combine business with pleasure, so I daresay there is. The dress code is business casual."

Micaela had no idea what that meant given the context, but she said nothing about that either and murmured that she wasn't sure whether Rekke could make it.

"People from beyond the world of politics are coming too. Intellectuals, free spirits, the kind of people Rekke usually likes. Do let him know that even Pontus Bremer has promised to put in an appearance."

"The author?"

"No less, and Mr. Bremer just gave me his solemn promise—for what that's worth—that he'd stay reasonably sober and avoid a fight with our poor Culture Minister, whose legs tremble at the mere sight of him."

"I don't know . . ." Micaela said tentatively, meaning to say that she didn't know whether Rekke would be able to put up with Pontus Bremer any more than the *poor* Culture Minister, but she let go of that too. "But I'll let him know. Five, you said?"

"Five o'clock. The Minister would greatly appreciate your attendance."

She hung up and made to go and tell Rekke, but as she glanced into the kitchen she saw him in there completely absorbed by his murder case and she resolved to put it off and escape into her own thoughts.

"Wrong number. I'm going to take a bath," she called out to him.

He merely nodded, transfixed by his computer, his left leg twitching nervously beneath the table.

FIFTEEN

Santander, July 1988

Pompe continued to stare at the waitress, then he leaned forward with a greedy look in his eyes.

"Not much of an ass on her," he said.

Dag wanted to hiss: well, leave her alone then. But he remained silent. He didn't even defend her by saying no, you thicko, can't you see she's wonderful? Far better than you deserve. He sat there dumbly, wishing he were anywhere else.

"So you didn't even know who Hank Williams was?"

Here it comes, Dag thought.

"What? No, not really," he said.

"You'll never be able to write anything good with these gaps in your knowledge. You'll never be able to raise your gaze to the stars. Hank Williams was a genius. Hillbilly Shakespeare."

"You said."

"Drank himself to death too," Pompe said, as if implying that no matter what else Williams had done, nothing lived up to this.

"Really?" Dag said wearily.

"Died at twenty-nine in the back seat of his Cadillac in West Virginia, hopped up on booze and painkillers, and no-one, I promise you no-one, sang about loneliness like him."

Pompe leaned forward a little more and began to sing in a put-on croaky voice. Dag turned his face away because of the breath and the saliva spattering him, which was why he didn't quite catch it. There was only one sentence he could make out properly: *I'm so lonesome, I could cry*, or perhaps *die*, and that was surely the truest thing he'd heard in a long time.

SIXTEEN

Rekke noticed neither his left leg twitching nor that he was mumbling to himself.

Had he been more alive to these tics he might have smelled a rat. Now, on the contrary, he felt unusually alert, and was able to picture the murder through borderline hallucinatory visions.

The killer must have stood above his victims, he decided, and that was important to him. He had most certainly felt threatened by the women's intellect and independence, and control was what he sought. Absolute power was the ultimate goal of his violence.

Aided by the injuries to the bodies and the positioning of the arms, Rekke thought he might be able to establish an order, a chronology. The murderer must initially have kicked the victims' heads and only when the women had sunk into unconsciousness and their hands, which they had shielded themselves with, had fallen slack by their sides, had he attacked their faces, brutally and at length until their features were obliterated. Afterward, he'd kicked the hips, the shoulders and the buttocks and naturally he must have stood somewhere on either side of the body.

Still, it was noticeable that he'd concentrated on the left-hand side. The violence perpetrated to the right-hand side was quite different.

The most flagrant thing was the fingers. They had been broken with such disturbing accuracy, and Rekke suspected it must either have happened early or late in the sequence of events. At the very end, when the anger had cooled and the women were dead, the murderer had knelt or crouched and marked his victims with a pocket knife which had not discernibly trembled in his hands.

"I'll find you," Rekke muttered, looking out of the window.

The blizzard was rattling the frames and he wondered what had become of Micaela, and then he recalled what she'd called out. In the distance, he could hear a bath running.

At that moment, his phone vibrated as a text message arrived. An email came too, also sent by Magnus, telling him not to forget about Kleeberger's reception later that day.

SEVENTEEN

Santander, July 1988

Sandra still had no end to her story, nor a proper beginning either, except for that sentence she'd written down in the morning about the stray dogs that came with the storm, but she needed a framework and a narrative arc. Cool it, she told herself.

Customers were streaming in and needing serving, and once again she made for the Swedish men, feeling just as nervous as before. The blond guy seemed to be singing, and she considered turning on her heel or continuing past them, but just then he turned his head and gave her a look that made a jolt of warmth pass through her.

"Oh, finally. Where have you been?" he said.

"I just popped to China," she said, wondering whether this was funny or plain silly, but the blond man laughed while his friend looked more tormented still.

"I'm jealous of China."

"Can I get you anything else? On the house," she said boldly.

The blond man grinned.

"How splendid. Make it champagne and oysters in that case. Actually, no. A whisky will do nicely, and a glass of milk for Dag."

"Knock it off."

She sensed that edge between them again and wondered whether to just go and get the whisky and perhaps another coffee, but she didn't want to let the opportunity go to waste and to be on the safe side she said to the two of them:

"Will I see you at the fiesta then? So we can discuss Lorca?"

"Definitely," said the one named Dag.

"Do you know anywhere good?" the blond one asked.

"La Mar on Peña Herbosa," she said.

"La Mar," he said. "Eight o'clock?"

"Perfect," she said, feeling a wave of excitement, or perhaps not just excitement.

She was also overcome by an unexpected uneasiness that mixed with the tension in the air, and she felt the one named Dag graze her foot as he silently mouthed a short word. *No* or perhaps *not*, or perhaps even a warning. But surely that couldn't be possible, and she searched for something good-humoured to say, anything.

"It'll be chaos," she said.

"Sounds fantastic," the blond one said. "Calm is so disturbing. What's your name?"

She said her name and blushed.

"They call me Pompe," he said. "Dag's Dag. He may be a little inhibited, but he's a nobleman no less. Personally, I'm more of a plebeian. You're gorgeous."

"What?"

She could barely take it in.

"Gorgeous," he repeated, standing up. For a moment, she thought he was going to put an arm around her waist and kiss her on the cheek, but his grin merely broadened and he made for the bathrooms, leaving her alone with Dag. She felt the urge to flee there and then.

She didn't want to know what he had to say. She was afraid he'd ruin it all, and so she made her excuses and hurried away while the one named Dag thought, I'm more. I'm better. Look at me.

EIGHTEEN

Two things happened at once as Micaela stood in the bathroom having just filled the tub: she felt a stabbing pain in her stomach and her mobile rang. These occurred so simultaneously that for a moment she thought it was the ringtone that had triggered the pain, and she sat down as a cold sweat prickled her face.

Overcome by cramp, she bent double, but it was a temporary crisis. When the phone rang again the worst of it had gone, and she answered with a hello that didn't sound too strained to her own ears.

"What's the matter, sweetheart?" Caspar said. "What's happened?"

"Nothing. Just out of breath."

"Sweetness, it sounds like you're in pain," he said kindly.

She still felt annoyed as she examined her reflection in the bathroom mirror, her teeth gritted. This was hardly her finest moment, but the colour was returning to her face and she was breathing steadily again.

"Nothing to worry about," she said.

"Are you sure about that? You sounded so . . ."

He hesitated, apparently afraid of her reaction, and as if proving him right she replied angrily.

"What?"

"Nothing. Would you like to have dinner with me?" he said.

She softened a little, thinking, of course I would. But the irritation didn't quite leave her, whether it was due to the pain or something else, and she thought back to the call she'd taken not long before on the landline.

"I'm afraid I've been invited to another thing," she said. At the Foreign Minister's house, she was about to say, before catching herself in an act of pure self-preservation.

Rekke and his circle were already a storm cloud in their relationship.

"Oh right, that's a pity. What thing?" Caspar said, clearly trying his best not to sound hurt.

"A reception," she said, and she was about to say something conciliatory or perhaps even change her mind when a fresh wave of pain arrived and she managed to cough up a "Sorry, I've got to hang up. So sorry. Kisses."

She sat down bent double on the toilet seat with her arms across her stomach, before clenching her jaw, taking off the dressing gown and testing the bathwater. It's not warm enough, she thought. I need heat. She got in anyway and drew more hot water while she heard Rekke pacing back and forth in the hall outside. He seemed agitated. And those conclusions he had up his sleeve: E refers to Epsilon in the Greek numeral system, which refers to the Epsilon category in the Huxley novel, blah blah blah. *Déformation professionnelle*, she thought.

It was Rekke who had introduced her to this concept. *Déformation professionnelle* referred to the fact that humankind tended to interpret the world far too much from its own knowledge or experiences, and she wondered whether that was exactly what Rekke was doing. Just because he was so ridiculously well-read didn't mean the killer had to be. On the other hand . . . he might be right. He was right all too often, at least when he wasn't manic. She looked anxiously down at her naked body. Were her boobs bigger than usual?

No, of course not, but she felt self-conscious all the same. She pictured the murderer in her mind's eye, and imagined him standing above his victims staring down at them, and that made her shiver as if she too were the subject of a wicked gaze. But it was probably the pain.

The pain was making her vulnerable. Micaela hugged her knees to her chin, but that didn't help. I can't be pregnant, she thought. That'd be a disaster. But no, that wasn't possible. Besides, surely pregnancy didn't announce itself through pain, unless she was already miscarrying. She opted to ignore it, which worked just fine. Warm water continued to gurgle from the tap, enveloping her, and her thoughts drifted to Caspar and his arms.

Perhaps she should call him and say that she'd like to see him. The Foreign Minister's reception would only make her uncomfortable, especially given how sore she felt. On the contrary, dinner with Caspar might be just the ticket, in place of a snobby event hosted by a toff of a cabinet minister where she'd only feel inferior, like an Epsilon, and that was mostly definitely not only because she was a policewoman in the junior ranks.

Her skin tone played its part, and Micaela looked at her body again almost in irritation, thinking that the only people who looked like her in a neighbourhood like this were the cleaners and couriers. Everyone else was white and stuck-up and looked at her as if she was on her way to unclog the drains and mop the floor. Not to mention Magnus, Rekke's brother. His contempt was almost enough to floor her, and he would definitely be at the reception acting as if he were king of it all. Fuck him. But take it easy, she thought, clutching her hands across her stomach. A new, better age was dawning.

A black man had been elected president of the United States, and perhaps the world was becoming more sensible in spite of itself, and a little less racist. Micaela dunked her head, reached for the shampoo bottle on the edge of the tub and washed her hair. Then she got out of the bath to talk to Rekke about that damn reception.

But first she needed to conceal the pain and worry with make-up, brush her hair and tie it into a tight bun, and straighten her back so it looked like she too was a member of the master race.

NINETEEN

Santander, July 1988

When did he suspect that something was badly wrong? It might have been in Reims.

He and Pompe had dined not far from the cathedral. They shared a bottle of champagne and their conversation was still almost that of equals.

Then Pompe got drunk and more personal, and queried what Dag's disposition was. At first, Dag didn't understand the question. Of course, it was about sex and what he was interested in.

"I don't know," he said, which was by and large true.

Back then, he hadn't got any further than that. He was happy if anyone wanted him—and if he didn't make a complete fool of himself. Pompe wasn't satisfied with that answer.

"Me, I'm a sadist," he said, downing his drink.

"A sadist," Dag said, feeling unsettled and inclined to change the topic. But Pompe wouldn't let up and explained at length that all men were. It was contingent on biology, he said.

"Admit it: you've dreamed of seeing them suffer."

Dag felt diminished by this superior attitude and resolved to get even and not duck the question. To examine himself honestly and unsparingly was, after all, his intellectual virtue. To hold Judgement Day over himself, as Ibsen had put it. Dag paused for thought. Did he want to see women suffer? Was that a part of his sexual fantasies in any way at all? He considered it—he really did—but no matter how much he probed himself he did not find any tendencies of that kind. He wanted to be liked, most of all, admired and loved, but seeing others suffer . . . No, he was much too busy trying not to suffer too much himself.

"I don't think so," he said.

"You're so fucking sanctimonious," Pompe snapped, and Dag already knew enough to know that sanctimonious was the worst thing Pompe could call someone, and he spent the rest of the evening resolving to be tougher.

He almost wanted to say: "Yes, you're right, I want to see women suffer." But he didn't go that far, thank goodness, although he surely said other things he didn't believe and that were solely intended to gain Pompe's approval, and that was one of the insights from that night. Pompe had power over him, especially when Pompe's drunkenness pivoted and became toxic, and after Reims that would happen earlier with each passing day, and that was scary and not just because Pompe was awful. It was infectious—Dag said dreadful things too sometimes, and he began to be afraid, including of himself. He could sense the ticking harbinger of violence, and in Santander the day had started in a worrying fashion.

"I've got to run away," he muttered, looking around the restaurant.

Pompe still hadn't come back and the waitress had vanished as soon as she'd been left alone with Dag, which in itself was a slap in the face that confirmed what he'd been feeling of late: his association with Pompe had made him invisible—or worse, people were uncomfortable in his presence; they avoided him. He bit his lip. No-one sees me, no-one cares.

He fell to self-pity; he couldn't help it. It was maddening, and where on earth was Pompe? Was he having a crafty drink out back? It wouldn't surprise him. Nothing about Pompe surprised him anymore, and for want of anything else to do he leafed through Pompe's copy of *Journey to the End of the Night* and his eye was caught by a sentence about no-one looking as ridiculous as the spectator who has strayed onto the stage.

Was that what he was? A spectator struggling to get into the spotlight, but who only felt stupid once there, because everyone knew that he really belonged in the first row. Once again, Dag watched the waitress and was again absorbed by her face, on the surface so friendly and attentive, but also different, seemingly glowing, as if she had an inner smile, a secret. As long as she wasn't thinking about Pompe. He really did need to warn her, but why would she listen? To a spectator? To a man who had been rendered invisible on Europe's roads?

Why indeed? She'd probably only take such a warning as jealousy, and here was Pompe coming back, drunk and malicious. More than ever, Dag wanted to tell him to get lost. Nevertheless, he smiled stiffly and hunched his shoulders as if to protect himself from attack.

"Do you think I can hit that?" Pompe said, glancing toward the waitress.

Over my dead body, Dag thought, but he said nothing. Instead, he looked down at his hands and wondered whether to ditch Pompe now or whether he should try and speak to the waitress first, no matter how silly he would seem. He had to do something.

TWENTY

It was very trying standing upright in front of the bathroom mirror getting ready, regardless of whether it was for the Foreign Minister or for Caspar. She was hurting so damn much that she applied a little extra makeup to be sure before tightening the cord of Rekke's dressing gown for all she was worth as if to vanquish the pain. Then she held her head high and left the bathroom, bumping into Rekke in the hall. He was clutching the copy of the literary magazine and peering at her intently. What the hell's wrong with you, she wanted to snap.

"What's up?"

"Oh nothing," he said, smiling kindly. "My dressing gown suits you. I like the train behind you. I have the sudden urge to bow."

"On you go then. I may need it."

He performed an absurdly elegant bow that he must have learned in his pianist years.

"Nicely done," Micaela said. "So you've solved the murder, have you?"

Rekke laughed in embarrassment.

"I was overconfident."

"There was a call from the Foreign Minister," she said. "Kleeberger's hosting a reception at his place on Tysta gatan today."

"I know. Shall we go together?"

She thought this over again.

"I think I'll stay at home."

"What a shame for me," he said. "Do you think Kleeberger wants anything in particular?"

"Sounded that way," Micaela said, suddenly contemplating him with equal intensity.

There was a new kind of presence in Rekke that she found unexpectedly attractive.

She felt the urge to do something dramatic.

"Are you in pain?" he said.

"Not at all," she said, disappointed in a way, and she dismissed her impulse.

Don't mess things up, she thought. Instead she asked:

"Is the blond man of letters in Santander still your main lead?"

"I believe so," Rekke said.

"Then I've got one suspect for you due to attend Kleeberger's do," she said.

He took a step closer.

"Capital! Who?"

"None other than Pontus Bremer," she said. "He's a perfect match. Wino. Blond. Clearly a narcissist. Überliterary."

"He does, however, write bombastic depictions of violence. Not at all authentic. *Haec mihi veri similia non videntur.*"

"Could be a cover," Micaela said, wondering whether she should join him for this reception anyway.

After all, she had been invited, and to visit the home of the Foreign Minister on a day like this—Obama's day—to raise a toast to new beginnings would be a grand thing.

She slipped into her room, relieved that she hadn't made a fool of herself with Rekke.

TWENTY-ONE

Santander, July 1988

The one named Dag paid in cash, and the men went off toward the harbour. She stared longingly at the blond man's back. Turn around, she thought, and indeed he did turn and blow a kiss toward her, and she waved in reply and then went back to work, strangely tense, as if something big and important was in motion.

Stop it, she told herself. It's just a date. Or not even that. Just a phrase. A handful of words that mean nothing: *Eight o'clock at La Mar.* He probably won't even come. If he'd meant it then surely he'd have repeated the time and place or checked that she would be there. But he'd simply made that ironic bowing gesture beside the table. No, nothing will come of it, she thought. I won't see him again, and that's just as well—nothing serious would ever come of it. It's best left well alone.

That didn't work, and instead of being realistic about it she began to daydream about a whole new sort of life where she'd have those kinds of conversations about Lorca and world literature all the time, and leave her dull, vacuous existence behind.

Who could blame her? Nothing happened in her life, nothing. And then up popped a figure like him who made the whole city pale by comparison. Please let him come to La Mar tonight, she pleaded. Pretty please let him like me, and let his friend stay at home. She wasn't quite sure why the latter part was so important, but she sensed that he would ruin their encounter. He'd wanted to say something that his friend couldn't be allowed to hear. Maybe she should have listened. There had been such entreaty in his expression, and in another context she would probably have thought him irresistible. He had kind, sad eyes, and a beautiful smile. But she hadn't made an effort to look at him. Her eyes were always drawn to the one named Pompe.

She repeated the name silently to herself, and with a dreamy gaze she watched him disappear toward the harbour as if he owned the city, or stood above it—as if he might at any moment do anything: dance, sing again, yank a flower from the beds lining the sidewalk. Maybe she was attracted to the wrong guy again, but no, she thought. No, there were no parallels with Roberto, none at all. She quickly looked around to check what that idiot was up to.

Roberto was wiping down a table by the windows, and for a moment she studied his muscular body, as if she wanted to glimpse the man who had attracted her not so long ago. But that man was gone, replaced by someone who was not only loathsome, but also dangerous.

The insane assault in the doorway came back to her like a shake to the shoulders and chest, and she made up her mind to ring Señora Delgado who owned the restaurant to tell her that this could go on no longer, she could no longer work under these conditions. I can't go on being afraid, there has to be an end to this. But there was too much to do, and to her left as she raised her gaze she once again saw that weather-beaten man with the silver cross and the guitar.

He looked at her as if he'd known her since childhood, even though she'd never seen him before, and that too made her skin crawl. Stop staring at me, stop staring at my legs, she thought. She longed to be in a place of calm privacy where she could sit and write about her stray.

TWENTY-TWO

Rekke retreated to the kitchen table as Micaela locked the front door from the outside as she left.

He had no idea who she was seeing; he didn't want to be forward and ask. But he'd sensed for some time that she was on her way out, which was of course perfectly natural. She'd been his lodger for four years, and she probably needed to tear herself free. But it still felt sad to him, and he wondered what it was that had happened moments before in the hall. What was that look she'd given him?

She was clearly in pain, and yet—hadn't she looked as if she wanted to wrench him toward her, or at least shake him up? Dash it, he was probably misinterpreting things again, or it was no more than wishful thinking. Rekke looked down at his hand. He was clutching the copy of the *London Review of Books*, and he flipped to page twelve where he read the introduction.

Fragments of Sandra Ramirez's short story had been published in the months following the murder, but at the time they had mostly been titillating and sensational features of the press coverage. No-one seemed to have regarded the short story as a work in its own right, and only now much later had the literary agent Carmen Balcells—under pressure from the girl's old Spanish teacher—taken it on and had it translated alongside a preface by Mario Vargas Llosa.

It transpired that there were three versions of the short story the girl had written during her final day alive. Therefore, it was possible to follow how the narrative had changed by comparing it with the excerpts in the case files, a fact that fascinated Rekke. He thought the process said something material about what had befallen the girl. The elements of magic realism hadn't been present in the original. They had emerged over the day—as had the old oak. That was a late addition, first appearing as a rather ordinary tree, then developing into an increasingly supernatural location the dogs were drawn to. He wondered what had led her down that path.

What was it that had precipitated this creative rush? Nervous and focused, Rekke skipped back and forth from the case file to the short story, and at last he found something. It wasn't much, not much at all. But somehow, it was tied up with Lorca, the Spanish poet. He rose and went into the library to retrieve his copy of the collected poems.

TWENTY-THREE

Santander, July 1988

When Sandra finished for the day, she decided to go to the record shop to listen to the Leonard Cohen take on Lorca. She got no further than the café down by the harbour; the phrases continued to run through her head and she felt compelled to sit down and write. She still had no beginning or end, but the stray dog was becoming ever clearer in her mind, and she sat down at a table closest to the water, feeling the bruises on her calves and at her temple where she'd hit the door frame. Then she opened her journal and wrote:

The Galgo had been kicked and beaten for as long as she could remember, at least as long as she had lacked a name. But now the kicks were such a natural part of her life that she was surprised if they didn't come. Why aren't you hitting me, she would think. Can't you even see me? She ran along the beach where she had once attacked a girl and seen the blood flow . . .

Sandra put down her pen and read through what she had written and wondered whether it held up as an introduction.

Not quite, she thought. It was better than the idea she'd first had, the one with the dogs arriving with the storm. She carried on, writing down the sentences that had come to her at the restaurant, and for some time she was in full flow. Then other things crept in. Not only self-doubt, but also unease. Was someone watching her? She raised her gaze and looked around, almost afraid of what she would discover—of course, it was Roberto she was thinking about, but not only him. There were other things too, less defined, like danger approaching with the fiesta and the people it brought, like that man with the silver cross whose gaze had touched her like a cold hand.

She shook the feeling off—or at least tried to—and ordered a cheese and tomato omelette. She was hungry—famished—and when the food arrived she ate with her left hand while writing with her right, but she was unable to regain her flow. That sense of unease wouldn't leave her. She twisted and turned on her chair, and all of a sudden she heard a man call out her name. The voice sounded both intimate and fearful, and it made her look up.

She couldn't understand where the cry had come from, and no-one made themselves known. There were people everywhere by now, and she saw several men down by the shore, including a young guy in black trousers held up with suspenders, but he and the others all behaved as if nothing had happened, which was weird. Surely you wouldn't call out and then feign ignorance? She wondered if she had misheard, but no, her name had been spoken loud and clear, and she wanted to get away from there. She asked for the bill, left a generous tip and departed with her notebook.

The streets were crowded now. Everywhere there were stalls being built and shutters lowered, and she nodded and smiled at acquaintances, but the anxiety wouldn't let up. Reaching Calle Santa Lucía, she thought about the attack again. It was mad, wasn't it? If Roberto was prepared to do that kind of thing in front of people, what might he do if they were alone? She looked around but saw nothing untoward, except that the whole city now felt threatening.

Was it Roberto who had called out? She didn't think so. Although the voice had been strained, possibly even intentionally distorted, it hadn't sounded like him. Perhaps it hadn't even been a Spaniard. Besides, it didn't make sense psychologically. Roberto was hardly the sort to shout timidly and then scurry away. He would step forward and grab her by the neck or arm. So who was it? The man with the silver cross? No, he didn't know her name. Pompe? No, not him either—he wouldn't hide afterward. He would have sung if he wanted attention, or done whatever the hell he liked. So who was it? Nobody, she concluded. A secret admirer. She smiled at the thought and tried to relax, but she couldn't find peace, and once again she pictured Roberto's stubborn hostility in her mind's eye and realized even more clearly how much the Swedes must have provoked him. They were in every respect his antithesis, and the mere thought that she'd allowed herself to be charmed by them had surely driven him insane.

She picked up the pace, thinking she could discern Roberto's scent, and she had the impression that he was there somewhere, and she decided to take his behaviour seriously, raise the alarm and change jobs. But no matter what she did, she could not turn around and confront him. That would only make it worse. Forward, she thought. Take cover in the record shop, borrow their phone and call Papá. Papá would come and pick her up on the Vespa.

But the temptation was too much and she turned around anyway and there was no Roberto there. It had all been in her imagination, and perhaps it was connected to the short story she was writing. She was becoming like her Galgo, and she felt hunted and abused too, although . . . wait. She drew breath, not sure she was seeing things right.

Ahead of her and slightly to the left was the Swedish man—the one who wasn't Pompe, the one named Dag—and he was looking at her, something wild and threatening in his gaze.

TWENTY-FOUR

I'll regret it if I don't go, Micaela decided, opening her closet and brushing the sleeve of a red H&M blazer that she thought might go with a black shirt and jeans to achieve business casual. She put on the outfit without any great enthusiasm but didn't get far. The pain in her stomach kept her by the closet, and then the phone rang.

"Hello?" she whimpered.

"How are you, my sweet?"

It was Caspar checking up on her.

"Okay."

"You've got me worried," he said. "You never usually—"

"What?" she interjected.

"Sound like that. Whatever's the trouble?"

Whatever's the trouble?

It sounded quaint, and Micaela softened despite the pain and despite the fact that the moment she had emerged from the bathroom and encountered Rekke in the hall had come back to her.

"Just a tummy ache," she said. And it hurts like fuck, she wanted to add, but she refrained from doing so.

"Oh, you poor thing. Are you still going to your party?" said Caspar.

She thought about this.

"I don't know," she said. "I feel kind of paralysed. Sorry if I sounded like a grump."

"That's what happens when it hurts."

Micaela smiled tenderly to herself.

"Thanks," she said. "So, Obama. Big deal, right?"

"For sure," he said. "I just watched his victory speech." Caspar mimicked his voice: "Change has come to America."

"We had a Spanish deputy commissioner around with an old murder case."

"Did you?"

It wasn't always easy to get Caspar interested in their investigations.

"They're looking for a killer who carves different numbers into his victims, as if he's demonstrating that they're no more than cattle to him."

"That's scary."

"And it seems like he murders intellectual women. The girl in Spain wrote . . ."

She felt a stabbing pain in her stomach.

"What did she write?" he said.

"A short story. Look, Caspar. Give me a couple of hours to rest up and I'll look in this evening. I miss you."

"That would be wonderful," he said. "I'll take care of you."

Micaela lay down on the bed, blazer and all, thinking she wouldn't budge an inch for a long time. But then she began to think about the murders and the carved E, and about the Epsilon people at the bottom of the hierarchy, and she dragged herself out of bed and into the kitchen to discuss the investigations with Rekke. He was no longer there, so she sat down and read the files for herself—perhaps mostly to forget how much pain she was in.

TWENTY-FIVE

Santander, July 1988

Dag had been rejected before. He'd encountered the full repertoire in his time, from polite smiles and friendly refusals to guarded comments, being ignored, icy cold, contempt, and harsh words like "get lost"—but this was worse.

The waitress looked afraid, and he felt a wave of humiliation and anger. For the first time, he'd broken free from Pompe's magic power. That should have paid off. Instead, he was seen as a stalker. The girl disappeared into a shop further up the street, and he wanted to kick a window to pieces just like Pompe on a bender. But the mere thought of the comparison made Dag calm down. "Pull yourself together," he muttered, looking the other way.

The place was swarming with people all waiting for the fiesta. It was two o'clock in the afternoon, but it felt later. After their visit to the restaurant, he and Pompe had retraced their footsteps to the parked car, and the walk had been nothing short of abominable. Pompe was in a ridiculously good mood and wouldn't stop talking about how he was going to do the waitress, while Dag wanted nothing more than to be swallowed by the ground beneath him. There was no hint that he would show some courage in the end, but things finally came to a head when Pompe headed for the driver's seat to get behind the wheel.

At first, Dag only meant to protest. The BMW was the most beautiful thing he owned, and Pompe driving it after his liquid breakfast was out of the question. But something changed; it suddenly felt like a rush through his body. He would rather sacrifice the car—his right arm too—than spend another second with Pompe.

"You go, I'll stay," he said.

Pompe didn't seem to understand.

"Are you kidding?"

"See you at the fiesta," Dag said, realising that the decision would not only entail Pompe driving the car back to Laredo but that after countless further drinks he would then drive it back here.

"So you're staying here then?"

Dag nodded.

"Off to a whorehouse, are we?"

The usual malice, but for once it was exactly what Dag needed. A single word of appeal would have made him back down. Now he braced himself against the insult and threw the car keys to Pompe, before beating a retreat from the parking lot, not even turning when Pompe shouted:

"Come on, stop messing around."

He simply shrugged and went on his way with determined footsteps, consumed by the feeling that he had won a battle. "Damn it," he muttered, thinking that the sky had brightened. He was even happy to be rid of the car. Fuck it, he thought, feeling unexpectedly relieved, as if the Beemer had been a burden all along.

It was good to be done with it. Let Pompe damn well crash it—what difference did it make to him? At last I'm free, but first . . .

He'd spotted the waitress ahead of him, her lips forming secret words. Without her, he would never have been so foolish. Without her, he would simply have got into the car next to Pompe and become even more suffocated and depressed.

That was why he'd gone back to the restaurant and resolved to make a fresh attempt at being seen. But then dejection had seeped back in and he'd thought bitterly, it doesn't matter whether I'm rid of Pompe, I still have to drag myself around, and he never dared to step up. There were too many people in the restaurant, and instead of making himself known he walked about the town looking in the shops. When he returned, he could no longer see her.

She was gone, and he decided to head for the railway station and get out. He'd leave it all behind: Pompe, the car, everything. Then he caught sight of her. She was in a café down by the harbour writing in a blue notebook, and he walked toward her before hesitating. To disturb her felt like a crime. She seemed so completely absorbed that he simply stopped and watched her right hand moving eagerly across the paper. What was she writing? The same words she had been muttering in the restaurant? He wanted to know—and perhaps help—and suddenly he called out her name. It was neither loud nor discreet, but more the act of a man who didn't know what he wanted, and he consequently took a couple of steps to one side as she raised her gaze.

He hid behind a couple of red barrels and let her disappear again, and now, not long after, he was standing in the street not far from the record shop she'd fled into. He felt angry and humiliated—but he didn't know what to do with his anger. It was one of those moments when every single tiny impulse might send him the right or wrong way, and by chance the madman from the restaurant appeared, coming along the sidewalk radiating the same hostility as when he'd attacked the waitress, and that spark became the ignition point.

Dag rushed toward the man with a fury that would have startled him had he seen it from the outside.

TWENTY-SIX

Rekke returned to the kitchen to find Micaela there, having changed into a red blazer and black shirt. He was touched to see her reading the Spanish case file.

Their best moments together had been spent investigating crimes. But he was also possessed by a melancholy feeling as if it were the last time she would be sitting in his kitchen.

"Find anything interesting?" he said.

She looked up and he noted the same strained expression and slightly bent posture she'd had earlier.

"This Roberto Ortega guy was lying during questioning," she said.

Rekke sat down opposite her.

"Is that so?" he said. "The good Deputy Commissioner was so certain that it was the right decision to let him go."

"And it may have been, but he wasn't telling the truth."

Rekke examined Micaela's hands.

"In what way?" he said.

"Roberto had been in a fight earlier that day, but he claimed not to know who it was with. I don't believe that."

"Why not?" Rekke said.

"There are witnesses to the argument—not the fight itself, but its origins. He claimed some tourist flew off the handle at him and went nuts. The tourist—a young foreign male—fled down an alley and Roberto gave chase, but no-one saw what happened after that and I don't buy Roberto's explanation."

"What did he say?"

"It's not credible that he was attacked for no reason."

"And he'd never laid eyes on the tourist before?"

"No, that's his claim. And they pushed him hard on that. The interrogator wanted to know if the fight had anything to do with Sandra, but he denied that outright. All he'd say was that it was some idiot picking a fight, and that the idiot in question was a Dutchman, or a German, and there was something weird about his lips, as if he had a harelip."

"A harelip?"

"He was oddly unspecific, and I don't know whether we can rely on that either. It's as if he offered up the first characteristic he could think of, and no-one else mentioned anything unusual about the guy's lip. There's something missing in this account."

Good work, Micaela, Rekke thought. Good work.

"And you saw that right away. I doff my cap to you," he said, performing another bow as he sat down.

He noticed her pupils were dilating.

"Did you read the girl's story?" he said.

She nodded.

"Quite striking, don't you think?"

"Truly. Do you think she was depressed?" said Micaela.

He shook his head.

"Quite the contrary. It takes distance from grief to describe it so well."

Rekke glanced at Micaela's blazer and shirt again.

"You're coming to Kleeberger's after all, then?" he said.

"Thinking about it," she said. "Stina Jonsdotter invited me too—improbable as that may seem."

He beamed.

"Well, what's the problem then?"

"It's just that I can't be bothered with your damn brother."

"Who can be bothered with Magnus? Why don't we deal with him together?" Rekke said, smiling at her.

Then he leaned forward and snatched the papers from the case file Micaela had been reading and became engrossed in them for a brief while before he finally stood up and went to his bedroom and also perused his closet.

But most of all, he was thinking about Sandra Ramirez and the Lorca-inspired lyrics that she'd listened to twenty years ago, presumably at around the same time as Roberto Ortega had been fighting with an unidentified man nearby.

TWENTY-SEVEN

Santander, July 1988

Sandra stepped into the record shop, but not with the same expectant energy she had anticipated. The walk here had riled her up, and she was thinking about the man named Dag. What had he wanted, and what was it she'd seen in his gaze? Something threatening? No, she thought. Perhaps all he wanted was to make contact.

"Well, hello there!"

She turned around. It was Toni, who had worked in the shop for as long as she could remember and who still seemed to be not a day over thirty with his boyish face and his long curly rock star hair that fell down over his dark eyes. Toni was known throughout the city as an encyclopaedia of pop music. Granted, there were whispers that he was a creep—that he stole birds' eggs and groped little girls in the shop's listening booth—but she figured it was mostly bullshit, and she felt safe in here. Toni wore a black T-shirt emblazoned with the word *Genesis* and dark skinny jeans.

“Can I help you?” he said.

“Yes, maybe,” she said. “But first . . .”

She didn’t even finish her sentence, taking a step back toward the door, even more convinced that Dag hadn’t meant her any harm.

He’d been nothing but sweet at the restaurant and had been about to tell her something. Perhaps she should hear what? Maybe she might be able to ferret out something about Pompe too.

“Won’t be a moment,” she said, and just then she heard a bang, a crash and a cry outside in the street.

From where she was standing, it didn’t seem especially alarming. That was why she hesitated, and that was why she missed crucial parts of the drama.

“What’s going on?” said Toni.

“I don’t know,” she said, stepping outside. At first she saw nothing—except that there was some ruckus and that people were standing still and watching.

For a moment she thought there was blood running down the gutter, then she realized it was red wine. Further down, opposite Cadelo, the restaurant in which her friend Ana worked at the weekends, there were shattered wine bottles lying on the ground—some ten or twenty. Immediately in front of them there was a truck with its rear doors open.

In the midst of the confusion there were two men, both burly and red-faced. One was bending down to prevent unbroken bottles from rolling away, while the other—with a huge belly—was standing in a lopsided, contorted position while bellowing toward the nearby alley: “I’ll kill you, you little shits.”

He shook his fist, but didn’t give chase, settling instead for shouting and gesticulating. Then he bent too and perhaps he looked afraid, as if the people he’d been roaring at were dangerous.

Should she ask what had happened? The same impulse that had made her give Dag the slip made her refrain now, and she turned to Toni, who had followed her outside.

"What happened?" he said.

She pointed to the devastation.

"Clumsy assholes," he said. "But they'll make quick work of it. The alkies can lick up the rest."

She smiled as if this were funny and then went back into the shop with him, wrapped up in anxious thoughts, although she soon pulled herself together. The fiesta was starting soon, more wine bottles would be smashed, and now she asked in a more lighthearted tone whether he had Leonard Cohen's new record, *I'm Your Man*.

"Now that's an album," he said, pleased by the question. "Came out in February. Want to have a listen?"

"Only to one song, actually. It's named 'Take This Waltz' and it's based on a Lorca poem."

Toni let out a low whistle and then went to flip through the records filed under the letter C before returning with a black-and-white sleeve with a picture of a man in his forties wearing a pin-striped suit. The man was eating a banana, which shone like a yellow emblem.

"Use number two," Toni said, extracting the vinyl record with his customary care before putting it on the turntable by the counter while she went into the number two listening booth, which was slightly bigger than the other one and had dusty grey curtains and a Freddie Mercury poster on the wall.

She put on the headphones that were hanging on a hook on the wall that was coming loose and then she waited. There was a crackle and then she heard an instrument she couldn't identify. Then came the melody. Cohen began to sing, but it all went too quickly for her—or perhaps she was drawn in by the music and could only make out the occasional lyric. As for what fascinating quip she would make about it, she was none the wiser. But then two lines captured her imagination. She saw a dark place where the men had stopped talking and were staring mutely into their glasses, and a waitress—perhaps it was her—was putting chairs on tables and trying to get the men to go home, but all of them merely looked back at her with the same vacant eyes. The vision triggered her imagination, and she wondered whether she might use it in her short story, although she wasn't sure where it would fit, and before long the song was over and she stood there confused.

Then she emerged and asked Toni to put it on a second time, and that was when she heard the line that gave her the end to her story, and which might have cost her her life.

TWENTY-EIGHT

Numbskulls, Micaela thought. This investigation raised far too many questions and there were way too many lousy witnesses. For example, whom had Roberto Ortega fought?

His opponent had emerged from the alleyway off the Calle Santa Lucía in Santander with his hands in front of his face before vanishing, according to detectives. But surely that couldn't be true? Fights were like stones thrown into water. They caused ripples. Two dramatic events in the same place were often linked, and here was something unresolved—especially the peculiar fact that the murder-victim-to-be had been close by and had seen the aftermath of the fight. There had to be a connection, Micaela thought as she read on. Then she stopped to listen, leaning forward with her head in her hands.

In the living room, Rekke was playing the piano, but it wasn't Chopin, Liszt, Beethoven, Schubert, Ravel or any other of his household deities. Instead, it was a melancholy piece, searching for something in its own way, and she stood up, placing a hand on her aching stomach. What should she do? She'd had an ambitious plan to attend the Minister's cocktail party and then head over to Caspar's and fall into his arms. But now she wasn't sure, and she went into the living room. Rekke stopped playing. He'd changed into black trousers, a white shirt and a grey checked jacket.

"What are you doing?" she said.

He turned to her with an amused smile.

"That is the question," he said. "But for a moment just now, I thought that somewhere among these keys there was the most beautiful melody that could ever be written."

Micaela giggled.

"I suppose it could be."

"But it's hidden in the labyrinth of infinity."

"I'm sure you'll find it if you stay here for another thousand years."

"Like the monkey hammering away on a typewriter for all eternity."

She moved closer.

"But what about when you find it? What will you do then?"

Rekke glanced at her playfully.

"I anticipate that I shall use it to stop all war. I can picture the scene now. People involved in the most murderous of activities, who have lost all decency, but suddenly they hear something—faintly at first—then louder, and then they stop fighting and become amazed, moved. You really are in pain."

"What?"

"You're leaning forward ever so slightly, your jaw is clenched, and your eyes are shiny."

"It's nothing to worry about," she said.

"Are you sure?"

"I'll gladly tag along to Kleeberger's for a little while, if that's what you've got all dressed up for."

His face lit up and he played a fanfare on the grand piano, perhaps not the most beautiful melody that could ever be written, but still a piece in an exuberant major key, and Micaela heard herself laughing and wondered whether she should bow to him as he had to her. She settled for saying:

"You'll have to protect me from your horrible brother."

"With my life."

Don't hurt yourself, she thought, before going into her room and putting on a pair of red high heels that she'd bought in Åhléns a couple of years ago but almost never worn. Then she heard the storm outside, took them off and put them in a plastic carrier bag, before gazing at the blizzard lashing around the street below. Perhaps her stomach felt better? Micaela decided it did. This was going to be a good day, she decided, and she lingered in front of the mirror by the door smiling at herself, as if to confirm that everything was now A-okay.

When she returned from her room, Rekke was no longer at the piano. He'd gone into his study and was deeply lost in thought in front of the computer with his jacket sleeves carelessly rolled up, and once again she studied his lanky figure.

"What are you doing?" she said.

"Giving some more consideration to the scene of the crime," he said without turning to her. His left leg was twitching.

"The old oak?"

"There's something significant about it."

Micaela looked down at her black socks, which were distressingly washed out.

"That's putting it mildly. The girl wrote about the tree and then got murdered there, of all places."

"It's strange," he said.

"She must have been there before."

"Yes, as a child. And probably later in life too."

"How autobiographical do you think the short story is?" she said.

"Fairly," said Rekke. "She's obviously been beaten and felt

abandoned, like the Galgo. But she also took inspiration elsewhere. Did you read the bit about her asking about a Leonard Cohen song in that record shop?"

Micaela nodded.

"And in that song—which is based on a Lorca poem—there's an interesting line about a tree, which might well have spoken to her. By the way, I think I forgot to compliment you on the jacket and blouse. But if I may . . ."

He stood up and smoothed out some wrinkles on the back of the blazer. She felt self-conscious.

"Is it business casual?"

"It's splendid. Did you have time to take a look at the literary Swede?"

Micaela looked out of the window.

"We're going to have to dress like we're climbing Everest," she said. "I haven't found anything yet, but there wasn't exactly a shortage of other things to look at. I think the guy in the record shop is sketchy—and he has a record. Anyway, what do you say? Time we were off? I'm not going to stay at Kleeberger's for long."

"We'll be in and out," said Rekke, linking arms with her.

TWENTY-NINE

Santander, July 1988

Dag fought as if he'd never done anything else, aided by an old reminiscence. Admittedly, it had been so long ago it hardly counted. It had been during middle school in Solna. But the muscle memory was there. It had happened on the compacted pile of snow shovelled together by the diggers in the playground; the boys would fight for their moment of triumph on the summit, beating their chests and yelling:

"King of the hill!"

Dag had been one of the youngest boys there—possibly also one of the most vulnerable since his father was a celebrity—and he generally got beaten up or had snow rubbed in his face. Nevertheless, he wanted in. It was masochism, to some extent. There was a self-pitying sweetness to taking the beatings, but most of all he wanted to show that he wasn't soft—and to his surprise, he wasn't at all. He rose in stature by that hill and fought with an abandon that left him both surprised and proud, and not infrequently—until the teachers put an end to it—he would end up on top of the mound of snow, kicking down all who approached.

Looking back, he could never square it with the rest of his character. But sometimes, like now, when he needed to summon strength, he would draw on that memory, although not just that. Pompe's barbs also sprang to mind, what had happened in La Rochelle, the attack on Sandra at the restaurant, all sorts of things, and from the very first moment he fought like a madman. He shoved the waiter.

"I saw what you did to her, you bastard," he hissed.

The guy began to throw punches right away and Dag fought back, and somewhere inside himself he knew that was exactly what he needed. There and then, he didn't care about the man's physical superiority, and he cared even less about the mess they were making around themselves as the men hauled boxes out of a truck. All Dag cared about was his anger, his sudden anger at his whole life, which was why he barely reacted when the waiter tripped over the men with their cases of wine and everything on the street came to a halt, while he just stood there ominously above the man.

"You leave her alone," he said, and he almost had time to feel proud of himself for being king of the hill again before the scene changed.

The waiter leapt up, out of his mind. Dag could feel it physically. The blood rushed from his upper body into his legs and he fled down an alley that stank of piss and booze and he meant to keep running. No-one on Earth would be able to catch up with him. But the alley terminated in a mottled gold wall covered in graffiti, and he looked in every direction, desperately searching for any way out and he was about to run back when he found the man before him, fists raised and teeth bared, and it seemed completely incomprehensible that Dag had actually attacked him. He didn't stand a chance.

"I'm just saying that you should leave her alone," Dag stuttered, wondering whether to try pushing past him.

"Why you care?" the man shouted in broken English, taking a rapid step toward him and shoving him violently against the wall, and afterward Dag could barely describe what had happened.

The world seemed to fade away and he fought for all he was worth, in no doubt about his physical inferiority. But he remained upright for a long time, intoxicated by the desire to cause harm and perhaps even to kill. Dag really did hate this man—and not only him. In a way, he was also pummeling Pompe in his mind, and he aimed kicks at throat and crotch until he slumped down against the wall without any sense of his own injuries. All he knew was that it was over. People from the street were approaching and the waiter made himself scarce. Only then did Dag notice how hot it had become.

The sun was high in the sky and close by he could hear rapid, shallow panting that sounded like that of an animal, but he was too dazed to be afraid. He squinted up, his gaze clouded. A lean stray dog was standing there looking at him, and then it squeezed through a hole in the wall Dag hadn't seen but which was too small for him. Otherwise he would have liked to follow it.

A feeling of shame washed over him, and with the shame came the pain—in his head, in his stomach, his cheeks and lips. "Shit," he muttered. There were footsteps approaching and someone shouting in Spanish. Dag definitely didn't want help.

He wanted to get away from there, to be alone. He felt humiliated, not only by the man who had beaten him but also by Sandra who had looked at him in fear, and in that moment he remembered what Pompe had said: "Admit it: you've dreamed of seeing them suffer." Maybe there was some truth to it, after all.

Then he got to his feet and emerged from the alley with his head bowed and his hands over his face.

THIRTY

Santander, July 1988

Sandra pulled back the curtain and told Toni to play the song yet again. She sat hunched forward on the stool in the booth waiting for Cohen's line about the tree, and when it came she misheard it through some twist of fate. She interpreted the word *doves* as *dogs*, which was hardly surprising given her own preoccupation.

A tree where dogs went to die? She shuddered. Right there, in the booth beneath the poster of Freddie Mercury and with Toni in the black Genesis T-shirt suspiciously close to the other side of the curtain, she knew how the short story would begin and end.

The Galgo would get sick and no longer care about the beatings, or even about finding food. The dog would make its way to the hill and find a place to die, a tree, like in the song. A sad, majestic tree, she thought. One the dog had seen before. Because in that moment she realized which tree it was.

She'd been there as a girl and carved her name into the trunk. But she didn't know if it was still there—tree or engraving—and she wondered whether to go there at once and find details to put into her story, something precise and beautiful about the branches or the trunk, and to get help to draw that powerful feeling the tree had evoked in her as a child. Then she decided to forget about it. Everything was different as a grown-up. The magic disappeared and the tree might not even be there any longer.

Perhaps all that would be left was a stump—a mouldering piece of wood in the ground. No, she thought. Best to stick to memory, and she thought about Mamá who had been with her that day at the oak. It must have been before Sandra was bitten. It felt that way from the light itself in her memory; she'd drunk juice from a flask, and in the distance she'd seen a man running, more as if he were fleeing something than working out, and it lent the memory an anxiety, a charge. But now she wasn't sure what she'd actually seen, and now the song was over once again and she didn't have anything to say about it except that it contained a line about a tree.

"Sorry, Toni!" she called out. "One more time," and then it came on again, and now she heard the full lyrics, which were about Vienna, so she gathered.

There were ten beautiful women in Vienna, a Viennese concert hall, a hall where love had never been, a shoulder where death would rest, and all sorts. And the singer—the voice of the poem—was sick. It really was beautiful, but all she could think of was her tree and her short story. That was why she removed the headphones and emerged back into the shop. Toni stared at her breasts and blinked as if spasming.

"You going to buy it then, or what? You can get the song as a single," he said. "I've still got a couple of copies left."

"Can't afford it."

He looked at her sceptically.

"You work all the time."

"I'm quitting," she said, a little taken aback at herself, but she realized at once that what she had said was true.

She couldn't stay at the restaurant, and the moment she had that thought, she became more forgiving of Dag. He wasn't the one who had upset her. It was Roberto who had scared her, and she made up her mind to go out and try and find the Swede—if only to find out more about his pal, Pompe. She said goodbye to Toni and stepped outside, only to become immediately aware of what she had just seen in the street. The burly men were still there dealing with the bottles, and she looked around anxiously. Further away, she spotted one of Mamá's friends, Elena.

Elena wore a white hat and blue blouse with epaulettes. Sandra walked toward her. Elena worked in the pharmacy and often exuded suspicion—as if she suspected everyone was out to trick her into handing over pills they hadn't been prescribed. But right now her expression was completely neutral, and she seemed younger.

"Sandra, I was just thinking about you," she said.

"Were you?"

"I've just seen José Ortega's eldest—that horrible boy."

"Roberto," she said.

"Yes, Roberto. He looked like he'd taken one heck of a beating."

"What do you mean?" Sandra said, not really understanding. Roberto wasn't the one who took a beating, he was the one who meted it out.

"He was bleeding from the mouth," Elena said.

Sandra asked whether Elena knew any more, but she'd only just got there and couldn't tell her anything else except that Roberto had been clutching his knuckles and had gone down toward the Plaza de Cañadio.

"I daresay he deserved it," she said. "I've heard such terrible stories about that boy—including what he did to you. Your mother told me. Oh Sandra, my dear, what's the matter? You look completely—"

"It's fine," she interrupted. "I agree. He deserved it."

It's just that someone will have to pay, she thought, and she nodded to Elena before setting off in the opposite direction, toward the Calle Lope de Vega. Once she had moved away, her thoughts returned to Dag. She wondered if he'd had anything to do with the fight—after all, he'd reacted so vehemently to Roberto's attack on her. Perhaps she had misjudged him, but no, it didn't add up. Dag couldn't have given Roberto a whipping; it was impossible. She would have to drop it until she knew more. Instead, she fantasized about the tree and her Galgo. Perhaps she could go to the oak later tonight—if it was still there—and write the final lines in situ, because surely it was at dusk that the dog would die, or perhaps by night as the stars shone and the fiesta unfolded in the city below.

She could ask Pompe about it when they met later, and seek his advice on the plot. Perhaps they could discuss the ending. She knew, of course, that she was letting herself get carried away. But she couldn't help it, and she picked up her journal and read her most recent sentence. *The attack on the girl led not to the liberation the Galgo had hoped for, but only to a gnawing sense of damnation and loneliness.*

Not bad, but now she needed a new beginning and a life story for the dog to have forgotten so that it could be recalled on its final day alive. Yes, that was exactly how it would go, she thought, deciding to head for the library on the Ruiz de Alda to finish her story there. But in the end, her eagerness was so great that she sat down at a sidewalk café table without noticing that there were eyes watching her.

THIRTY-ONE

It might only have been early November, but it felt like the middle of January. The wind was whipping in sideways, and Micaela was shivering and her stomach ached and she was annoyed with Rekke. There was something off about him; he was walking with his coat open and his arms spread as if trying to embrace the blizzard.

When a truck drove too close to them outside the French embassy on Narvavägen and spattered him in slush, he merely shook his head and theatrically muttered a couple of words in Latin.

"Are you alright?" Micaela said.

"Quite alright," he said, peering down cheerfully at his sodden trousers.

"Why do we live in this frightful country?" she said.

"We want to be tormented," Rekke said, grinning like a child, and she had the impression he was exaggerating and maybe feverish, but she let him be and focused on hugging her quilted jacket even closer while she proceeded forward bent double against the wind.

Not long afterward, they reached Karlavägen and turned right and then left onto Tysta gatan, a quiet and secluded street for the rich who preferred not to lounge about down on Strandvägen, but still wanted to demonstrate that they'd chosen their address with care, and Micaela hardly needed to seek out the right door.

On a stone step illuminated by the flickering glow of lanterns leading up to the front door of a recently renovated building she spotted the Security Service personnel and regular coppers—who were all conspicuously freezing—although not to the same extent as the young woman clutching the guest list. Her gloves were much too thin and she'd not even had the sense to put on a hat, presumably so as to avoid ruining her recently coiffed curls. The woman recognized Rekke and ticked the two of them off the list.

"Your brother hasn't arrived yet," she said.

"Capital," he said. "Best if you don't let him in at all."

The woman laughed as if this were the funniest thing she had ever heard, and then they took the elevator to the fourth floor and passed by two more security heavies before entering a large apartment that was furnished in a somewhat antiquated style with expensive works of art adorning the walls. It was already crowded inside, and there was an ample cohort of white-coated servers carrying trays of canapés and champagne. Micaela had barely had time to put on her high heels and snatch a glass before a fair-haired woman in her forties approached them and exclaimed with equal parts amusement and annoyance:

"That man touched my bottom!"

"I'm sorry," Rekke said, turning in the direction the woman was pointing to see none other than Pontus Bremer towering above all the others with his shock of blond hair, his loud voice cutting through the hubbub.

"No, no," he was saying. "When intellectuals flirt with party politics then they should be warded off with a cat-o'-nine-tails. The very point is that we're free and can say whatever we like."

"But for goodness' sake, surely that doesn't mean you need to sound off whenever you like," said an elderly woman next to Bremer, whereupon the group around him burst into laughter and the woman by Rekke and Micaela, who was wearing a shimmering blue, close-fitting dress and had beautiful blue eyes, also giggled.

"Well," she said. "I suppose I'll have to consider it an honour. Have you seen his play at the Royal Dramatic?"

"No, not yet," said Rekke.

"Well, I daresay there's no rush, either. It's caused such a stir that it'll no doubt run and run. You're Professor Rekke, aren't you?" the woman said, and Micaela reflected that in this company, at least, her rear was quite safe given that this killjoy would never do anything inappropriate.

"Alas I am," Rekke said. "And this is my good friend, Micaela Vargas, another free thinker. And you work in the world of finance, do you not?"

"What?!" the woman said with a laugh. "How do you know?"

"Tone of voice, attire, spirit and then of course there is the bracelet with the dollar sign. Sophisticated, yet ever so slightly vulgar chic. I imagine you've done quite well out of the financial crisis."

"I confess: I'm a hedge fund manager. Downturns are often my best friends, but there are people I know . . . It's so tragic. Don't remind me. Might I be so bold as to request a favour, Professor?"

"Naturally," he said.

"Could you and your sharp wits go over to Pontus Bremer and say something devastating. Avenge me."

Micaela felt lost, looking for a way to join the conversation.

"He won't be able to do that—he's much too polite," she said.

The woman glanced at Rekke in amusement.

"Is that true?"

"*Comitas onerosa est.* Courtesy may occasionally impede the bandying of words, although they tend to flow more easily with the impudent."

"Pontus Bremer is impudence personified. And just take a look at his haircut. Meticulously tousled to within an inch of its life."

"Now, now," said Rekke. "I like the tweed jacket and the red trousers, and I must admit that he has given us a couple of classics, as well as a couple of refreshing cultural brouhahas. But I shall see what I can do. I have another matter to discuss with him. It was a pleasure speaking with you, Mrs . . ."

"Odelbäck. Renée. I'm one of your brother's advisors, I suppose you might say. On matters financial."

"Well then, I hope you give him some bad advice."

"I'll have him bankrupt the exchequer if you can take Pontus Bremer down a peg or two."

Rekke smiled, and he and Micaela proceeded onward together but they didn't get far. Ambassador so-and-so wanted to greet him, and Rekke had a reply for everyone. "Oh, you've just been in Egypt," he said to a bald man in a brown jacket, before making an almost incomprehensible observation to which the guy responded with a laugh, seeming enlivened. But Micaela still thought Rekke was being over the top. Then Kleeberger himself appeared. The Minister really had taken the business casual thing seriously and wore a red cashmere sweater with a hole at the elbow.

"Hans," he said. "I'm delighted you could make it." He turned to the staff behind him. "Do be sure to top up these glasses—I don't want any downcast faces here." He lowered his voice. "Magnus did have a matter he wished to trouble you with—if he deigns to put in an appearance."

"I suspected as much," said Rekke. "You do know Micaela, don't you?"

Kleeberger turned toward her and offered a hand with a twinkle in his eye.

"I don't believe we've had the pleasure," he said. "But naturally one hears the dispatches. A charming girl—quick-witted too. The work you're doing out in the suburbs—most important."

"Thank you; it's an honour to be here," she said, feeling stupid.

"The honour is all mine," Kleeberger said. "Hans, I wonder if we might talk shop later. I fear Magnus may once again have led me up the garden path."

Rekke laughed.

"Surely not? Although I expect he's made himself indispensable to you, Mats."

Kleeberger pulled a face.

"Yes, unfortunately so. What an incorrigible man."

"What does he want?"

"He'll have to tell you that himself, and of course you may do as you please, Hans. It's really none of my business. By the by, I saw you bump into Renée Odelbäck. Confound her too! I think she's managed to persuade Magnus to play the markets, and it's going to make us all look bad. Hang it all, it's time to get this party started. Hans . . . it shames me to ask . . ."

The Minister of Foreign Affairs peered down into his champagne glass.

"But apparently you are doing so nonetheless?"

"Well, yes. If you wouldn't mind playing something beautiful by Beethoven or Schubert—or whoever—so that we can drown out Pontus Bremer and those other loudmouths and create a bit of reverence in here for a change. I've had it tuned and everything. You can send your bill to the Ministry."

"Ha!" Rekke said, putting a hand on Kleeberger's shoulder

and then heading toward the famous author in the living room while Micaela glanced back.

She shouldn't have, because at that moment Magnus Rekke came through the front door in a black coat covered in snow which he handed to one of the girls as he signalled for champagne, and quickly. His cheeks were rosy and his eyes glazed as if he'd already had enough to drink.

His smile was manifestly satisfied, and it was at once obvious to all that he was important. Guests came to attention in front of him, much as they did with Kleeberger. Magnus barely noticed them. Instead, to Micaela's surprise he fixed his gaze on her.

At first she thought she must be mistaken. There's someone behind me, she deduced. A minister. Some hotshot. To Magnus, she was an Epsilon. But now he was approaching her, and she resolved to be steely. Don't give him a fucking thing, she told herself. Not even a smile. Nada.

"Micaela, you're looking radiant," he said. "You should wear a nice jacket like that more often. It suits you." He insolently pulled it open by the lapel to reveal the H&M label inside. "Well, blow me down—and I've been shelling out a fortune on my suits. Mind you, it's good that you're pitching in to keep the Bangladeshi child labourers busy."

"What do you want?"

"Nothing. I just happen to think that you and I should be on better terms," he said, and for a brief moment she thought that was really what had brought him over—that he wanted her on his side in some conflict he intended to embark upon with his brother.

"Say what you have to say or leave me alone."

But when he let it drop it hit her like a ton of bricks and she found herself struggling to breathe.

THIRTY-TWO

Santander, July 1988

Dag could only see the city through the cracks between his fingers. But despite the aches and pains in his body, he quickly stepped into the street and turned left—away from the crowd. His abdomen and chest hurt, and his mouth and brow were bleeding. But most of all, there was a sense of humiliation roaring through him. He'd fought for her, practically risked his life for her, and for what? Nothing, he thought.

It was so unfair. My God . . . He could barely walk so he slowed down. He was thirsty and dizzy and he staggered down toward the harbour until he reached a fountain with a tap beside it and he drank at length, feeling the small basin in front of the fountain itself drawing him into it.

A moment later, he dipped his head into it, and it wasn't anything like he expected—the sun had warmed the water and dirt got into his eyes. But as he rinsed his face and his blood swirled into the pool, he came to life. The whole day came back to him in a scattergun series of images, and as he raised his head, which was now soaked down to his shirt collar, the world around him no longer looked as hostile. It suddenly seemed possible to get through the day, and he smoothed down his hair and wiped his cheeks and eyes and felt amidst all the pain and disappointment a sense of relief at being free of Pompe. It was as if he had rid himself of a burden, a toxin in his body, and he tried smiling at a little girl holding a balloon and eating an ice cream beside the fountain, which went surprisingly well.

His cheeks didn't tense like before; that was one of the discoveries he'd made in the last week with Pompe. Everything became heavy. Talking was heavy, walking was heavy, and he was disinclined to smile.

Much later on, he would identify this as a symptom of depression. But back then, it was as if Pompe himself had settled into his body, and as he walked back toward the city centre he felt cautiously hopeful and thought about Sandra again without the earlier bitterness. And just what did he have to be ashamed of? Nothing.

He'd fought with a man who was stronger and more brutal, and who should have crushed him, and he'd done it for a young woman who perhaps didn't even want to be acquainted with him. That was a big deal, right? Perhaps even somewhat heroic. He decided it was, and felt a thirst that could only be quenched with beer—it had been a long time since he'd felt that. Pompe had deprived him of that joy, and he proceeded to look for a charming open-air bar, unwittingly taking the same route back. Suddenly, he realized he was passing the alley that had been the scene of his battle.

He became intensely nervous but quickly calmed down. Normality had returned to the street, and most of the shards of glass had been swept up. He became absorbed in his thoughts. Should he buy a notebook and sit down to write too? Perhaps it would open the floodgates? Language had been his enemy of late. He'd become stuck on phrasing and linguistic detail. It had been as if he were dreaming of a style he was incapable of realising.

But now he had something to tell, and perhaps he might flee his compulsive nature. Ahead of him in the street he saw a slight man with long black hair and skinny legs who was staring suspiciously at something. He was perhaps thirty-five years old and rather shabby-looking, to Dag's eyes. There were rings on his fingers and he wore a black top emblazoned with the word *Genesis*. Dag passed him, silently branding him a weirdo without quite understanding why. A moment later, his heart was in his mouth.

On a chair by the sidewalk, he spotted a slender back that he immediately recognized. The waitress was hunched over a book lying on a small round table, and her hand was clutching a pen, but it wasn't writing. She seemed to be thinking, and although Dag felt the uneasiness return, he realized he couldn't let this opportunity slip through his fingers.

He had to repair the situation, he told himself as he went over—fortified by his fight and the water he'd splashed over his face, and perhaps by that shabby guy too, as if Dag saw it as his duty to protect her from all creeps.

"Sorry to bother you," he said.

She turned and looked at him, not in horror as she had done earlier in the street, but rather in astonishment. He continued in a rather awkward way:

"I'm sorry for scaring you before. There was something I wanted to say. I—"

"What's happened? You're bleeding," she said, cutting him off.

He put a hand to his lip.

"I don't think he should be allowed to knock you around like that."

"Have you been fighting with Roberto?"

He nodded and her eyes widened, and he looked at her and

could feel how incredibly fragile that moment was. The slightest critical glance from her and he would lose it. His whole body was screaming out for recognition.

"All I said to him was that he shouldn't hit you," he said. "He lost his shit."

"Oh my God," she said.

She stared at him in even greater amazement.

"Yeah, it was pretty crazy," he said, touching his ear and cheek and hoping for a smile, or perhaps even an outstretched hand. But she remained wary and his body tensed.

"Are you hurt?"

Her voice sounded uncertain.

"A little," he said, suppressing the impulse to tell her all the places that hurt. "What are you writing?"

She gave him a look that was difficult to interpret.

"Is it really true?" she said. "Did you fight him?"

"It's true."

"And did he say anything afterward, or . . . ?"

"No, he simply left. I gave pretty much as good as I got."

"Damn."

He looked down at the table, not sure what to say.

"Is it a story?" he said.

She closed the book.

"Yes," she said after a moment's hesitation. "It's about a Galgo."

"A what?"

"A dog," she said. "A very tormented dog that flees into the hills to die."

"Cool," he said, grateful for the information, and with a vague and irrational sense of identifying with the dog in question. "Do you mind if I sit down?" he said, and she nodded and he took a deep breath and smiled without his cheeks tightening.

THIRTY-THREE

It's fortunate I'm so damn talented, Pontus Bremer thought. He had no idea what he was going to say—and he loved it.

He tended to fling a few provocative words out there, any old ones at all, certain that he would be able to follow up with an argument and dazzle people as he muddled through, and in the event that anyone identified a hole in his rationale he would deploy self-deprecation, a wild association, an obscure literary reference or a risqué intimation and emerge triumphant nonetheless. He crushed them with his brilliance and his lack of inhibition, and it really didn't matter whether they were pretentious novelists, bean counters or, as was the case here, Foreign Office fops with their slicked-back hair. He outshone them all.

"So you think Obama is going to fail," said a pert woman beside him.

"Exactly," he said. "He's much too good of a writer."

"What are you getting at?"

"It's quite straightforward," said Pontus Bremer, cocking his head to one side—one of his classic moves—and quickly trying to work out why it was quite straightforward. "You see," he said, raising his voice, "I read the book about his father—well, the absence of his father—and it was brilliant. A significant biography." Confound it, he really did detest praising other writers, but he kept going nonetheless. "And that worries me. We great writers . . ." he said with a playful wink, "we great writers twist and turn everything, we pause for brief moments, and we see as much anxiety in an unexpected movement of the hand or a shadow on the retina as we do in falling share prices and Middle East crises." Nice work, Pontus. Nice work, indeed. "We linger on the small stuff, and that's why we're bad decision-makers." Hell, he'd give them that, even though he'd undoubtedly be a far better decision-maker than any of the political buffoons in this place. "A good politician is more or less the opposite. He's simple, rectilinear." Bremer lowered his voice. "Like Kleeberger over there," he said, eliciting a well-deserved and horrified giggle from the group. "Or even more so someone like Ronald Reagan. He shot from the hip and won the Cold War, while thinkers like Obama and I . . . we vacillate like Hamlet. We see that something is rotten in the state, but when we come to correct that, all we do is make one hell of a mess."

Further well-deserved laughter. He contemplated whether to topple a glass or vase in order to exemplify his comments. He settled for grinning, at which point he caught sight of a tall gentleman with hawkish features gazing at him in amusement. The man had big blue eyes that seemed to see straight through him.

"Or perhaps you disagree?" Bremer said.

"Most interesting," the man said. "And we might observe how well things went for Bush—another cowboy lacking in literary inclinations. But that was quite something to listen to—straight from the hip, no? And with some sweeping flourishes. You've been to the café on Banérgatan."

"What makes you think that?" Bremer said in amazement.

"I'd know the crumbs from their rye anywhere." The man gently brushed a couple of said stowaways from Bremer's collar. "But I myself have a question—now that the rectilinear Foreign Minister finds himself in such grand company," he added without lowering his voice at all.

"It was only a joke," Bremer said self-consciously.

"Was it indeed? It certainly invigorated me. But then again, I happen to know who the real organ-grinder is at the Ministry of Foreign Affairs, and alas, he's not rectilinear at all—although he's most certainly a lousy author. *Si libet, licet.* Do as you please—his only rule."

"I'm not sure I . . ."

"My apologies, I'm babbling. You might say I was tasked with this intervention by a lady who was recently embarrassed. Incidentally, allow me to congratulate you on your success at the Royal Dramatic. Sold out until the summer, I hear. And a film adaptation of your novel in the pipeline too."

"What? Oh, yes . . . They're shooting it now. Morton Production."

Bremer tried to regain his composure while the man continued talking:

"How magnificent. Well, my question is quite simply whether you are well-read in depictions of violence in contemporary Swedish literature?"

Bremer could not fathom why this man made him feel like a fish out of water. He resolved to regain the initiative.

"An excellent question, and directed to the right person. But perhaps we should introduce ourselves first," he said, noticing that a group was gathering around them, scenting a duel.

"My name is Hans Rekke. Reader rather than writer. Former pianist and psychologist."

"And now master detective," said a female onlooker.

"Largely an amateur," the man said. "But I am actually asking in relation to one of my private investigations concerning a cold case."

"Oh!" Bremer replied. "Is this an invitation to join one of your investigations? You flatter me, Hans."

"Professor Rekke," bellowed an older gentleman in the gathering.

"My humble apologies Professor; naturally your title must be included. It's a good job I don't need to 'sir' you; I'm not sure I'd be able to pull that off. I met the King just the other week and addressed him as 'you' seven times in a row until the marshal of court was overcome by a serious coughing fit," he said, awaiting scattered laughter. "But how thrilling, Professor! What are we looking for—a writer, or someone who has drawn inspiration from literary depictions of violence?"

"I should say a writer," Rekke said. "Someone who writes about sadistic tendencies toward women with greater insight than others, and who may—this is merely a guess—once have portrayed an abused stray dog that dies beside an old tree, possibly during a festival."

Pontus Bremer shuddered, experiencing a wave of anxiety which he dismissed.

"A sadist," he said, lingering on the word. "We all have to be sadists in this line of work—completely uninhibited. We can't show consideration to anyone at all; we can only follow our inner voice."

The Professor made as if to conceal a yawn with his hand.

"I'm sorry I'm boring you," Bremer said, "and I'll gladly contradict myself at once. Swedish writers are false opportunists who never utter a word of truth about anything that would cast them in a bad light, and given the current political climate it's impossible to write honestly about anything—let alone men's fantasies about women. Everyone becomes mendacious and ingratiating simply to avoid riling up feminists and the critics. Granted, there are exceptions. I myself once wrote about the time I attempted to strangle my little sister, which was one of the most pleasurable moments of my life. I think of it often," he said, hoping to both shock and amuse, and largely failing on both counts. With a brief spark of interest Rekke remarked:

"Just like Bergman in *The Magic Lantern*."

Bremer swore silently—drat, was that stolen? He needed to get it together. That was his usual modus operandi: take any question whatsoever and guide the answer to himself. But it hadn't worked this time, and once again he was overcome by an icy sense of déjà vu: a stray dog dying by an old tree, a sadistic voice whispering in the night. There was something in that.

"You'll have to give me more details first," he said, before suggesting that he and the Professor step outside, and he couldn't help but make a sneering remark on his way out in an attempt to restore his self-esteem:

"A private detective, eh? Don't you lot spend most of your time following cheating husbands?"

"Alas, that's not really my forte, but I'm sure it's very interesting," the Professor said, sounding amused.

THIRTY-FOUR

From the hall, Magnus Rekke noticed Pontus Bremer looking supercilious and muttering a few snide words to his brother. Good luck with that. Few people saw through narcissists like Hans; he knew them like no one else. As far as Magnus was concerned, Pontus was welcome to try and thrust his dagger into Hans, but he didn't have the time to think about that now. He needed to handle the Latina.

"Say what you have to say or leave me alone," she said with a surprising degree of superiority.

Sure, Magnus thought. You do you, girlie. I've been to the wrong side of the tracks too.

"Perhaps we might have a chat about your new boyfriend," he said, mentally adding a *touché*.

She was at once on her guard.

"How do you know about him?"

"It's my job," he said. "And all I'd like to ask you—*entre nous*, of course—is which side of the Iranian revolution you think he comes down on?"

She glared hostilely at him.

"Obviously he's against the mullahs. He's an exile; he hates the regime in Tehran."

Magnus elected to remain silent for a while so that she might consider the question further.

"Just what are you suggesting?" she said.

He liked her anger—it was a sign that he had her in his power, and once again he chose his words carefully.

"It's our belief that Caspar Amiri is engaged in industrial espionage on behalf of the Iranian regime, and that he is targeting those of his compatriots who have sought a safe haven in this country. But we lack unequivocal evidence. If you were to assist us in this matter, I could have a quiet word with your superiors to secure you your promotion to Inspector at long last. Because surely it's only your crook of a brother who's got your career on the skids? It's hardly because of you—or is it?"

Magnus peered at her, curious to see how she took the jibe. She surprised him by smiling a cold, hostile smile that bore witness to admirable self-control, and he was reluctantly impressed. He could even sense what his brother saw in this girl, and he was overcome by an impulse to touch her—to press himself close. But at that moment, he felt a cold chill at his fly and he realized she'd thrown the contents of her champagne glass toward his crotch.

"I expect Kleeberger can lend you a pair of trousers. Or you could just say you've wet yourself," she said, before making off toward Hans and Pontus Bremer, leaving Magnus muttering profanities in her wake.

THIRTY-FIVE

Santander, July 1988

She looked at the man named Dag, who had been beaten black-and-blue and was now sitting next to her at the table, and wondered whether she dared tell him about her short story after all. Surely it couldn't hurt, Sandra thought, and perhaps she'd also understand a little more herself to boot.

"When I was little, I was badly bitten by a Galgo. I nearly bled to death," she said. She hesitated, but she was immediately strengthened by his reaction.

He gazed at her with such curiosity that the words tumbled out, and she told him in detail what she planned to do with the story.

"Wow," he said afterward. "I wish I'd thought of that."

Sandra smiled, suddenly feeling proud.

"This tree," he continued, "is there anything magical about it?"

"I don't know," she said. "Should there be?"

He raised a hand to his bruised face.

"Maybe," he said. "Some small thing that the dogs can sense but people can't."

"Something divine?"

She noticed that his eyes were sparkling in a completely different way to how they had appeared in the restaurant.

"Maybe there's an opening to another world, a crack right beside it, or in the trunk."

"Okay," she said, amused.

"Maybe it's nighttime in our world and day in the other, which is why the light seeps through."

"Doesn't that make it another story, though?"

"I think it could be beautiful, and we don't need to know whether it's happening in real life or simply in the dog's head."

"That's true."

His gaze became bolder.

"Or the tree's roots are connected to hell itself," he said.

"You mean the tree's evil?"

He held out his hands and smiled, as if compensating for its malice.

"Possibly."

"Wouldn't that make my dog evil too, since it's drawn there?"

"Or being by the tree makes you evil. It's like the tree brings out the worst in us—twists our thoughts down into the darkness."

"Like the hotel in *The Shining*."

He laughed.

"Exactly."

"What's the dog going to be named?"

"I'm not quite sure," she said. "For a while, I was thinking maybe Corazón—but now I think maybe it should be nameless. It's trying to remember what it was once called when it had a master, but it never does—not even at the point of death."

"Tragic," he said.

She looked at his split lip.

"I can't believe you fought Roberto. How did you survive?"

"It's unfathomable. But honestly?" he said. "I think it did me some good."

Sandra pulled her chair closer.

"How?"

"A little bit of life came back to me with that fight. The last few weeks have been utter hell, although perhaps I shouldn't be telling you that," he said.

"What's happened?" she said.

"I've felt a bit like your stray—constantly being kicked."

It occurred to her that she wasn't pleased to hear that, and she asked:

"Is it your friend? Pompe?"

"He's nasty, and I'm diminishing in his company. I've been shrinking to nothing, but now I'm—" He cut himself short.

Growing, he thought.

"I understand," Sandra said, feeling even more clearly that it was Pompe she wanted to be with.

She couldn't believe he was nasty. There was probably just something going on between the two of them.

"But you like him," said Dag.

"He seems interesting, but I don't know," she said.

"No," he said, laying his hand on the table, and she didn't know what to do.

She wanted to take his hand in hers and continue talking about the tree and the fight with Roberto, but that felt wrong. Her thoughts about Pompe had come between them. At the same time, a sentence came to her—an obvious turn of phrase that allowed her to picture the old tree in her mind's eye. *Two bolts of lightning had split the trunk, and yet its branches reached up as if praying to the sky with thirty supplicant arms.*

A moment later, new sentences began to bubble to the surface and she felt unexpectedly excited. She found herself caught up in a rush of inspiration and it was clear to her that the oak really did need to be magical, and perhaps even evil, tied to the underworld, despite its branches reaching skyward, and without being aware of it she stood up.

"Are you leaving?" said the one named Dag, and she looked at him in confusion. He looked devastatingly unhappy, and she definitely didn't intend to leave.

She wanted to stay here and talk. She liked him now, not as much as Pompe, but there was no doubt about it: he'd given her story new heft.

And yet she said:

"Yes, sorry. I've got to write."

"No," he said with such despair that she didn't know what to do.

But it was as if the fever in her mind made the decision for her, which was why all she did was say thanks for the help, followed by a "See you." Then she left, muttering sentences to herself again, without hearing that he was calling after her more and more angrily.

THIRTY-SIX

After he had provided Pontus Bremer with further details on the murder in Santander, Rekke slipped away into the throng and sought out Micaela—but she had vanished. He moved from room to room, scanning each one and swearing silently. He should have taken better care of her, and why had he bothered with Bremer? That chatterbox could quite clearly do nothing to help; his question had been a cry into the void.

"Hans?"

He heard his brother's voice behind him and reluctantly turned around. It was even more crowded now, people everywhere chattering away like birds, and he reached out for a champagne refill to draw strength for this conversation.

"Magnus," he said, scrutinising him, and in that moment Rekke was flooded with so many impressions that it felt as if he had been blinded.

I have to calm down, he thought. His gaze was quite still, and without quite knowing what he wanted to say, he opened with:

"Your trousers."

Even as he said these two words, he understood. The trousers were too short and tight, and were unbuttoned at the waist. Magnus pulled a face.

"I had a small accident and had to borrow a pair of Kleeberger's. I had no idea the rogue was so thin," he said.

"You hit the bottle early today."

"A small toast to Obama."

Toasting yourself, more like, Rekke thought.

"But you're looking magnificent, Hans," Magnus said. "I can't believe we have the same genes. You look as if you could run the Stockholm Marathon tomorrow. Did Pontus Bremer get what was coming to him?"

"Magnus, what do you want?" said Rekke.

Magnus looked around and checked that no-one was listening.

"I should like to request a small favour that may amuse you in your further study of grandiose personalities. Perhaps you're free right now? If so, I could accompany you to the detention facility right away."

"Am I meeting a criminal or do you wish to incarcerate me?"

Magnus laughed.

"I should like you to talk to a woman who has caused all manner of headaches for the CIA. I want to know what she's up to. The prosecutor says we can only hold her for another twenty-four hours."

"*Quis est?*" said Hans.

"Gina Mo Anderson. I think you'll find her stimulating."

Rekke recalled what he knew about her.

"Traumatized, in all likelihood."

"I surmise she doesn't hurt easily. She shakes off most things provided the sun is allowed to shine on her. But she has indeed been in captivity for some time now. Are you interested?"

Rekke surveyed the gathering, still searching for Micaela.

"You didn't happen to address a few poorly chosen words to my lodger just now, did you?"

Magnus responded to this question by trying to adjust the position of Kleeberger's trousers.

"For goodness' sake, Magnus, what did you say?"

"Nothing really, but she was the cause of my little accident. Tough girl. You really should make an overture before it's too late."

"Leave her alone," Rekke hissed.

"I'll make amends for everything if you do me this favour."

"Why should I lift a finger for you?"

Magnus licked his lips nervously.

"Gina Mo can have the shirt off anyone's back," he said. "It's as if she assumes a new personality with everyone she meets. No-one understands her and she revels in it. It'll take a man of your calibre to see through her."

Rekke glanced toward Kleeberger, who was watching them with a worried expression.

"I don't feel like it," he said.

"Please, I beg of you. Name your price."

Peace, Rekke thought. Peace from machinations and power play.

"She's a journalist at heart, around forty years of age, no?" he said to his own surprise.

His brain was apparently happy to seize every opportunity to return to the Santander murder investigation, which surprised him.

"Quite. She would have done well in journalism if she'd felt so inclined. But she's been constantly drawn to war zones, guerillas and all kinds of dramatic events," said Magnus.

"Okay," Rekke said.

"Okay to what?"

"I'll meet her," Rekke said, but first he needed to find out how Micaela was doing.

. . .

Micaela had returned home through the storm and was now at the kitchen table, still feeling cold, and once again reading the Spanish case files. She kept discovering new things. For instance, there was the record shop guy—Toni Molina—whom she'd mentioned to Rekke. She couldn't help but feel he hadn't been telling the truth, either. Witnesses had seen him following Sandra Ramirez. Yet he categorically denied it. "I just had to pop out to get the lay of the land," he'd said, quite clearly concealing something. It was probably nothing big, but still. He had a previous conviction for sexual harassment and had once been reported to the police for rape. There was something going on there. But she was struggling to focus. Magnus's words came back to her.

Had Caspar lied to her? Was he really affiliated with the Iranian regime? No, she thought. That was impossible. Caspar had told her in detail how his family's life had been ruined by Khomeini's rise to power, and how they'd fled as a matter of urgency. Magnus must have been lying. He probably just wanted to get at her and by extension Rekke. She tried to forget about it and ploughed on through the files to see whether she could find any further traces of the Swedes. But they were few and far between. The detectives had been focused on Roberto Ortega for far too long at the expense of all other suspects. The world beyond him seemed to have vanished, existing only in the periphery. "Idiots," she muttered, thinking back to Magnus Rekke again.

She pictured his horrid, soaking wet crotch. What a liar. The only thing was . . . How did Magnus even know that she was with Caspar? It wasn't as if they'd advertized it with their Facebook status. Wasn't the very fact that this information had reached Magnus a sign that Caspar was suspicious in some way? Erroneously, perhaps—Magnus had wanted her help after all—but still . . . Why otherwise would Magnus have spent time on it?

She carried on reading the file, but the words were dancing before her eyes so she stood up. She was going to see Caspar; she'd promised. Perhaps she could subtly bring the issue up and fish a little, if only to confirm that it was a load of nonsense. She listened for sounds in the stairwell.

The elevator arrived. Was it Rekke? She suddenly felt furious with him, as if it were all his fault. Which it was. He'd promised to protect her from Magnus. But the idiot had flitted away in excitement at the party, and she decided to tell him off for it and headed for the door and saw him stumble in with exaggerated movements and snow covering his coat. At that moment, she felt a stab of pain in her abdomen and her legs gave way, and all of a sudden she found herself in Rekke's arms.

She hated herself for that.

THIRTY-SEVEN

Pontus Bremer greeted a cocksure fellow who also went by the name Rekke, and whom he recognized from the news, but he didn't feel like talking anymore. He was done with the party. He wanted to go home or settle down alone in a bar and think over what had actually happened. What were these demons that had been awakened within him? It was beyond his ken. He went into the stairwell, past the security service heavies and an elderly but chic lady smoking quietly in a corner, and at that moment his phone rang.

It was Per Morton. Pontus loved talking to Per. Per was the producer overseeing the movie adaptation of his novel *The Wrath of Illusion*, and Per never had bad news, only enthusiasm: "Pontus, this is going to be so good. The script is so brilliant, the starlets are ten metres off the ground." Per always put him in a good mood, and there was something boyish, a little impish, about him that brought Pontus down to a level he loved to regress to. Damn it, no-one could be an exalted intellectual all the time! Still, right now he couldn't even bring himself to talk to Per. The indeterminate demons—or the memories, probably damn repressed ones at that—continued to torment him and matters weren't improved when he stepped out into the street.

The storm was wild. It was impossible to even think in the face of it, except to reflect that Sweden should detach itself and move south like an old ocean liner. The blizzard took over his whole organism and he walked bent double down Narvavägen, swearing as he kicked at the snow. But before long, he saw a tempting glow to his left. It was that French wine bar he'd been into a few times, and as he staggered inside, snowy and cold, stamping his shoes, he was met by a young waiter who greeted him with:

"Oh, this is an honour! Come into the warmth, Monsieur Bremer."

He usually loved to be welcomed like this. He was almost hurt when not received in this way, or even worse—God forbid—when people didn't recognize him at all. Uneducated yokels, he would think. Illiterates. Haven't you ever even opened a book in your life? But this time he wanted to remain anonymous, so he neglected to make a grand entrance where he made the other patrons understand that they were encountering Sweden's greatest living writer. Instead, he took a seat toward the back, ordered a beer, took off his coat and pulled out his notebook.

"People are like orangutans," he wrote, without meaning anything by it. It was no more than a scribble. He could as well have drawn a cube or an angry old man. But they all had their impact, the orangutans, the beer and the muffled hum of the bar. His thoughts began to organize themselves, and slowly—as if making his way through a fog—he understood what had been awakened in him during his conversation with Professor Rekke.

It was an encounter with Dag Wrangel—it must have been five or six years back, or perhaps more. Ten at most. Back before Dag had made his name, when all he'd published was a collection of poetry that no-one cared about. He was a nothing, a pretentious lightweight. But there was nothing wrong with his sense of ambition. He had the fervour of Strindberg himself, determined to become a writer to be reckoned with, and that was what had gripped Pontus. Well, truth be told he'd mostly been gripped by Dag's admiration, and on a whim he'd taken him to the grand watering hole that was Konstnärsbaren after a tedious publishing party at the offices of Wahlström & Widstrand.

At the bar, Pontus had drunk like a fish as a gesture of fraternity, and had briefly held forth on what it took to become a great man of letters, and a great man in general. Dag had soaked up every single word. Well, more of them than he should have, given what that damn epigone had subsequently achieved. But later on, when they were drunk, Pontus had asked whether Dag had an idea for a novel he wanted to run by him. That was when Dag had squirmed and then outlined a story that was not altogether coherent; it sprawled with elements of fantasy, and it came back to Pontus now with a terrifying undertone to it. Cool it, he told himself; don't get bogged down in speculation.

Dag was a kind person; some might even say excessively kind. What a pushover, Pontus sneered. But the pushovers were the worst, and he remembered that he'd stayed there to listen and afterward had thought in shock, damn, I didn't think you had it in you.

It was a murder story, he recalled: a harrowing story of a girl—practically a fay—who without knowing it was writing the story of her own death, and—just as she had predicted—she was killed beside an old tree that was connected to the underworld. Pontus couldn't recall quite how the murder itself occurred or who the murderer was, but what he did remember was the fervour in Dag's voice as he whispered the details like evil spells.

How many pitches for novels had Pontus heard in his life?

About seven thousand, he figured, and there had surely been nothing special about this one. Nevertheless, it had stayed with him, less because of the narrative and more because of the tone in which it was told, the feeling. But perhaps the strangest thing of all was Dag's transformation. After being such a fawning lapdog all night, he'd assumed a jittery authority, as if describing a personal experience that had been marinating within him for years, and now, long after the fact, Pontus couldn't help thinking about what the Professor had told him about the murder in Spain. There were disturbing similarities, and what was worse: he remembered Dag's expression afterward. The gaze that hinted at an abyss of guilt and horror.

Pontus Bremer drank his beer, overcome by intense unease. Surely Dag couldn't be a murderer? That would be . . . He didn't conclude that thought, but instead ordered another beer and looked around the joint. A chick in a blue cardigan was staring at him with an impudent countenance. He nodded to her and sipped his drink, lost again in his thoughts. He didn't know a kinder soul than Dag. But kind souls had done terrible things before. It was the most inhibited wretches who bottled it up the most. People like himself always got everything out immediately.

"I saw your play."

Pontus turned around; it was the impudent-looking chick.

"Thanks, that's very kind," he said absentmindedly.

"I thought it was outrageous and sexist," the girl said, and he thought, my God, can't I ever be left in peace? He was tempted to say, "If it's sexist then that's only because girls like you are so thick," but instead he thought of Dag, the tree and the Spanish girl, and said:

"I'm sorry."

The woman looked at him sceptically.

"You have my word," he said. "I'll pull myself together and never hurt anyone again, and I'll only write about sunsets and innocent leaves swirling around in the wind. As it happens, I shan't even finish my beer in order to demonstrate that I've now chosen the right path. Adieu and amen. Take up thy bed and walk."

Then he laid a couple of banknotes on the table and set out to hunt for a dive bar where the crowd was so uneducated and slovenly that they'd never even heard of Pontus Bremer.

THIRTY-EIGHT

Micaela disappeared down the hall with the same hunched shoulders she'd had earlier, and Rekke wondered what was the matter. She'd thrown herself into his arms like a drowning woman reaching for a branch, but she still hadn't wanted to talk except to say that Magnus had generally spouted a load of bullshit. She said she didn't care, and added she was going to lie down and read the Spanish case files.

"Let's have a cup of coffee," Rekke said. "I spoke to that scamp Pontus Bremer."

She turned around and repeated the word *scamp* back at him, as if it was the stupidest thing he'd ever said, which perhaps it was. The word felt as dated as he did, and Rekke gazed sadly after her as she left and slammed the door behind her. Outside, the blizzard was rattling the city and Rekke looked down at his hands. They were clutching Gina Mo Anderson's security file. He had half an hour to review it before a car from the ministry came to pick him up and take him to the prison.

"I can't do it," he muttered.

Still, speed-reading was a specialty of his, and the file wasn't even that thick—not for someone who'd been held for four years as a suspected terrorist. So Rekke decided to have a drink first, a chaser, just a drop of red, what with him being as good as off the opiates, as good as . . . "Don't tempt me," he murmured, and he felt a tremor run from his shoulder to his heart, and once again he thought about Micaela's embrace moments earlier, as if something in it might be able to heal him better than all the drugs and wine out there.

He skipped the drink after all and aimlessly paced back and forth in the apartment before sitting down at the kitchen table and opening the file: Gina Mo Anderson, born 1966, forty-two years old, American father, Swedish mother, troublemaker, groupie, abortions at a young age, car thefts. He raised his gaze, thinking about the opiates again. A little bodily peace wouldn't do any harm. He wouldn't be questioning anyone in this delicate state. No, enough of that. He read on. A talented student in the midst of everything else and a dazzling stage presence, presenter on ZTV, intern at *Aftonbladet*, widely read columnist at *Metro* but exposed as having copied two columns without sustaining any lasting damage, except that she made her way abroad to areas of conflict and became more of an activist than a reporter. Frequently on television, witty, charismatic, left-wing, committed to the developing world and Palestine, but with populist leanings and a tendency to fake or sex up her quotes. Those cribbed columns were no accident, Rekke thought. Not that it ruled out the possibility that she sometimes had interesting things to say. But by and large, she blurted out generalist and audience-pleasing lines that stuck in his craw, and he longingly ran his hand over the copy of the *London Review of Books*, tempted to read the murdered girl's short story again.

He dutifully returned to the file, distracted at first, and then he did a double take. After 9/11, Gina Mo had travelled to Afghanistan and reported from there with her usual tendentiousness, and with an increasingly antagonistic tone toward the United States and the War on Terror. At the same time, she had secretly—and this was interesting—been searching for Osama bin Laden. Duplicity, it seemed. A rapprochement with Al Qaeda but also an infiltration of the terrorist group. An undercover investigation, she'd claimed. But it was hard to tell what was true and what was not.

In January 2004 she'd fallen silent. There followed reports that she had been apprehended by the CIA, imprisoned and tortured. Now—some four years later—she'd been released and transported to Sweden, where she intended to hold a press conference. There was no doubt about what Magnus wanted.

He wanted to know what damage she might cause him and the government, and Rekke didn't give a damn about that. But, he decided, it might nonetheless be interesting to meet Gina Mo. Manipulative and intelligent people remained a favourite subject of his, which was precisely why he should calm himself down with a couple of pills. "No," he muttered. For once he mustered a firmness of character. He stood up, filled with conflicting impulses, and remembered Micaela's embrace at the door. He remembered the drama of the movement—as if it were a parting, or the opposite, a flight into his arms.

Then he went and tapped on her door.

"How are we getting on?"

Micaela snapped "Leave me alone" in reply and then Rekke left her to it and not long after that the front door slammed shut. That man, she thought. He shouldn't have settled for that, he should have come in anyway and listened to her. He was so tentative. She couldn't bear it.

If she'd thrown herself at him like she had with Rekke when he came in, Caspar would have picked her up and carried her to bed. But . . . Micaela swore. She couldn't shake what Magnus had said. The words burrowed into her, seeking resistance. Hadn't Caspar said he was pleased about Obama's victory? Surely no-one working for the Iranians would be? No, she decided. Some-one like that would demand that she wear a veil and would have a fourteenth-century outlook on women—although he could be faking it. That was what spies did. She bit her lip and called Caspar.

"On my way. Sorry it took a while," she said.

"Hurrah," he said enthusiastically. "Are you feeling any better?"

"I think so," she said, adding a "Miss you."

"Me too," he said, and she convinced herself that Magnus Rekke had only wanted to hurt her.

She really did miss him, and she was going to leave right away. Yet she took the detour via the kitchen and became entangled in the Spanish case files and once again began to read the victim's short story. In this version—written in the morning immediately after her shift had ended—the attack on a girl who was probably the author herself was described, but she then disappeared from the story. After that, it was solely about the Galgo and all the kicks and blows it sustained during its lonely wanderings through the town.

The second and third versions contained everything from the first, but had a more driven style. They both revolved around the old oak, which had only been introduced in the second draft. From the very beginning, it was said that the strays inexplicably lay down and died beside the tree, and the reader was also told that the hero of the story, the anonymous Galgo, would end its days at the foot of the oak. After that, the story went back in time and the Galgo recalled its old life as a beloved racing dog, or rather, as an increasingly unloved racing dog.

The Galgo was beaten and tortured and eventually lowered

into a well before being saved by a firefighter and embarking upon life without a master. It was hard not to feel for the mutt, especially given the girl's own fate, but the real point of interest was of course whether the story offered any clues about the murder.

At any rate, it wasn't impossible that what had happened to the dog provided some indication of the author's final day alive. But I'll have to deal with that later, Micaela thought. Now she needed to get going, and just as she had stood up and put on her shoes and coat, something unexpected occurred to her. Something that made her freeze and then return to the kitchen table.

THIRTY-NINE

Dag Wrangel alighted at the Mariatorget Tunnelbana station and emerged onto Swedenborgsgatan. The snowstorm cut right through to his bones and burned his cheeks.

He turned up his collar and looked down at the street and squeezed the mobile phone in his pocket. No call from home, thank goodness. Viktor, his son, tended to call once every ten minutes. It was barely possible to leave him for a second, even though he had his piano—his only friend, some might have said—not that he had mastered it, poor kid.

Viktor spent every waking hour playing, but was still stuck on Chopin's most basic waltzes and nocturnes. It was incomprehensible, really. He was stuck treading water and whenever they'd had boys his age who played classical music come around it had been so painful. They had all made so much more progress, while Viktor just stuck at the same piece month in, month out, which was confirmation enough that the boy was different.

Dag couldn't bear it—he lived for his son. And, of course, for writing. Not well but masterfully. Anything else was meaningless, in his view, and that meant that he was constantly getting hung up on turns of phrase and other minutiae. Admittedly, he'd garnered some appreciation. There had been the prize from the Society of the Nine, two short-listings for the August Prize, and the nod from the Swedish Academy. But he also knew that his books lacked something crucial. Natural reasons precluded him from approaching his true pain points—the ones that roused him in the small hours, panting with anxiety.

He was forced to remain silent about his unfathomable crime, only ever allowing it to slip out as grief in his prose, and he spent most of his time at home with his wife Andrea and their son. Only occasionally did he give lectures or join panels. Today, he was due to speak at the Church of Saint Mary Magdalene in Södermalm, not that it much mattered given that no-one would turn up in this foul weather anyway.

Dag would be addressing empty pews and would once again be alone at the signing table. He tightened his coat with a sigh. People rarely came at all these days; there had been a bit of excitement after his book about his father came out, but now he was being forgotten again. The phone in his pocket rang. That was a sort of nice feeling—Viktor hadn't rung in twenty minutes and Dag was almost starting to miss his anxious calls. Good grief; a glance at the screen showed him it wasn't Viktor. The realisation ran through him like a jolt. It was Pontus Bremer.

The gilded world was calling, and Dag was instantly nervous. Of course, you could say what you liked about Pontus Bremer and how his hubris made him careless. There was hardly a sentence in his oeuvre that Dag himself would have loosed upon the world; he could easily have edited his books down by half, and Dag would certainly have removed ninety per cent of his metaphors.

Nevertheless, there was no escaping the fact that Pontus was larger than life itself. He dominated every room he entered, and every writer—minor authors, as Pontus would have described them—knew their reputations would be bolstered simply by being seen with him. Dag was unfortunately no different. No matter how much he considered himself to be a better writer, he shrunk alongside Pontus and he was also flattered by his company. It was absurd, but there was no escaping it, and Dag was about to answer when he realized that he was so cold that his fingers were unable to press the buttons on his mobile. He'd have to take it later and he hurried toward the churchyard, past the tombstones that always made him feel intensely uneasy, and entered the church, where his misgivings were immediately realized.

It was resoundingly empty, with only a few old ladies in the front pews. His self-esteem dropped even further as he nodded in embarrassment to the vicar, a fairly young woman wearing high heels and a blue corduroy jacket over her clerical collar.

"Looks like we'll mostly be talking to each other today," he said, proffering a hand.

"Oh, I'm sure more people will be here soon," she said encouragingly. "Why don't we give them fifteen minutes' grace?"

He nodded and stepped aside to call Pontus Bremer back, reflecting that the culture-vultures would have braved any storm going for Pontus. It would have been a full house for Pontus, and the audience would have brought their snapshots and autograph books, and the women would have had crazed looks on their faces and given him their phone numbers. But for Dag, they were at best politely interested.

Then he felt a little hopeful anyway. Perhaps Pontus had a job for him—or perhaps even an accolade or an appointment. After all, the government had asked Pontus to help compile a cultural canon, and provided he wasn't planning to fill it completely with his own books then maybe . . . What did he know? Perhaps the day was about to turn.

"Hello, it's Dag," he said. "You rang."

Pontus, the noisiest man on Earth, answered in a whisper that turned him to ice:

"A detective—a Professor Rekke—contacted me about an old murder in Spain."

FORTY

Micaela was looking at the case file again, wearing her quilted jacket and shoes, and she tore out several pages and put them down together with the autopsy report on the Danish victim before going into Rekke's study.

The room was as much of a disordered mess as usual, filled with stacks of papers and books, while the young ballerina was in her usual spot by the door, bowing to her. Micaela had never liked that statue, which was presumably why it was in here. But there were fine oil paintings of musicians hanging on the walls, and a couple of framed photos of Rekke himself as a young man on stage that she occasionally looked at furtively.

Not that the idiot had ever realized as much, but he'd been a dreamboat back then, so damn sophisticated in his tailcoats and tuxedo jackets that it was borderline offensive. She put these thoughts aside and went over to the aged fax machine, which doubled as a printer. Lying in the print tray was an old article about Gina Mo Anderson. Micaela wondered what Rekke had to do with her. Hadn't she been locked up in the US for ages?

She dropped the thought and jotted down a couple of lines

to Jonas Beijer, a colleague of hers who worked on the murder squad in Solna. *Jonas, sorry, I know you've got a lot going on. But it'd be great if you could take a look at this and see whether anything like it has happened here or elsewhere in the Nordics. Can't help but see similarities with the murder of Järvinen, that Finnish journalist, a few years ago. She certainly seemed to have been kicked and beaten the same way.*

Not that she supposed Jonas would turn up anything new. No matter how careless the Spanish detectives had been to start with, they must have done a proper job once they had let Roberto Ortega go. But the years had gone by and the Finnish murder—which had suddenly sprung to mind—might have flown under Corales's radar. It wouldn't do any harm for Jonas to take a look at it and run some database searches. She added: *Rekke thinks it might be a Swedish serial killer.*

The key word here, she reflected, wasn't *Swedish* or *serial killer*, but *Rekke*. No matter how much he bugged people at the station, and no matter how much they called him ridiculous and out of touch, they would always perk up when his name was mentioned. She had learned to deploy it when it suited her.

She brought up Rekke's name when people were ignoring her—whether it was because she was an immigrant, too young, had a crook for a brother or all of the above. It might not have been her most dignified trait, but you played the hand you were dealt. She sent her fax. Then she let it go. She needed to get out of the apartment, so she took the elevator downstairs and went outside. It hadn't got any warmer.

On her way to the Tunnelbana station, leaning into the snowstorm, she thought again about the girl's short story. In it, or rather in the second version of it—in a section that had later been deleted—the Galgo met another stray, another lost soul wandering around the town, and it was that dog which reminded the Galgo of the old oak and said the tree was sacred. The encounter was described as being beautiful at first, offering respite. But then something happened—it was unclear what. The other dog began to growl angrily and became threatening and, startled, the Galgo fled up toward the hill.

Was this a rendering of Sandra Ramirez's first encounter with her killer? Micaela mulled this over as she hurried on through the wind to Östermalmstorg station.

It was twenty past seven in the evening. She put a hand to her stomach; the pain would not let up.

FORTY-ONE

Santander, July 1988

Sandra had written a clean copy of the short story at the kitchen table, and the Galgo had once again died beside the old oak. She felt a twinge of euphoria.

Maybe she really could become a writer. Maybe her short story would one day be acclaimed as her first literary work. She couldn't help but dream about it, imagining herself commenting on the decision to portray the stray that had attacked her.

"It was an interesting change in perspective," she'd say modestly, not giving too much away.

Mamá was vacuuming the hall. She'd probably mop it too. She always went to absurd lengths to spring-clean before the fiesta. Outside in the courtyard Sandra could hear shouting, and she stood up to look through the window. The little boys were playing soccer and waving their arms, and she was possessed by a strong desire to live life to the fullest and to join the party that was coming to life in the city. She called to her mother, her voice rising above the vacuum cleaner:

"Mamá, what time is it?"

Half past six already, apparently. Practically eight o'clock, in other words. Feeling stressed, Sandra glanced down at her blue jeans. What was she going to wear?

She had no idea and so she went to the room that she shared with her little brother, opened the closet and gingerly handled the three dresses Papá had given her. She'd never worn them outside the house. Her legs, especially the left one, were covered in scars and indentations around the heel and thighs. She really did hate them, although she sometimes loved them too, as if her legs were her true self.

"No way," she said under her breath.

Her sexual experiences were limited: three of them, to be precise. And each time she'd had to consider when to tell them. Before she took off her trousers, or long before that, while they were still only kissing, or even when they had just started dating? *I have really ugly scars on my legs.* She usually opted for the latter and prepared them for the shock from the get-go. With a little luck, like with Manuel, the boys were pleasantly surprised: "That's not so bad. You're still really beautiful."

"No way," she repeated, pulling out the pale blue dress that she liked best.

Then she undressed, put on the frock and examined her reflection in the mirror on the inside of the closet door. It had a crack running down its left side from one of her brother's tantrums, and she felt some momentary anguish as if the crack ran through her too, but then she suddenly smiled contentedly. The short story had given her a kinder outlook on herself, and she felt unexpectedly intrepid. She put on a pair of high-heeled sandals and then made it as far as the hall in her dress before she returned hastily to find a pair of tights to wear with it.

Then she left, never to return.

FORTY-TWO

Rekke was escorted along the hallway by two prison officers. He heard pounding against a cell door in the distance and a stifled profanity. There was the smell of tobacco and disinfectant, and on the floor there was a dead fly and a scrap of paper torn from a brown envelope.

Meeting suspects or prisoners that he'd read about had always been an interesting experience. It was a bit like opening the door to Señor Corales that morning. His expectations met and mingled with reality, and his senses were heightened and enhanced. But this felt different. A flood of disparate thoughts entered his consciousness before he'd even gone into the cell, and he pictured Pontus Bremer in his mind's eye.

That annoyed him. This was nothing to do with Pontus. But Bremer wouldn't go, and suddenly Rekke realized why. A flash of darkness had crossed the writer's face, a shadow that Rekke had interpreted as a sign of uncertainty or a moment of torment, but now he suspected it meant Bremer had been hiding something. I must talk to him, Rekke decided. The prison officers opened the door and the faint scent of perfume drifted toward him and he straightened up and smiled.

"Well, this is a pleasure. Good afternoon. My name is Hans Rekke," he said, proffering his hand.

Gina Mo stood up in a graceful movement. She was clearly tired, marked by her years behind bars and the lack of sunlight, but she'd been provided with a change of clothes in her cell. She was wearing tight-fitting jeans and a low-cut blue blouse, and she wore her hair down and had meticulously and boldly applied makeup to her face. She held her head high like an icy queen, and it had an effect and she knew it. And she enjoyed it.

It felt as if she were looking for a showdown. She wanted to show who she was and convey her status as a star and make it clear that no-one could touch her. But something unexpected happened.

The austere, regal face broke into a big smile, as if she wanted to impart that she'd been expecting a dull bureaucrat but had instead received an equal. It was skilfully done, Rekke thought. Clearly quite deliberate. She wanted him to feel special, chosen.

"I'm Gina Mo," she said, meeting his gaze. "Love the jacket."

"Thanks," he said. "You yourself are looking radiant. But do sit down, for heaven's sake."

The prison officers left, locking the door behind them, and he and Gina Mo both put off talking as they looked at each other. He noted the pale, anaemic skin tone under her makeup and the calculating look in her eyes.

"It grieves me that you've been badly treated," said Rekke.

"I never expected justice in this world," she said.

"But in the next one?"

She leaned forward with what was a deliberately seductive movement.

"Nor there. Are you related to Magnus Rekke?"

"My brother, alas," he said.

She laughed.

"So he sent you?"

Rekke saw a vindictive glint in Gina Mo's eye and knew that Magnus had just cause for his concerns.

"Yes, he did," he said.

She smiled wryly.

"Is your brother afraid?"

"A little, I daresay. I'm glad you were able to see the doctor just now," Rekke said.

"What?"

"Your left arm," he said.

She put a hand to her arm.

"The cuff left a mark," Rekke said. "I expect your blood pressure was a little high. But that's only natural given what you've been through, and I'm glad he gave you some benzo—ten grams of diazepam, by the looks of it."

She looked at him suspiciously.

"He told you?"

"Not at all, but I can see it in your eyes and hear it in your voice, just as I can tell your joints ache and that you do narrow push-ups with your hands turned inward."

"Are you some sort of genius?" she said.

He leaned forward.

"I see people's weaknesses just like you do—but I've changed."

She looked curious. "In what way?"

"I've become more like you. I have my own agenda, while as far as my brother goes I have no illusions left, and I'm happy to see him sweat. I assume he hasn't lifted a finger to secure your release."

"He's lifted an awful lot of fingers," she said. "To keep me locked up. He wanted to ingratiate himself with his pals at the CIA."

But there's something else too, Rekke thought.

"I look forward to hearing about it," he said. "I should think you have a speech prepared for your press conference?"

"It would be a shame to pass up the chance with the world lending its ear," Gina Mo said.

"I suppose so."

"Or are you going to make sure I do some extra time just for that?"

"Oh, I don't think you need to worry on that count. You've been treated badly enough as it is," Rekke said.

"I have. But I'm strong."

"Without doubt—complex too. You fight for the little person, but you're drawn to the strong ones with no limits."

"Is there something wrong with that?" she said.

"No, it's just interesting."

You're drawn to those like you, Rekke thought.

"Aren't you a strong person yourself?" said Gina Mo.

"Not especially," he said. "And I think you know that. You saw my weakness even as I came through the door. But I'm also interested in the grandiose."

She smiled derisively.

"As specimens, I imagine?"

"I suppose I'm drawn to them too. But what attracts me the most is puzzles. You said you knew where bin Laden was," he said.

"I know who's protecting him," said Gina Mo.

"I should imagine you've had to sing every word you know on that matter. I read about what they did to you."

"But no-one believes me. No-one believes there would be such monumental cynicism."

Rekke looked her in the eye, convinced she was bluffing, and another thought occurred to him. It was surely an idiotic notion, another cry into the void.

"I remain cautiously sceptical," he said. "But there's one thing I'm fairly sure of: you have a special ability to track down these kinds of personalities. It seems to have been a lifelong yearning for you."

She looked at him in curiosity.

"Well, I've been damn unlucky as far as boyfriends go."

He laughed amiably.

"I'm sorry to hear that. But that wasn't what I had in mind. What's the situation in your own trade, journalism? Are there a lot of them?"

She looked at him in surprise.

"You're looking for psychopaths?" she said, and he nodded reluctantly.

"Yes, someone who is violent to women and enjoys it. About your age, or a little older. Blond hair, probably thinning. This person may have . . ." he said, looking down at Gina Mo's hands which seemed older than the rest of her, "once broken someone's finger. Snapped it like it was a twig."

"Broken a finger?" she said, laying a hand provocatively on Rekke's thigh.

FORTY-THREE

Caspar opened the door and Micaela's first thought was it was no wonder she'd fallen for him. He was exceptionally handsome in his white turtleneck with his hair combed back so that his prominent features were accentuated, and she liked the tenderness of his gaze.

"You poor thing," he said. "I'll take care of you."

He'd dimmed the lights, laid out a buffet of Persian appetizers on the coffee table and opened a bottle of red wine, but she passed no comment. Instead, she kissed him and put a hand around his waist and led him into the bedroom, which was perhaps not a great idea given what she'd heard or indeed how her stomach felt. Still, she did it anyway. Worse still was that Rekke was in her thoughts, as if it were him she were embracing. She removed Caspar's turtleneck—suddenly eager—and pushed him onto the bed, managing to completely forget Rekke and her aches.

Afterward, she lay with her leg across Caspar's thigh and her arm on his chest and thought, let it stay like this for a while; forget what Magnus said. But of course, that was a forlorn hope. Apparently she just had to destroy everything.

"Why did you actually leave Iran?" she said.

He looked at her in surprise.

"I already said—why do you ask? We risked getting into trouble."

"I thought you were a little imprecise," she said, and yes, she could have expressed herself better and said she was just curious, but the turn of phrase was spontaneous. She noticed at once that he'd taken offence.

He pushed her away.

"What do you mean?"

"Nothing."

"There's clearly something you want to say," he said, giving her a look she didn't recognize, and she took refuge in an innocent expression.

Something had torn open between them and her kissing him on the neck didn't help. He was out of kilter and she saw no way to repair the situation. Instead—provoked by his irritability—she got up and put on her panties and shirt, and said she needed the bathroom. Which was true, so she thought. She was in pain and wanted to be alone.

But she never did make it to the loo. She turned right and went to Caspar's desk in the living room and began to search the drawers, briskly and methodically, noticing at once that one of them was locked, which alerted her. She briefly glanced over what she had found. There was nothing of any value so far as she could tell. Insurance policies, old bills, a few pictures of Caspar and his mum, and a Persian name, Mina Nazari, scrawled on a piece of paper. Beneath that there was a phone number and two times, 1:23 p.m. and 11:21 p.m., in addition to a couple of illegible notes. Then she heard footsteps—rapid ones—and she memorized the name and shut the drawer, although not quickly enough. She turned around to see Caspar standing some five metres away in his blue underwear with his hands on his hips and his mouth open, and then it dawned on her: if she'd been a fool earlier, that was nothing compared to what she was now, and she managed to blurt out a "Sorry, I was just . . ." but she couldn't think of an explanation. There wasn't one either, and she stared at him in desperation, looking for hopeful signs—preferably confusion, indifference, anything that suggested he wasn't thinking the same thing she was—signs that it was all a paranoid fantasy of Magnus Rekke's.

"What are you doing?" he said.

She didn't have time to reply. His body tensed as he moved toward her with a look on his face she'd never seen before, and she raised her fists to defend herself.

FORTY-FOUR

Dag Wrangel was under the impression he was doing well at keeping his expression neutral, but the vicar, who had seen many people in times of crisis, came over to him and put an arm around his shoulders.

"Has someone died?" she said.

Dag shook his head. "No, I just . . ."

But he couldn't get any more words out, because someone *had* died, even if it had been more than twenty years ago. Right now I need to focus, he told himself. What had he actually told Pontus Bremer? "No, I don't recall that. I don't know anything about that. I'm afraid I can't talk right now—I'm about to do a talk. But why don't we have a pint later? Sounds exciting."

Exciting.

He remembered the blood on his hands and his trousers. It was an intolerable memory. Not a day, barely even a minute, had passed by without him feeling hellish guilt, but he'd thought it was behind him. It had been so long. He put his hands to his throat. He needed to get out of here, needed to think. It couldn't all be ruined. He had Viktor and Andrea—a whole life that might not be perfect, but was beautiful all the same. He had to fight for it.

"Is everything alright? You've gone pale," the vicar said.

"Huh? No, nothing to worry about," Dag said, his brain grinding away. What could he do? Anything, he thought. Apart from contacting Pompe again. He'd rather die. A series of options flickered through his mind's eye. Perhaps it would be alright, perhaps they didn't really know anything.

Surely him pitching it at Pontus Bremer that one time wasn't enough; he might have read about the story in the papers and been captivated. But there was a Professor Rekke looking into it. A Rekke that he recalled his father telling him about long ago—a pianist, if he remembered correctly—and with a celestial sense for detail.

"Would you prefer to postpone?" the vicar said, and two seconds ago he would have said, "Yes, I've got to get out of here right now," but his brain was already working like a criminal's.

I must not arouse suspicion, he thought. I must remain calm.

"No, everything's fine. Nothing to worry about. We've been having a few issues with our son—he has such terrible bouts of anxiety. Sometimes he even hurts himself. But my wife is handling it."

After all, it was the truth. Viktor could go quite crazy when he didn't get to play his piano.

He'd pummel walls and smash up chairs and himself too. Sick with worry, Dag sought out help. It was as if his son wasn't made for this life. All he could do was tinkle away on the piano without gaining any particular aptitude for it, not that it mattered now. Now that it was all going to be ruined.

"I understand," the vicar said, putting a hand on Dag's arm, and he recoiled, surprised that someone was still being kind to him.

FORTY-FIVE

Santander, July 1988

Something strange happened to Sandra after she'd finished writing up her story and had gone out into the town in her pale blue dress. She bought a new notebook from the bookshop on the Plaza de Pombo and sat down on a lounge chair on the sandy Playa de Los Peligros to write some more while waiting for eight o'clock to come around.

But she wasn't able to pour out many words; she felt drained. She'd given the story of the Galgo her all, so she shut the notebook and gazed at the beach. There was almost no-one here now, just a few kids playing volleyball down by the water's edge and an elderly couple walking past. Not long after that, she gave a start, feeling ill at ease. Sitting immediately to her right was the weather-beaten man with the silver cross she'd seen that morning at the restaurant. His amused gaze to sea made her realize he had been watching her and was barely bothering to hide it, and she immediately felt afraid.

She wanted to leave, but she also wanted to understand who

he might be. He was perhaps forty-five years of age and had a well-drawn, almost beautiful face, and he was strikingly thin. Underneath his unbuttoned khaki shirt, she saw that he had veins visible even on his stomach, and, just as in the restaurant, by his side was a guitar with red and blue stickers on it. His salt-and-pepper hair was tied back in a ponytail. The eyebrows were jet-black, as if he'd added kohl to them, his lips were dry and a little chapped, and her impulse to walk away only intensified.

Yet she stayed sitting there, completely still, looking down at her legs. Obviously it was crazy to wear tights at the beach. She shouldn't have gone out in the dress, she should have worn trousers as usual, and without knowing why—perhaps just to show that she knew she was being watched—she nodded at him.

He nodded back, stood up and moved toward her. What should she do? She would just have to let it happen.

"*Disculpe*, sorry to disturb you," he said in broken Spanish. "Is your name Lola?"

She shook her head in confusion and then he added even more incomprehensibly:

"I'm sorry. I thought you were from Holland. I grew up in The Hague."

He said this in such a matter-of-fact way that she wondered whether it was a left-field pickup line. She'd already noticed on the walk here that men were looking at her differently. It was as if the dress made her more visible, and she had been pleased then and had felt as if life was getting started, but now she felt exposed.

"Oh really?" she said, meaning to add that she was writing and didn't want to be disturbed, but she didn't want to appear rude and risk provoking him.

"Don't be afraid, dear girl," the man said, as if he could sense her nervousness. "I only wanted to say hello. You looked so beautiful and far away. Are you going on a date tonight?"

She shook her head again. Then she realized it might be better to say yes, and it was the truth too. Well, she hoped it was the truth. She was longing to see Pompe more than she was willing to admit to herself.

"Well, yes, actually," she said. "I think so."

The man squatted beside her; his legs too were sinewy and slim. He smelled of cologne and tobacco.

"You think so," he said. "Then you need luck—it might be a magical evening if all goes well, which is why . . ." He slipped a hand in his pocket and she thought he was going to try to sell her something.

"I don't have any . . ." she began.

He put a finger to his lips and gently took hold of her wrist and she fell silent, mostly afraid, but also a little curious in spite of herself. He smiled knowingly while his eyes said *look at this.* Then he performed a conjuring movement with his fingers and suddenly there was a silver coin in his hand, and she couldn't help but say, "Wow."

It was as if the man had plucked the coin out of thin air.

"It's a talisman to bring good luck," he said, placing the coin in her hand.

There was a hole through its centre and a picture of a young man with long hair—Spain's patron saint Santiago, she guessed, although the apostle didn't look altogether friendly and bore a resemblance to the man himself.

"Take it," he said. "It will protect you from danger."

She became thoughtful at this, preferring to return the coin, but the man withdrew his hand.

"Why would there be any danger?" she said.

"You never know, but the coin brings you good luck. And you're beautiful as a spring morning. Nothing can go wrong."

She looked down at the coin and absorbed the compliment. She'd never been described as "beautiful as a spring morning" before, but the man was clearly exaggerating beyond belief. There was a theatrical air about him. Perhaps he lived down here by the beach and made a living doing tricks and sleights of hand.

"I can't take it. Though it's very pretty," she said, which wasn't altogether true but it wasn't a cheap coin either. It wasn't just some knickknack; this was proper craftsmanship with weight to it.

"Think of it as a loan," the man said. "I'll be here tomorrow. Return the coin to me and let me know how it went. I look forward to hearing about it."

Then he stood up and retreated toward his guitar, and she decided to leave too. It was approaching eight o'clock and she picked up her notebook while squeezing the coin in her left hand.

FORTY-SIX

Rekke gently removed Gina Mo's hand from his leg and met her gaze.

"And why do you want to hear about the psychopaths in my industry?" she said.

"It's a subject that interests me," he said. "But I've also fallen into the bad habit of crying into the wilderness—for want of anything else to do, I believe. At any rate, it amuses me more than establishing whether my brother might find himself in some trouble."

Her gaze became less challenging; perhaps she was interested.

"And you're looking for a man my age—or a little older—who's violent toward women and might have snapped a finger like others snap a twig?"

Rekke smiled wistfully at the naïveté of his question.

"Perhaps," he said. "I'm looking for a suspect who may have a background in your profession and has literary leanings, but who may also be quite a different type of person today."

"Sounds tricky."

"But if I'm on the right track then he moves gracefully and—if we're charitable—bears a resemblance to Mick Jagger. He has pronounced cheekbones and unusually plump lips. He has, or had, a drinking problem."

"We're talking about a rapist?"

"Worse than that."

Gina Mo fell silent, thoughtful.

"The basic premise is that this man was on the Cantabrian coast in the summer of 1988, but it's entirely possible that he's concealed this fact as much as possible."

"I'm guessing something terrible happened there?" Gina Mo said.

"Yes," said Rekke. "A girl was murdered. The man smoked unfiltered Gauloises back then and read Camus, and he liked Cohen and Lorca. If I'm looking for the right man, the world at large should by now have noted his grandiose aura, but also his misogyny, even if I'm sure it's well concealed behind beautiful words, alongside his tepid conscience, amorality, abundance of lies and presumably also a surfeit of threats and malice."

Gina Mo laughed as if this characterisation were amusing.

"I know him," she said.

"In the general sense?"

She looked pensive.

"No, in specific terms too. But I'd say the worst of them have left journalism."

"What makes you say that?"

"Because there's not enough money in muckraking. The most enterprising and amoral set up production companies, publishing houses or agencies where they're masters of their own world."

"Is there anyone particular you have in mind?" said Rekke.

"Maybe," she said, and it occurred to him that there was a considerable risk she would take this opportunity to smear an enemy.

"Bit of a looker, you said?"

He nodded.

"And secretly a sadist?"

"Most definitely," he said.

"I know a guy."

"Indeed?" Rekke said, already sick of himself. No-one tracks down murderers by asking people to name the biggest asshole they can think of.

"But I don't know his name," she said. "I can't even remember what he looks like, apart from being handsome—and powerful too."

Rekke raised an eyebrow.

"What are you getting at?"

"I've only heard stories about him. Seems he has shit hot lawyers who square things with his victims and get them to sign gagging orders."

"So that his name doesn't get out?"

"Well, not to me at any rate. But I've had stuff going on, and I haven't had time to look into it. This individual came to mind while you were talking about fingers being snapped like twigs. It's been years since I heard about it."

Rekke leaned in closer.

"And what exactly was it you heard?"

Gina Mo looked as if she were considering what she might ask for in exchange.

"I'm not sure how much I dare say."

"Come on," Rekke said, glancing at the cell walls as if to imply this was no place for her to play hard to get.

"Well, fine," she said. "Maria Rogestam's a fellow stringer I've known for years. She used to be based in Lebanon and reported on Israel and Palestine. But like more or less every other idiot these days she wanted to write whodunnits so she took a sabbatical, went home to Sweden and I didn't hear from her for a long time. Then, by chance, I bumped into her at the Södersjukhuset hospital. She looked like hell. Her hand was bandaged, face covered in bruises, but she refused to say what had happened, and only when I bought her a cup of coffee did it slip out that she'd been head-over-fucking-heels with some dreamboat guy. The only thing was that this guy could suddenly turn into a completely different person, and one night he'd apparently broken her fingers and given her a kicking. But it wasn't the assault itself that was the worst part, she said."

"What was the worst part?"

"His reaction afterward. He exhibited no remorse. In fact, his voice got quieter and became calm and controlled. Completely emotionless. He explained—in detail, I believe—how he'd ruin her career if she reported him or uttered a word about what had happened. She said it was like he'd done it a hundred times before, as if he were embarking on something formal and routine. Then he sent a lawyer her way who offered a ton of cash and told her to sign a nondisclosure agreement."

"And did she?"

"She didn't dare do anything else. The guy had loads of influential friends. He knew everybody, she said."

"You must have wondered who it was," said Rekke.

"Of course," Gina Mo said. "But I had so much on my own plate back then and I left the country not long after. But I think it was someone powerful in the literary world."

"What makes you say that?"

"Maria kept harping on about her book—her debut—which was coming out in the autumn. This individual who had beaten her seemed to hold sway over the publishing process, and she was afraid of him and not just physically. It seemed as if he had the power to crush her career, or so she said."

A torrent of excitement flashed through Rekke, but he did his best to suppress it. It was too simple, he thought.

"Thank you," he said. "I'll have to take a closer look at this."

He held her gaze and noted that vindictiveness in her eyes once again.

"Would you like to know something about my brother?" he said.

She nodded.

"You've got him worried. And do you know what I think?"

She shook her head.

"You've got something on him."

She smiled mysteriously.

"And I think you're going to give it your all at the press conference. I wish you the very best in your endeavour, and offer my congratulations on your freedom. Make the most of it. You've been mistreated, and for that I'm very sorry."

She gazed back at him almost tenderly.

"I'll cope."

"I expect you will. And do you know what?" he said.

"No."

"I'm glad I was able to meet you. I shall cross-check your information at once and will naturally be at pains to protect you as my source."

"That won't be necessary," she said.

But it is necessary for me, Rekke reflected, to recognize that the information came from you in particular and that you may wish to manipulate me. Perhaps you already know who this person is, and want to strengthen my convictions by letting me find his name by myself.

He felt a sudden impatience.

"Thank you for seeing me. I shall prepare my brother for your attacks," he said, standing up.

Gina Mo also stood up, perhaps a little disappointed that the visit was already at an end, and said she would monitor the news. Then Rekke summoned the prison officers and told them he was ready to leave.

FORTY-SEVEN

Caspar stopped, taken aback by Micaela's reaction. She realized that she was standing as if she wanted to defend herself with violence, and she lowered her fists and shoulders.

"What are you doing?" he hissed, moving as if to grab her by the arm.

She took a step back.

"I'm sorry."

"What is it you think? That I'm pushing drugs like your boys in Husby?" he said, and normally that would have bothered her intensely, but right now she sucked the words up greedily.

Was that what Caspar thought? That even here she was playing cops and robbers and had taken the chance to check up on him, because it was in her nature?

"I'm sorry," she said again.

"It's unhinged. You came straight in here. You said you were going to the bathroom?"

Micaela tried to look a little more relaxed.

"I'm just curious about you," she said. "You haven't told me much."

He appeared to be ruminating over whether there was any logic to what she had said.

"You could have asked."

"I get that. I saw some lovely pictures of you and your mum."

And one of your drawers is locked, she wanted to say. And you jot down times next to Persian names.

"What do you say? Why don't we have a bite to eat and try and make up? You've really outdone yourself," she said, pointing toward Caspar's spread and the bottle of wine on the coffee table.

"I have no secrets," he said.

But I do, Micaela thought, picturing Magnus Rekke's face. Then she padded toward the coffee table. At that moment, she heard a faint beep from her phone in the bedroom and she wanted to go and check it, but she was afraid to upset Caspar. The situation was so fragile.

"Come on sweetheart, I'm starving. And I could really go for a glass of wine too," she added hastily when he didn't answer or come toward her.

"Don't you want to check your texts first," he said.

"No, they'll keep," she said. "Come on, let's eat. And Caspar . . ." She took a deep breath. "I really am sorry. Truly, it's an occupational hazard."

"Is there something you haven't told me?" he said.

Play the innocent, she told herself. Pretend nothing has happened.

"Of course not. I just never know when to let things go."

"Then you won't mind if I read that text message for you."

Micaela hesitated. She didn't like the turn the conversation had taken, but she couldn't very well say no now that he'd seen her going through his desk.

"Go for it," she said, telling him her PIN.

He went into the bedroom and she tried to work out whether

there could be anything revealing or generally catastrophic that might have been sent to her. But if there was, she had no idea what that might be. Magnus Rekke would never text her about this, and it wasn't like she had any other men on the go. No, there was surely no danger. It was probably just Mamá or Vanessa. Or maybe Rekke to say he'd turned up a new lead. But when Caspar didn't return she grew worried nonetheless.

"It's from someone calling you *darling*," he said.

She exhaled.

"That'll be Jonas Beijer on the murder squad. He's always called me that. What does he say?"

Caspar fell silent.

"It's about a murder," he said, and she forgot about Caspar and the whole situation she'd found herself in.

"What does he say?" she said.

"Read it for yourself," Caspar said, throwing the phone to her, and when she read it she wanted to leave right away and get to work.

"Well I'll be damned," she muttered.

FORTY-EIGHT

Magnus Rekke picked up after one ring. He was back at home and had taken off Kleeberger's trousers and lain down to sober up, but it seemed getting any rest was out of the question. The phone was always ringing off the hook—to hell with all of them. But this time it was Hans, and he perked up, picturing Gina Mo in his mind's eye again.

She'd been in quite a state when they'd met inside a small annex at Guantánamo Bay where the Americans were holding her and a couple of other female inmates. She'd been sitting on a plain wooden bench in a visiting room with a window overlooking a burned-out field, clad in a red jumpsuit that fit tightly over her hips but was baggy everywhere else. Her head was shaved, her face lean and pale, but her eyes shone with an intense, dark glow. Her deportment was that of a queen, and Magnus made up his mind to really help her.

It went without saying that Gina Mo wasn't quite all there—she made up facts and would have sold her soul for a headline—but she was hardly a terrorist either. She was simply a woman drawn to guerillas and big drama, and he found her theories—

hearsay, really—about bin Laden intriguing. Perhaps bin Laden really was being protected by Pakistani intelligence, no matter how much Pakistan pretended to be an American ally in the War on Terror. Stranger things had happened. It would actually make sense in a way, given that the man had utterly vanished, leaving no trace. He remembered smiling back at the woman on the bench.

Gina Mo nodded in reply and jerked her head as if she still had long hair to toss back, and Magnus felt a pang of longing, which was unlike him. He'd never sought out power for those kinds of benefits. For Christ's sake, he was no Clinton. But there was something so attractive about that combination of vulnerability and pride that he put an arm around her and said he'd take care of her and secure her freedom. As she gazed at him seductively—as she apparently did with all men—Magnus clasped her by the hips and told her he'd take her to a decent hotel when she got out. That was it.

Nevertheless, it was a horrifying moment, and not because she was angry or even offended. On the contrary, she looked at him triumphantly, as if she'd discovered a weakness beyond what she'd hoped for. That was far worse. She'd spotted a deplorable trait in him, and had rejoiced as if it were another weapon for her to use, and it was in that moment he'd changed his mind.

He wasn't going to give her one iota of help. Quite the reverse—he would ensure the Americans held her for as long as possible, which was hardly so strange given that the standard operating procedure in politics was to save your own skin. In order to make it more morally straightforward he convinced himself that Gina Mo was genuinely dangerous. He persuaded himself that he'd been naïve before. It was impossible to move so intimately in guerilla circles without being drawn into their games. No, she belonged under lock and key, which was why it was such a damned nuisance they were now being forced to let her go.

"Well?" he said to his brother on the phone. "What did you find out?"

Hans remained silent—teasing him, of course—and Magnus got out of bed, picked up Kleeberger's trousers and put them in the trash. No-one that slight should be allowed to go unpunished.

"That she's got something on you," said Hans at last.

"She's lying," he said.

"But you haven't done much to secure her freedom. Quite the contrary, it seems."

"It may not have been my best work," Magnus said. "But she doesn't know anything about that."

"Are you so sure of that?" said Hans. "She's got a great attorney—Richard Brookman. I daresay he has his own CIA contacts?"

"Richard Brookman can go to hell," Magnus said, pushing Kleeberger's trousers even further into the trash for good measure.

"What are you doing?" said Hans. "There's a rustling sound."

Hans could fuck off too, for that matter.

"What do you think is going to happen?" he said more pathetically than he'd planned to.

"You'll pull through it quite unfairly provided that you . . ."

"What?"

Magnus wiped the residue of coffee grounds and yogurt from his hands.

"Haven't done something really stupid."

"I do what I have to and nothing more," he said pompously. It sounded a little absurd even to his ears.

"I think you're secretly flattered to be back in the soup," said Hans.

"Bullshit," Magnus said, but he thought, yes, perhaps. I'm sure I can put this to some good use.

"Who do you know in the world of publishing that knows every secret and machination in the industry?"

"What? Why do you ask?"

"I have my reasons," Hans said.

Magnus was still lingering on Gina Mo.

"Does she seem vindictive?"

"After four years' detention without trial, what do you think?" Hans said, and then Magnus muttered "Idiot" and hung up and returned to the wine cooler to uncork a fresh bottle of white.

He'd find a way to strike back, somehow.

FORTY-NINE

Pontus Bremer returned home to his apartment on Stockholm's Nybrogatan hoping that Micki, his wife, wouldn't be in. But of course she was. She was wearing an apron and she greeted him with a kiss and a compliment.

"Back already? I thought it was going to be quite a do at Kleeberger's."

"Nothing but a load of sticks-in-the-mud," he said. "Are we expecting visitors?"

Micki moved her lips nervously.

"Emma and Viktoria are coming over."

"Damn it," he said.

"I'm sorry, I thought . . ." she mumbled, looking so guilty that he couldn't help but be gentle and flash her a theatrical smile.

A fetching young wife like her came with its advantages. It impressed his colleagues and the gossip columns. But sometimes it felt like he was being punished for his sins, especially when she invited her friends over. It was like having a pack of chattering schoolgirls in the house. Their platitudes drove him to distraction.

"It's okay, babe. I'll pop down to Teatergrillen for a bite to eat."

"No, stay. There's enough food to go around."

"No, it's alright," he said, wondering whether to tell her something about the party with his usual bombast, simply to restore balance. But he didn't feel like it.

All he said was:

"You've met Dag Wrangel, haven't you?"

"Love the man," she said.

Of course you fucking do, you fawning, overfamiliar fangirl.

"Why do you ask?" she said.

He paused for thought.

"Just wondered. Didn't he use to give you weird looks?"

She suddenly smiled tenderly and came toward him as he pondered whether to remove his coat or not.

"My sweet, surely you're not jealous of Dag Wrangel?" she said, kissing him lightly on the mouth.

"I'm not . . ." he said, offended, but she didn't let him finish.

"I like Dag," she said, "because he takes an interest in me and isn't a self-centred prick like most of the rest of your colleagues. But come on! He's hardly Pontus Bremer, is he? That boy's no man."

That softened him up right away.

He loved it when she spoke about him in the third person, and while he was happy to be a man he preferred most of all to be Pontus Bremer. A concept, an institution. He kissed her back.

"Sorry, it was just something about him that came up," he said.

She was immediately curious.

"What?"

He didn't bother to shrug off his coat and figured he might as well get going at once. If he uttered a word of what he was thinking, Emma and Viktoria would know about it in an instant and it would be all over Facebook before he knew it.

"It's complicated," he said.

"Come on, you've started so now you have to finish," she said, and it bugged him that she used such threadbare turns of phrase. *That boy's no man. I've started so I'll finish.* That was no way for the wife of a wordsmith of his calibre to express herself.

"A rumour," he said. "Well, hardly even that. Just a trivial thing that occurred to me. I have to check it out first."

Then he took off his shoes and coat before going into his study to look up the name he'd extracted from Professor Rekke: Sandra Ramirez, murdered on the night of July twelfth, 1988, in Santander, Spain. Come on, Pontus said to his computer. I don't have time for any of this Spanish bollocks. Give me something nice in Swedish or English. A moment later he gasped. Great Scott! The *London Review of Books*!

How could he have missed this? Published only six months earlier—with a preface by Mario Vargas Llosa. It was almost too much, and he instinctively felt envious. When was the last time the *London Review of Books* had been in touch with him? Never! Fuck them. But then he calmed down.

The story had doubtless been published for sentimental reasons. Who wouldn't want to indulge a murdered young woman? Although heaven knew why it was in print now, so long after the fact. Whatever. Let's see how you lay your scene, little girl. He began to read.

A storm blew up that night, bringing with it the strays, tortured, forsaken and malnourished.

Not bad, he thought, before realising the story was about a tree, an old oak with a trunk split down the middle by two bolts of lightning, and whose branches reached into the sky as if praying with thirty arms.

Not so bad either. He might almost have written it himself. He carried on, searching for shortcomings in the text like he always did when reading authors who'd experienced vexing success. He forgot all about the world and himself, and didn't even register the noise of Emma and Viktoria's arrival. He was completely engrossed, reading the story from start to finish some two or three times, not only reluctantly impressed but also unpleasantly affected. The story resembled Dag's old pitch, and Pontus's thoughts anxiously skipped back and forth.

Oh Dag, what have you done? Surely you don't harbour such brutality that you'd kick a young woman to death? It's impossible. Then again . . . what did he know? Nothing. As he liked to say, man had three selves: a public self, a private self and a secret self. As for Dag, what to say about him? He was so damn nice that even Micki loved him; there had to be a darkness beneath the surface. Pontus resolved to look into the matter. It might be another scalp for his belt, and surely he should be able to solve this without Rekke—because who could beat him when it came to acuity? Hardly that damn Professor.

There was the sound of laughter from the kitchen. My darling girls, what simple little lives you lead, he thought, while here sits Pontus Bremer, grappling with the big questions. Well, what was he going to do?

He remembered Dag's voice on the phone earlier. His voice had sunk and cracked, as if he were plunging into a black hole. But then he'd crawled out of it again and feigned nonchalance as he suggested a drink. Was that an option now? Going out for a pint with Dag to gauge where he was at?

Pontus stood up and sauntered through to the girls in the kitchen, and in that moment the tree in the story came back to him—the tree the strays went to die by, and where thoughts descended into gnawing solitude. Had the Spanish girl felt like that too—that the world completely lacked mercy? Pontus stopped in the hall.

He made up his mind to escape the gossiping girls' giggles in the kitchen and head down to Teatergrillen to call Dag. Maybe he could squeeze the truth out of him.

FIFTY

Santander, July 1988

Sandra clasped the coin in her hand as she pushed her way toward La Mar. There were people everywhere, everyone seemed cheery and expectant, and the men were smiling at her and some were even whistling. She felt like Cinderella transformed by an enchanted dress, and she smiled back and wanted to embrace them all.

It was ten past eight; she was pleased to be a little late. She didn't want to seem too keen, and she was hardly even nervous. She was as ready as she ever would be to meet someone like Pompe. She was bubbling with a newfound confidence. She had lots to tell—the coin was a story in itself—and truth be told she wasn't at all worried that he wouldn't show.

He's coming, she thought. Now everything is going my way. Why would he pass up a chance like this? To meet someone like her? Suddenly, she felt special and allowed herself to feel intoxicated by that feeling.

Ouch! A man had trodden on her foot. It was Stefano, a friend from school she'd always liked from a distance. He kissed her on the lips without asking permission and said:

"Sorry! You're looking beautiful tonight, Sandra," and she smiled in return and laughed, as if this were something that happened to her on a daily basis.

"That dress looks amazing on you," said Stefano's friend Javier, and he kissed her too, smelling of booze and fiesta. The whole city smelled of fiesta and intoxication, and everyone suddenly seemed to love her and that was wonderful and nothing else and she didn't even bother looking for Pompe.

She simply let life come at her, hugging strangers, imagining that somewhere here, not far away, he was watching it all and thinking, look at how fêted she is, embracing people all over the place. She's not the way I imagined she was. But when Sandra raised her gaze and looked around, she couldn't see him. She didn't allow herself to be discouraged. It was only twenty past and it might be fun to linger here for a while. There was no rush. She decided to go into the restaurant and buy a drink. Why not get drunk like everyone else? She pushed her way through the crowd, eagerly at first, and then she froze. Standing by the bar was Roberto, his face black-and-blue like Dag's, and when he spotted her his gaze and body both tensed, and he took a step toward her and her happiness was so shallow that it was gone in a second to be replaced by downright fear.

FIFTY-ONE

Micaela read Jonas Beijer's text one more time:

Darling, how thrilling! Fuck me . . . Jenni—that murder victim in Helsinki last year—was assaulted that exact same way AND her shoulder was marked too. But not with a number. It was some other weird shit. Call me?

She raised her gaze and saw that Caspar was watching her, and she wondered how to handle this. She wanted to get out of here and call Jonas, but Caspar had just sat down and they hadn't had the bottle of wine and their meal yet, and the atmosphere was already challenging. She couldn't dash off right away.

"Just an exciting work thing," she said.

"Oh yeah?" he said acidly, which annoyed her, but what did she expect?

"I told you about that murder in Spain. The girl who was beaten to death. We think it could be a serial killer, and this is a lead on another potential victim."

"Gosh," he said, attempting to sound interested. "How gruesome."

"But I'll deal with that later. Why don't we get dressed, drink some wine and have a bite to eat?" she said, even though she was no longer hungry.

He stood up. His expression was troubled as he glanced toward the desk by the window. Please don't bring up the rummaging through the drawers again, she thought. She could hardly explain it a second time without mentioning the real reason for her curiosity, and then she'd ruin everything. Micaela took a sip of wine and helped herself to some food while her mind continued to race.

"It's as if you're somewhere else," he said.

"You too," she said.

"Is it so strange that I'm a little shocked? You could have asked if there was anything in my drawers you were particularly interested in."

She bit the bullet.

"I could. But I think . . ."

The pounding in her head would not subside and she felt a stabbing pain in her stomach. Might it be the world's worst PMS, she thought.

"What is it that you think?"

She'd have to spit it out.

"I've got to go."

"What?"

"I'm sorry. I can't stop thinking about that text. There's something . . ." she said before cutting herself short because that final sentence wasn't addressed to Caspar but herself.

There was something in the Spanish case files that didn't add up, was what she wanted to say. There was something there that neither she nor Rekke had understood yet. But Micaela pushed this aside, stood up and was hit by the sensation that she didn't really know Caspar at all.

He was giving her a look that was difficult to interpret.

"I'll call you later," she said, going into the bedroom and dressing while listening for footsteps that never came, and she wondered whether he'd gone to the desk to see what she'd touched.

Outside the window, the blizzard was howling as she did up her trousers and smoothed her hair before emerging again, unsure what to expect. But Caspar received her with open arms in the living room and told her he was sorry and said she could rummage through his drawers all she liked.

He had no secrets; not from her. But he was out of sorts too, he said. There was a lot on at work for him as well.

"Not exactly serial killers, but still pretty pressing stuff," he said with a smile.

Then they parted on friendly terms, or at least they did a good job of pretending to, and she went out of the door of his apartment and while she was descending the stairs she called Jonas Beijer.

He picked up after one ring and said: "Darling, how I've missed you. The stuff you sent me? Dynamite."

And she said:

"I know, right?" as she walked toward the door to the street, but when she saw the storm beyond it she lingered in the hallway.

"Tell me about the Finnish murder," she said. "Did you work the case?"

"Just a sec," he said. Someone was making a noise in the background and he yelled "Calm down!" before seeming to close a door. "I wasn't really involved," he said, "but a couple of my colleagues were because for a while there was a suspected Swedish connection. On the night she was murdered, Jenni Järvinen had been to a party thrown by a Dutch businessman who made his fortune in hospitality, but had by then moved to Helsinki and was trying to get into movies and publishing in the Nordics. There were plenty of Swedes at his do: screenwriters, agents, producers and one or two celebs, and it wasn't unreasonable to assume the killer was someone Järvinen met at the party."

"But that wasn't the case?"

"Not that anyone could prove. At around ten o'clock, Järvinen took a cab alone to her parents' place in Espoo, which was right down by the water and empty at the time. She unquestionably made it into the house. She turned on the lights in the kitchen and living room and got out some bread and a beer, if I remember correctly. But she must have gone out again—without locking up. She was barefoot, as far as we know, and wearing an ochre dress. A rather short one. She was found dead in the morning next to an old pine tree by the rocks not far away, badly beaten."

"The case is still open, isn't it?"

"Yes, but I wouldn't leap to the conclusion that it's the same killer you're looking for. Järvinen had taken kicks to the throat and hips. The back of her head had been caved in, as if it had been smashed against the rocks. But there was no sign of the same elaborate sadism or the excessive violence from your cases, which could admittedly be because the killer was interrupted. The mark that I mentioned was only half there, as if the murderer didn't have time to finish it off."

"What was it?"

"It was an incomplete letter O, or I suppose you might say it was an upside down U. Hard to say. It wasn't very even. Blood must have been pouring out which would have made it a harder job. But it was still carved pretty deeply."

Micaela sat down on the bottom step and gazed at the storm through the glass-fronted main door. Something was bothering her, and it wasn't just her stomach, which was now aching even more. It was something else. Then she understood.

"So they didn't carve it into her post mortem?" she said.

"No, but the killer might have thought she was dead. He might have been shocked at the blood. It's hard to say."

"Could you email me the pictures from the autopsy and whatever you can turn up from the investigation?"

"Give me some time to sort it. There's something else I've got to ask you first."

He hesitated.

"Yes?" she said.

"The detectives knew about the Danish woman—Regina. They worked with the Aarhus police, but I don't think they knew about the Spanish case. How did you two come across it?"

"Rekke had a visitor."

"He should start charging."

She smiled.

"He doesn't have it in him. Do you have the names of the Swedes who were at that party?"

"That agent guy everyone's always talking about nonstop, Oliver Popov, was there. And Per Morton too, the owner of Morton Production. And there was the crime writer Olof Eriksson, and a few others I don't remember. Junior staffers."

"Did everyone have alibis?"

Jonas was silent for a second or two.

"Yes, it seems so—although a couple of them provided each other with alibis. And there never was enough evidence."

"Do you think it might be any of them?" Micaela said.

Jonas hesitated again.

"Fuck knows. There was something off about that Popov geezer. He was so arrogant under questioning, and there were loads of rumours that he'd turned violent before. But it seems doubtful that he'd kill a woman like that. He had powerful friends vouching for him, and there were no forensics to tie him to the murder, and he'd got no priors, even if—"

Micaela interrupted him.

"Just a minute."

A taxi was crawling through the snow in the street outside and at that same moment she heard someone running down the stairs behind her. Then she saw it was Caspar, who stared back at her in uncomfortable surprise.

"Sorry, Jonas," she said. "There's something I've got to take care of. Can you send over whatever you've got and we'll talk later."

She hung up and stared at Caspar, who looked like he'd been caught red-handed.

"You're still here?" he said, startled.

"It was so miserable outside I ended up waiting for a bit. Where are *you* off to?" she said.

"I'm seeing a friend," he said hesitantly, standing still, but then he bit his lip and dashed past her with guilt-laden steps and she stood up, determined to stop him and talk this out.

But her legs wouldn't carry her; she felt another infernal stabbing pain in her stomach, and she bent double like a jackknife and swore and probably called out after him. But she didn't know for sure.

She collapsed in pain in the stairwell, just inside the main door, and lay there paralysed on the concrete floor, gasping for air.

FIFTY-TWO

Rekke didn't notice it himself, but he spoke faster upon his return home and moved more frantically. He was on the phone and writing emails simultaneously. He was reading the case files and Googling simultaneously, he was doing all sorts of things simultaneously, and he realized more quickly than he could have hoped who it was that had probably broken the young author's fingers, the woman Gina Mo had told him about.

It was his old publisher at Natur & Kultur who had put out his nonfiction work that set him on the right track.

"A rot's set into the industry," the publisher told him on the phone, describing a shift in the publishing world, a commercialisation of sorts, more aggressive negotiations pertaining to saleable bodies of work, but also a brutalisation, he said. Threats were levelled and junior staffers abused, but no-one did anything about it, he said. Far too many people at the major publishing houses benefitted from this new order, and no complaints had been made. It was difficult to act on hearsay, and perhaps no-one wanted to act either, given that most of the top dogs had personal relationships—based on reciprocity and loyalties—with the driving force behind this change, who went by the name of Oliver Popov.

Popov was the owner of an eponymous literary agency and a wine importer of some significance, particularly of Californian varieties. He was forty-four years old and had previously been a screenwriter at Morton Production. He'd started his own business in the mid-nineties and quickly become successful, at least in part, if Rekke understood correctly, because he'd gone against the cautious and polite etiquette that characterized the publishing world. Popov had appeared on the scene with a new and frenzied abandon, and while many were horrified, even more were enchanted. All the anxious intellectuals were suddenly charmed by this grandiose brigand, as Rekke's publisher put it, which was no surprise and merely basic psychology. The overcultured often longed secretly for the savage and lawless, Rekke reflected, and he would ordinarily not have given it a second thought, but a couple of details made him linger on the topic. These included the online pictures of Popov, who was blond and had a high hairline, and while he was fit and powerfully built, there was a gracious, almost feminine air to him that matched the witness statements pertaining to the literary Swede who had drunk so heavily in the Santander restaurant in 1988. Then, of course, there were the broken fingers.

Both Sandra Ramirez and the Danish woman Regina Lassen had had their fingers snapped, and while he wasn't able to have it confirmed, Rekke found details to suggest that Popov and the bandaged crime writer whom Mo had crossed paths with at the Stockholm hospital had been an item. According to several sources, Popov had been violent toward former girlfriends, and it was known that he used aggressive lawyers to buy people's silence. A short piece in the trade publication *Dagens Media* noted that a broadsheet journalist by the name of Gustaf Nordlund at *Svenska Dagbladet* had carried out a major investigation into Popov that never saw the light of day. Without giving it any further thought, Rekke called the reporter.

He wasn't able to reach him and so he left a message on both his mobile voicemail and his desk answer machine, and it was then, as he was rattling about his study, that he discovered that Micaela had sent a fax to Jonas Beijer.

Might that turn up more than Corales had found? It wouldn't surprise him. There was more buried beneath the surface. He was sure of it. He stared at the pictures of Popov again. His eyes were dark and cold, his smile slightly lopsided and derisive. I know that kind of personality, Rekke thought. "Easy now," he muttered. So far, he knew nothing.

The phone rang. It was Gustaf Nordlund from *Svenska Dagbladet.*

"Professor," Nordlund said. "This is an honour. I saw you at the Stockholm Concert Hall when I was a child. You played Bartók."

Am I that old already, Rekke thought, but fortunately Nordlund sounded as if he were terribly young.

"How nice," he said. "I always enjoy your articles and I'd be happy to share a story if you could help me out with something."

"Go on then," said Nordlund. "I recall you sat completely still as you played."

"Movement should come from within, as my teacher always said. I just met Gina Mo Anderson," Rekke said.

The reporter was clearly flummoxed.

"How did you pull that off?"

"She's due to be released and will be holding a press conference. It'll be on the wires first thing tomorrow. I should think you'll get the scoop if you write it up now."

"Thank you," Nordlund said. "Why's she being released and where is she?"

"I'll tell you," Rekke said. "But first I'd like some information. You know Oliver Popov?"

Gustaf Nordlund laughed.

"That bastard? Do I ever! But I don't suppose anyone will be able to take him down now," he added.

"Why would that be?"

"Because he managed to sell the Prime Minister's book for a record-breaking sum and he has lots of new friends in the government."

Doubtless including Magnus, Rekke thought.

"What did you have on him?" he said.

"What didn't I have?" Nordlund said. "But the editor-in-chief backed down. He got scared. That's what Popov and his lawyers do best—make people nervous."

"Was it Popov who broke Maria Rogestam's fingers?"

"It's murky," Nordlund said. "But it would follow the pattern. Popov meets women that he has power over and then he turns violent. When they push back he doesn't budge an inch—instead he goes onto the front foot and says he'll crush them if they take it any further. He's a master of breaking people with words, and he never shouts in those situations. He always delivers his threats in a controlled whisper. No-one is allowed to make others feel as small as he does. Somehow, he manages to shift the guilt onto his victims."

"Has he ever danced?"

"I beg your pardon?"

"Danced. Ballet, preferably. Something that taught him to stretch his back and gave him a graceful stride."

Gustaf Nordlund was silent for a moment.

"I don't know about that. But he does have an unusual gait—walks with his shoulders pushed out and a slightly awkward stride. He really does know how to work a room, and unless he sinks them, he makes the people he meets feel very seen. He can flatter anyone, and I think he's a damn good salesman. What's your angle?"

"An old crime," said Rekke. "I read he stopped drinking."

Gustaf Nordlund laughed.

"I'm not sure that's always an unqualified success, and it can't be entirely straightforward being off the wagon and a leading wine importer all at the same time. But he's definitely cut back. An old friend of mine told me he'd done the most terrible things while drunk. Apparently he could completely lose it. He's more controlled these days."

"Has he become kinder too?"

"Definitely not," the reporter said. "Only more calculating and more manipulative. He thinks he can do anything these days, and he brags about it. 'I'm invincible,' he says. 'No-one can get to me.' The guy's as high as a kite on his own hubris."

"And no-one says anything?"

"No-one dares, and there are way too many people making money off him. Well, fine. There are a few. Linda Olofsson and Eva Stark—you know, the crime writers—have both distanced themselves from Popov. And Dag Wrangel seems to be an ardent hater, although even Dag seems afraid."

"Do you know what he was up to during the summers of the late eighties?" said Rekke.

"Only that he went to journalism school at Poppius and that he travelled Europe. But he had to buckle down too. He's not from money. His old man . . ." Nordlund said.

But Rekke didn't catch the rest because at that moment the doorbell rang, and not just once but persistently. Then the door flew open and his old housekeeper, Mrs. Hansson, stormed into the apartment, visibly worked up.

"Gustaf, I'm going to have to call you back," Rekke said as he gazed at Mrs. Hansson, who had taken up a position in front of him, red-cheeked, hands on hips.

"No!" Nordlund said. "You promised me a story."

Rekke took a deep breath.

"And you've got it," he said. "Call Gina Mo's lawyer, Richard Brookman. He'll tell you more. Give him my best."

Then he rang off and gave his attention to Mrs. Hansson. The woman was seventy-four years old and had a bad back and achy joints, but often managed—as she did now—to look worried and crackle with energy. She wore a long skirt and a woolly sweater and had her hair in a bun.

"Out with it," he said. "What's happened?"

"They've rushed Micaela to the Karolinska hospital. She's in a bad way. They say she's in critical condition."

FIFTY-THREE

Santander, July 1988

Sandra had no idea that wicked eyes were watching her.

She didn't know that those eyes could make out the scars through her tights and longed to add new ones—let alone that the same person, the same man, was studying her hands and found them so beautiful that he wanted to hold them in his, lovingly, smiling, as if they were as precious as the baby chick he'd once picked up out of a nest as a child.

The chick had felt so warm and had been ticking away with nerves and he hadn't been able to resist the temptation to squeeze, so he'd crushed it in his hands. But she didn't know anything about that. She was just glad that Roberto had missed in his lunge toward her and that the whole bar had come to her rescue and protected her from him. She was happy that the evening was smiling on her, and that everyone was being so friendly and paying her compliments. The fiesta had gotten off to such an auspicious start. The only thing was that time was passing and there was no Pompe, and eventually that began to niggle at her. Her gaze revealed her change in mood. All the men smiling at her and looking at her were no longer people in their own right. Instead, they distinguished themselves solely by not being Pompe, and it cast a gloomier light on the evening. She made up her mind to leave La Mar.

It was by then a quarter past nine and her tights were itchy, and she was missing her short story and her stray, and she felt as if she didn't belong in these crowds. She wanted to be alone and to write. Might Pompe be the same? He'd seemed so straightforward that morning, but perhaps he also preferred calm seclusion. Of course, it was impossible to know.

She became tense, aware for the first time that evening—or worried, rather—that she was being watched, but when she turned around she could see nothing out of the ordinary. All she saw was the throng of people pushing past while cacophonies of music blared from the various restaurants' speakers and collided with each other. She was seized by paranoia. But everything was probably fine, she told herself. Roberto was nowhere to be seen, nor were any other threatening figures, but there—Good God . . . She gasped. Standing behind a stand selling wine and cheese, hidden behind a group of teenage boys in Barcelona shirts, was Dag.

He'd obviously been watching her for a long time, and it felt a bit much—as if he were spying on her again. But he reassured her by smiling shyly, and she walked hesitantly toward him.

"Hi," she said.

"Hi," he said, breathing a little heavily.

He looked down at her hands.

"Thanks for your help with the story," she said. "I finished it when I got home. It was all about the magic tree."

He looked up at her face.

"Did you make it evil?" he said.

"Really evil," she said. "Just like you suggested."

He smiled.

"If I get it published, I'll be sure to thank you," she said, and then immediately felt silly. The road to publication was a long one; it would be a good while before she would even show it to anyone else.

But Dag beamed and asked if he could buy her a drink and she wanted to say yes. She felt lonely and uncomfortable in the crowd, and she remembered how pleasant their conversation had been earlier that day, and she didn't really have anywhere to be. But she managed to ruin it.

"Where's Pompe?" she said, instead of answering his question.

"I don't know. I'm just glad to be rid of him," Dag said, moving closer to her as if he wanted to kiss her or to stroke her hair, which didn't really bother her that much.

Nevertheless, she drew back. It was as if her body could only drive her away, and perhaps she was afraid Roberto might see her and Dag together, and perhaps Pompe too. At any rate, she mumbled a "See you later" and left Dag as quickly and insensitively as she had done that afternoon, and perhaps that was when the evening turned and became threatening and dangerous for real.

FIFTY-FOUR

Early the next morning, Micaela lay in a bed at the Karolinska hospital in a room she was sharing with a young woman who'd had a late miscarriage. The girl kept crying.

"He'll be devastated," she said, as if she weren't the object of sympathy in this instance. She was pretty and petite, but despite constantly referring to her boyfriend—the father of the child she had lost—he never did turn up and Micaela half-heartedly attempted to offer comfort. She didn't do a very good job of it.

Micaela had also lost a child; a foetus she'd had no idea she was carrying and that she had never wanted, and which had implanted outside the womb, causing her fallopian tube to rupture. That was why she'd been in so much pain. She'd had an ectopic pregnancy, and now she was disinclined to think about it. All she remembered was lying in the stairwell of Caspar's block and feeling as if she was going to shatter into pieces when an old man with a greying beard and kind eyes had bent down over her. The man had called an ambulance and not long after she'd been carried on a stretcher and she'd roused herself for a bit and called Rekke—not Mamá, definitely not Caspar, no, fucking Rekke—but that hopeless idiot had been on the phone.

Instead, she'd dialled Mrs. Hansson's number; she was a bit like a mother to them both. But as Mrs. Hansson had picked up, Micaela had suffered from a fresh bout of convulsions and a female paramedic had taken the phone from her and explained where they were going. Later she got through to Rekke after all and told him that if he was going to come and visit her anyway, he might like to bring her laptop and log in to see what Jonas Beijer had sent her. Despite the pain, she was mostly concentrating on the old murder investigation. Perhaps it was an escape. She was in such agony that it didn't surprise her in the slightest when they took her straight into surgery, and now she'd been awake for a while and had spoken to a nurse and been told that Rekke had been in the hallway outside all night working away, which she supposed should have touched her. Instead, she was furious, angry at his solicitude and angry at the girl in the next bed who wouldn't stop crying and most of all she was angry at Caspar who had stolen away in his taxi like a thief in the night. And she was angry that her stomach still hurt, and that she felt numb and exhausted, and that she couldn't take in what had happened.

"I don't know what I'm going to say. I just don't know," the girl in the next bed said.

"For Christ's sake—call him and tell him already," Micaela snapped. Then it hit her that this was something else they had in common. She couldn't face calling her partner. Or maybe she could, but she wasn't feeling like it. She didn't want to tell Caspar that she'd been carrying his child, even if she hadn't been doing it properly. Instead, she thought about that name she'd seen in his desk drawer—Mina Nazari. But then she let go of that too and stared toward the window and the darkness beyond it. The blizzard had abated, but it looked grimly cold out there. She looked at the time. A quarter past seven. She pressed the call button and immediately felt guilty. The nurse probably had other things to be getting on with, and they were probably understaffed at this hour. But the nurse appeared and Micaela explained that she would like to see her visitor.

"Oh, he will be pleased," the nurse said, and moments later Rekke appeared in the doorway dressed in the same suit he'd worn to Kleeberger's the day before, her computer under his arm.

But there was something different about him. His limbs were restless, and he grasped the hand of the weeping girl and offered his condolences, telling her it was fortunate she was a long-distance runner: "It might help a little in banishing the darkness." Then he turned toward Micaela and had just bent down to hug her when the girl in the next bed said:

"How did you know I run?"

"I can hear it in your breathing," he said. "You've got a low pulse, despite your loss. You're stronger than you think."

"Am I?" said the girl, but Rekke barely seemed to notice.

He sat down on the chair at Micaela's bedside and scrutinized her with a nervous smile before opening her laptop and logging in. He was unshaven and red-eyed, and while he looked intensely focused, he jumped when a cart bumped into the wall in the hallway outside. He seemed to be experiencing sensory overload, and appeared ready to leap up from the chair at any moment.

"My brave girl," he said. "How are you?"

"How are *you*?" she said somewhat provocatively, because his hypersensitivity was making her nervous.

He looked confused, as if something else had occurred to him, but he gave a composed answer.

"I'm a little manic again. I'm seeing a bit too much, hearing a bit too much. But it has its advantages. I took a look at what your colleague sent you."

She smiled reluctantly. She hadn't seen him manic in a long time, and this looked like a modest bout. He didn't seem to be on the brink of turning the world upside down, just a little more excessively intense, which was perhaps no bad thing—provided she had it in her to slow him down. In his manic spells, he sometimes saw more clearly than ever, but he also made more mistakes. The constant doubt that both slowed him down and enhanced his focus in his depressive episodes vanished.

"Then I shall have to remain sceptical," she said.

"Once again, you get to be my Sancho Panza. But I'm worried about you. You've lost a child."

"Not a child I knew I had."

"And the father?"

Micaela closed her eyes and asked Rekke to draw the curtain separating her and the girl, and he did this while once again examining the girl with his nervous smile, as if he'd spotted something else besides her being a runner.

"He doesn't know anything," Micaela said.

"Shouldn't he?"

She paused for thought.

"No, it was all a mistake. I've come to suspect he's an idiot."

"Aren't we all?"

"Well, you are. You should get back on the lithium."

"A gloomy medicine," Rekke said.

"Better than opiates and benzos," she snorted.

"You were in a bad way."

"I know," she said. "But that's exactly why I need something else to think about. I've come to think it might be risky for us to focus too much on these literary Swedes. There are other suspects in the investigation."

Rekke didn't appear to take her words seriously.

"Perhaps," he said. "But now we have these murders in Aarhus and Espoo too. They suggest a Nordic connection, and perhaps a connection to journalism—to writing."

"I suppose so," she said thoughtfully. "Järvinen—the Finn—her shoulder was marked too, wasn't it? With an incomplete letter O."

Rekke shut his eyes and didn't answer immediately. For a while, Micaela fell to listening once again to the girl's sobs and the sound of distant voices in the hallway. Then she hauled herself up in bed.

"It's not an incomplete letter O," Rekke said. "It's not even an upside down U. It's a new number. A hieroglyph."

FIFTY-FIVE

Pontus Bremer woke up at six o'clock in the morning with a smile on his lips. His night at Teatergrillen had gone exactly as hoped. He'd received the welcome he deserved: tributes and slaps on the back and a couple of drinks on the house "because it's an honour to have you here." A shady billionaire he knew from the business pages had bowed, while a dark-haired girl of about twenty, whom he would have hit on had he not been so occupied playing the dignified man of letters, had wanted him to sign her book.

He laughed at that. It's almost enough to scare a man, he thought: here I lie as Pontus Bremer. Ha ha. It took less than that to leave some people on edge. Then it didn't feel quite as much fun, although it was always like that on hungover mornings. For the first few minutes, the alcohol lingered on as a shield across the heart, affording protection from anguish, which was definitely the case that morning.

Getting up, he donned jeans and T-shirt, went to the kitchen and took in the aftermath of Micki's girls' night. A shiver of annoyance ran down his spine. "They might have tidied up after themselves," he muttered, as he loaded glasses and plates into the dishwasher and emptied the trash. In that moment, his second call with Dag Wrangel came back to him. It must have been shortly before closing time. It had been a brief discussion, and the hum of the bar in the background had meant he'd barely been able to hear, and he couldn't remember quite what he'd said himself either—only that he'd prattled on about the murder in Santander and the Spanish girl's short story. But he remembered the panic he'd instilled.

He remembered the silence and the rising terror it contained, which had in turn transmitted itself to him, and he'd murmured an apology and figured he'd drop the whole thing. He recalled Dag's whisper that he had it all wrong, which Pontus had reacted to as well. He didn't have a damn clue what he'd said, only that he'd imagined the worst. Given the late hour, Dag must have been calling long after his family had turned in. Suddenly it hit Pontus.

He'd met said family not long ago, in passing: the wife, Andrea, who really didn't seem to deserve a disaster, and the boy. What was his name? Viktor, that was it. Viktor, who sat at the piano and played basic pieces with such melancholy that it sounded as if he were fifty rather than eleven. Not that it mattered, damn it.

Pontus hated children. Children were self-absorbed and boring and thank God he didn't have any of his own and he really should dismiss any urge to be considerate on that count. If Dag was mixed up in a murder—if he was—then the truth had to come out.

"I'm going to call Professor Rekke," he said aloud to himself.

"Huh . . . what was that you said?"

Micki had woken up and come into the kitchen in a dishevelled state.

"Nothing," he said. "Forget about it. I'm trying out formulations for my novel."

. . .

Rekke's gaze wandered. There were still stoic sobs audible from beyond the curtain. In the hallway outside, a hospital cart rattled past.

"It's quite elementary," he said. "It's hard to understand how they missed it. Take a look." He turned the computer toward Micaela, and she stared at a dead, mottled, black-and-blue hand.

"The fingers on the left hand are broken toward the base, just like they were on Lassen and Ramirez," he said. "And here . . ." He changed the image and a bruised shoulder appeared with a deep wound showing dark edges. There was something primitive, ancient even, about it, she thought. The carving looked like a basic pot that had been turned upside down.

"It's like an upside down U," he said. "But it's hardly an unfinished letter O as your colleague suggested. On the contrary, the markings at the bottom show that the movement was intended to stop right there. This and nothing else was what he wanted to show."

"What does it mean?" said Micaela. "Is it an old symbol?"

A beep signalled the arrival of a text message on the phone in Rekke's pocket and made him jump. He fumbled for the phone.

"Leave it."

He looked thoughtful.

"Of course," he said. "And given the injuries and what we already know, I would venture to say with some certainty that it's a new number but an older model."

"Go on," she said, on tenterhooks.

"Which is logical, in its way. The killer has gone back in time from the Roman to the Greek numeral system. It only seems natural he would have ended up with the Egyptian one."

"Egyptian?" Micaela said, gazing at the carving, once again

consumed by the feeling that she was looking at something ancient.

"Exactly," he said. "Their numbering system emerged more than five thousand years ago. Straight lines, sticks, denoted the numbers one, two, three, four—all the way up to nine. Then they created other symbols with ten as the base for bigger numbers. A drawing of a frog stood in for one hundred thousand. One finger was ten thousand, a lotus flower was one thousand, a coiled rope was one hundred."

"I see," she said.

"And a simple picture of a hoof was ten," he said, pointing to the carving. "It looked just like that—an upside down U."

"Oh my God," she said.

It began to sink in.

"The tenth victim," she said.

He nodded.

"Unless he's overgenerous in his counting."

"You think he might be exaggerating?"

Rekke's pocket beeped again as another message arrived, but now he didn't seem to care.

"It had crossed my mind," he said. "Ten is a lot of bodies. We would have heard more about them."

"Why would he lie about the number of victims?" said Micaela.

A melancholy smile played across Rekke's lips.

"Perhaps for the same reason that he kills. There's a void inside him and he fills it by showing off his power—preferably more power than he has. In fact, I feel I have a quite clear conception of him. And do you know what I think, Micaela?"

She looked at him in curiosity.

"He mourns the fact that his murders aren't more renowned, and I thought I might assist him on that point," Rekke said.

"You mean by going to the press?"

"Or we tell him to his face."

Micaela stared at him in astonishment.

"So you know who it is?"

Rekke leaned forward. His leg was twitching.

"I'm fairly certain that Jenni Järvinen met the killer at the Helsinki party she attended the evening before her murder. Your Finnish colleagues compiled a list of those who attended, and I see one name that is of interest."

Micaela sat up in bed.

"What name would that be?" She felt suddenly excited. "Jonas Beijer mentioned the party was thrown by a Dutch businessman."

"Indeed, a man by the name of Klaas Martens. Peculiar fellow. He's an old hippie who made his fortune in freesheet newspapers and now wants to invest in Nordic show business. But the name I refer to is Popov—Oliver Popov—the literary agent and importer of expensive Californian wines."

"Popov," she said.

It rang a bell.

"Russian ancestry on his father's side," Rekke said. "But he's perfectly Swedish. He grew up in Gärdet in Stockholm in modest circumstances."

"What makes him interesting?"

"First and foremost, his character. He's violent, deceitful and unscrupulous, and he's known to have spoken to Järvinen only a few hours before the murder."

Micaela touched the dressing on her belly.

"He must have been questioned thoroughly."

"Oh yes, several times. He was incredibly confident—even a little threatening in a disturbingly familiar way. But he was eventually ruled out because he had an alibi."

"Which is problematic, right?"

"That's my hypothesis. His alibi was provided by two people: a friend and a former employee. But I know he's lying—partly through force of habit. Lies are his professional modus operandi and his way of life. But I believe there's also something more serious here. He previously broke two fingers of a young woman."

Her body tensed.

"Really?" she said.

"Yes, I think so," he said. "We're having lunch later today. It feels high time I published my old case notes—a hotshot like him should be able to secure me the biggest advance."

She stared at Rekke in bafflement.

"What?"

"Well, that's what I'll tell him, anyway."

"How are you going to get him to give himself away?"

Rekke looked down at his hands.

"I have my stratagems. But I am a little worried . . ."

"What is it you're worried about?" said Micaela.

"That I may have stirred things up. I may have made one or two more phone calls than I should, I may have set things in motion. I'm afraid that . . ."

He looked pensive and gestured toward the phone that had beeped.

Micaela too looked down at Rekke's nervous hands.

"Are you really going to meet this agent in your state?" she said.

Rekke gave her a wry smile.

"I'll play it calm," he said. "Use my old tricks. I think Popov has people covering for him. He has a worrying degree of control over his employees and those close to him."

Rekke's pocket beeped again.

"Damn, you're popular all of a sudden," she said.

"I can't bear it."

"See who it is. You're making me nervous."

He pulled out the phone but seemed to be focused on other things and lost in his thoughts.

"And?" said Micaela.

"It's Pontus Bremer," Rekke said. "He's sent three text messages."

"What does he say?"

"That he knows an author who knows something about the murder in Spain."

"Isn't he just trying to look important?"

"Perhaps, or maybe—"

"Well, call him then," she interjected.

"I'll ring from the hallway," he said. "I'll tell you about it later."

Micaela nodded and grabbed her computer and searched online for the Persian name that Caspar had jotted down. At first she couldn't find anything, which left her strangely relieved. But then she froze.

She'd spotted the name mentioned in a brief article in *Expressen* and it was in the worst possible way. She thumped the bedside table disconsolately.

FIFTY-SIX

Dag Wrangel had managed to snatch some sleep, which was a miracle. In those first hours after Pontus's nighttime call, he had lain there shaking. Then at last he'd succumbed to exhaustion and apparently it was now morning, and Andrea was up and on the phone to one of her thousand underlings.

Beyond her in the living room, Viktor was at the piano: Ba, dam, dom, dim, triddili, it went—over and over again. It drove Dag crazy. It was tragic, and yet another sign that something wasn't right. They were on the waiting list for an assessment—not that it mattered anymore. Soon, Dag would probably be missing his former worries with the desperate certitude of the incarcerated.

"I'll drop him a line right away," Andrea said on the phone, and regardless of what it was about he didn't doubt it.

No-one was as efficient as Andrea; that pained him too. He didn't deserve her. Not before and certainly not now. She was too intelligent and capable, and despite her workload she was constantly at his beck and call. In a way, she handicapped him, and the mere thought that she would soon know his darkest secret was something he couldn't handle.

"You're such a lovely person," she'd said only the other day with so much affection in her gaze that he'd almost believed her. But nothing was further from the truth.

He was a *creep* and nothing else. A *wretch*, a *cockroach*. He sat up in bed and bent double, his arms wrapped around his chest. Ba, dam, dom, Viktor went. "Shut up!" he wanted to bellow. From the street, the sound of a pneumatic drill penetrated the apartment and blended with the anxiety coursing through his veins. *You pig, you piece of shit—you repulsive murderer.* The torrent of whispered words in his head wouldn't stop. But he bit the bullet, gathered underwear, a freshly ironed shirt and a pair of suit trousers and went to the bathroom where he showered and dressed before going to the kitchen, where he found Andrea.

Off the phone now, she wore a green dress with small yellow giraffes on it, which was unobtrusively sexy. On another day, he would have drawn her to him, grasping her by the hips. Now, all he could do was stare at her in horror as she set out jam and pancakes and called Viktor—not that he stopped playing for that. He just carried on with the same bar, and for the umpteenth time Dag decided it was high time they replaced his piano teacher. It couldn't go on like this, it simply couldn't. He had to move on, otherwise they'd all go insane. But then Viktor rose from the piano stool and padded to the kitchen table as if nothing had happened, and nothing was going to happen. Dag could have shot himself for less. Damn Pontus. Wasn't being Sweden's most famous author enough? Did he really have to play the detective too?

"Bravo, Viktor. I thought I was going to have to carry you over," Andrea said.

"Can I eat at the piano?" said Viktor.

"No. Remember what Boris said. The piano doesn't like your

crumbs," Andrea said, hunched over her laptop on the kitchen table, presumably writing the email she'd promised to send. As yet she didn't seem to have noticed him, which was damn lucky.

She always saw when Dag was out of sorts, and right now he was doubtless radiating fear. Just to be sure, he looked away and opened the fridge since he figured it was best to feign hunger—but he didn't get far.

Andrea exclaimed:

"No, Viktor! Not on the carpet."

She leapt up and moistened a tea towel before crouching down to wipe off the jam. Was it all going to come tumbling down around his ears, Dag wondered. Was she about to look at him with loathing and fear, as if he might hurt her too? He wanted to rush back to the bathroom and lock the door behind him, but at that moment Andrea stood up again and glanced at him fondly.

"Someone's looking very smart. You got meetings today?"

He shook his head, looking unfailingly tormented, and obviously she noticed that but as luck had it Viktor spilled some more jam and Andrea crouched back down and Dag covered his face with his hands for a couple of seconds while he gathered strength.

"You run along to the office," he said. "I'll handle it."

"Viktor could clean it up himself."

If he weren't so different, Dag thought, putting his hands to his throat. But Andrea didn't seem to recognize how bad it was. Instead, she stood up and kissed him.

"I'll be off then—I've got a crazy day. But dinner's ready. You just need to boil the potatoes in the pan and fry the mushrooms and onions on the plate in the fridge."

She went into the hall with her eyes glued to a document she'd taken from the bureau, and of course her phone rang again. Presumably, she was going to read and talk at once; she was an unparalleled phenomenon. She tended to get more done on her way to the office than Dag managed in a day. But to his surprise, she didn't answer. She turned around sharply and smiled so sweetly that it made his heart ache.

"A strange thing happened this morning," she said.

"Oh?" he said, hopeful that this *strange thing*, whatever it might be, would provide him with a momentary distraction.

"An old friend of yours called. Said he was a big admirer of us both. Quite a charmer. But he said you were angry with him, which was why he was calling me. He said he had happy news."

"Oh really?" Dag said as neutrally as possible.

"He said you'd done a road trip in Europe together and been great friends and I pretended to know what he was talking about—but I don't recall you ever mentioning him. Pompe was his name. Seems to be a bit of a big shot. Oh Dag, what's the matter?"

"Nothing," he said as he began to clear up in Viktor's wake on the table and the floor.

The anxiety rushed in with such force that he couldn't say a word, let alone stand up. That was why he didn't manage to tell Andrea that on no account was she to meet Pompe.

He watched her leave with a confused expression and asked himself when the real pain would come and floor him completely.

FIFTY-SEVEN

Pontus Bremer was on his way back from the kitchen to his study and generous library when the Professor called back, and in that moment all his doubts vanished. What did he care about Dag and his family? Nothing. On the contrary, he felt proud. He was on his way to solving an important murder case. He would become even more emphatically Pontus Bremer—the author who saw through everything.

"You have something to tell me," the Professor said down the line.

Pontus felt an irresistible desire to begin by telling him something of his qualities.

"I have an almost photographic memory," he said.

"Is that so?"

The Professor seemed completely uninterested, which irked him.

"And given that I read two books a day, I have a rather astonishing overview of the Swedish literary scene."

"You said you knew about an author who might know something about the murder in Spain."

Pontus did not allow himself to be discouraged.

"Of course, most of what gets written is abysmal," he said. "Then there's the rest, which is pretty lousy too," he said. "But here and there we find things that contain traces of authenticity, like fragments that have inadvertently had a brush with divinity and retain a spark of it."

"I see," said Rekke.

"You find it in the middle layer in those who aren't important but aren't altogether meaningless either. Writers lacking in powers of observation but who, by virtue of the archetypes they depict, give us the truth—or a picture of it—like the shadow of a cloud."

Like the shadow of a cloud, Pontus thought. Damn it, I'm on fire.

"Is it one of these flawed literary witnesses that you have in mind?" Rekke said.

"Exactly. But I doubt you'll have heard of him."

"Try me."

"He also lacks the rather more dubious talent that helps us to cut through the noise of the media landscape; it's a talent that I have only reluctantly acquired. Sometimes we have to sell ourselves to—"

"Who?" the Professor interrupted.

"Dag Wrangel."

"I know him," the Professor said unexpectedly. "I read his bildungsroman. Such a wonderful melody to the language."

"I should say his prose is rather overworked, a little stiff even," Pontus hastened to say, feeling a desire to retreat from Dag; after all, who could expect anything else if he were about to finger him as a possible murder suspect?

"What brings him to mind?"

"Well . . ." Pontus said.

"Yes?"

There was a new fervour about the Professor that bothered him, but what did Pontus care about that? He spat it all out without any of the reservations he'd felt the night before. In fact, something akin to bloodlust simmered to the surface in his account.

"Interesting," Rekke said afterward, more alert now. "Do you have any idea whether he was in Santander in 1988?"

"No, but I can find out."

Rekke was silent for a moment.

"Hold off on that," he said. "I mentioned that there were two Swedes, didn't I? One of them was a blond-haired heavy drinker with a receding hairline, who walked with grace as if he were a dancer. Some witnesses said he reminded them of Mick Jagger."

Pontus wondered where this was going.

"Do you know a man named Oliver Popov?" Rekke said.

Pontus recoiled.

"Naturally," he said. "Everyone in publishing does."

"Do you know whether Popov and Dag Wrangel have ever been friends?"

A thousand thoughts flitted through Pontus's head.

"I find that hard to imagine," he said tentatively. "They're completely different. Popov is forthright and with-it and extraordinarily commercial, while Dag is delicate, narrow in literary terms and rather weak and oversensitive."

Just the sort of person Popov would love to exploit, Pontus added to himself, but he didn't say that part out loud.

"The strange thing is," said Rekke, "that another source just mentioned Wrangel's name to me. They told me that Wrangel hated Popov."

A memory resurfaced in Pontus Bremer's mind.

"I've never cared for Popov myself, Professor. He represents all those trashy genre fiction writers flooding the market and peddling their flops," he said, feeling a sudden pang of envy toward all those trashy authors, because while they might not be able to write and most of them were focused on looking good on Facebook, Popov had secured them plenty of lucrative advances for the sales of their foreign rights.

"But there's something on your mind?" Rekke said, as if able to see through him.

"Yes," said Pontus. "But it was more of a feeling I had. It was at the August Prize gala a couple of years ago. I happened to see Dag as Popov walked by. His reaction was downright physical, as if he'd just seen a ghost or something genuinely unpleasant, while Popov's face lit up as if he were enjoying the situation."

"I see," said Rekke. "And what do you think of Popov? Personally, I mean."

Pontus received the question with reluctance—perhaps because he too had stared into Popov's ice-cold eyes and had the feeling he was looking at a predator ready to pounce, but most of all because Per Morton, who was producing the film adaptation of his novel and whom Pontus liked, always put up a defence of Popov. "He's just like you, Pontus—a guy with no inhibitions," was what Per Morton had once said, praising the agent's irreverence and ability to formulate uncomfortable truths.

"I'm not quite sure what I think," he said. "I don't know him. But Dag . . ." Pontus added, eager to change the subject, "well, it feels like he's on the verge of a breakdown."

"The man's something of a depressive and ridden with guilt, if I'm remembering his book correctly," Rekke said. "But he's passionate too. Every sentence was finely crafted, and as you said, he presumably has a heightened state of sensitivity. The perfect victim, perhaps. But I might be way off the mark."

"Your reputation would suggest you're usually right."

"I'm constantly wrong," Rekke said unexpectedly. "But thank you for your information, it's most valuable."

Then the Professor curtly hung up, leaving Pontus clutching his phone and not knowing exactly what to feel, except that his skin was crawling with unease again, but this time not because of Dag and his family. Rather, it was Popov who loomed large like a threatening shadow, because this much Pontus knew: that man was not someone you wanted to clash with. He was merciless.

Then he shrugged, muttered the word “rot” and went into his study to do his ten pages. Inspiration was for weaklings.

FIFTY-EIGHT

Santander, July 1988

There were people everywhere, which made getting around almost impossible. Sandra no longer expected to see Pompe. She wandered back and forth feeling at a loss, occasionally allowing herself to be stopped by strangers or acquaintances without being drawn into the festivities. She'd run out of steam and was longing for bed, but she didn't feel like setting off into the backstreets that would lead her home.

She could feel Roberto's eyes on the back of her neck, and she thought about the punch he'd thrown her way at La Mar. It had missed, but it had been so powerful she'd felt winded by it, and she didn't want to risk an encounter with him without the protection of the crowd. The church tower in the distance told her that it was already a quarter to twelve. Time was flying by tonight, and she wanted to go home.

In front of her, a young man was handing out samples of a new juice. His stare was annoying, and she looked down at her legs and her sheer tights, and was reminded of her stray. In the short story, the dog longed to be close to the humans. It was with people that it had once felt safe. But when it did get close, it always got frightened. Life beckoned it with a promise that it could no longer fulfil, and perhaps the same was true for her too. The fiesta would have been best at a distance. Now it was simply importunate and shrill.

Sandra raised her gaze, relieved to have circumvented the juice guy. At that moment, a firecracker went off behind her and she ducked to the right, her heart pounding, before taking a left and continuing to think about the stray and about Dag and his eyes as she had left him.

"For God's sake," she muttered.

She should have stayed and had a drink with Dag, but now it felt as if he were against her too. She was always making the wrong decision, wasn't she? Leaving when she should have stayed, going right when she should have taken a left or gone straight ahead. Where on earth was she? She didn't recognize anything. Despite her intentions, she'd ended up in a side street with no bars or stalls, and when yet another firecracker exploded further away she jumped and decided to turn back, but first she bent down to take off her sandals.

"Bella, bella! Has my amulet not brought you luck?"

Sandra turned around and saw the man from the beach nearby. He seemed younger now. He was holding his guitar and wore a hat. He was squinting at her as if the sun was still shining, and his skin was leathery and seamed with deep furrows.

"What? No, not yet," she said.

"I can see that. You're still alone—but perhaps I can help you with that?"

He smiled kindly, but that didn't help much and she wondered anxiously where his charm was. Hadn't she been holding it before? How was she going to explain to him that she'd lost it?

"That's okay," she said. "I'm going home."

"Not now—not on the first night of the fiesta. It's almost midnight, and that's when the spell takes effect."

"Isn't it meant to be at midnight the spell gets broken?"

"Not in this fairy tale," he said.

She felt increasingly worried, and looked around in the hope of spotting someone who might help her.

"You haven't been following me, have you?" she said.

"No, no. But I saw you back there and you seemed lost. And like a girl too beautiful to be alone."

"I'm not alone; I just want to go home. I'm tired."

"You seem lively enough to me," the man said, taking a step toward her with his guitar. She began to rummage in her handbag to see if his amulet was there. She wanted to throw it at him and never see him again, never see people again, just concentrate on writing. That was what she was meant for.

"Is he bothering you?"

A voice in English spoke from a couple of metres behind them, and even before she knew who it was, a feeling of liberation shot through her and she looked up and saw him standing there, his body a little off-centre, that irresistible smile.

"Yes, a little," she said, smiling in reply.

"Okay, I'll sort it out," Pompe said, turning to the man. Quite what happened she didn't understand, except that Pompe said a few polite words, "Leave the lady alone," or something to that effect, but there must have been more to it, something he did with his eyes or body, because the man from the beach suddenly seemed afraid and beat a hasty retreat, and a moment later she and Pompe were alone.

"Finally," he said.

"Finally," she said, already thinking that she wanted to take him away from the fiesta and people's prying eyes, up into the hills, and perhaps to show him the old oak if it was still there and able to tell her anything.

FIFTY-NINE

When Rekke returned, Micaela was sitting up in bed glaring at her laptop. But although he immediately realized that something had happened, he gazed past her, picturing Sandra Ramirez's corpse.

He saw the beatings, the bruises, the scratches, the broken fingers on the left hand, the entire unsettling rainbow landscape, and he noted in his mind's eye what had been his very first thought. There was something disparate, strange even, about the injuries. Not necessarily the result of two attackers, but a feeling of discrepancy in the violence meted out, as if the murderer had changed method and shifted from a raw ruthlessness to a more cautious, restrained form of violence.

"Hello, hello? What's happened here then?" he said.

Micaela didn't look up. All she muttered was "Idiot" while keeping her glare fixed on the screen.

"Who's the idiot?"

She looked up.

"You!"

"Me?"

"I think so, but above all . . ." She hesitated and slammed the laptop shut. "I'm thinking of my boyfriend Caspar, the father of the child I've lost."

"What's he done?"

"I looked up a name he'd written down and made notes about. And just now I discovered that the name belongs to an Iranian woman living in Stockholm who burned her veil to protest against the Iranian regime's oppression of women."

"Which means?"

"The only reason I was even going through Caspar's drawers and found that name was because Magnus claimed Caspar had a sketchy security classification and might be an Iranian spy, and that really bothered me because Caspar has always portrayed himself as a refugee in exile and as deeply critical of the mullahs."

Rekke bit his lip.

"For Magnus, the truth is highly instrumental," he said. "There was a purpose behind him blurting that out."

"Of course, but if it's true then it's true."

"How did he know that you and Caspar were connected?"

She glanced irritably at him.

"That's what Magnus does, isn't it? Finds things out."

"He only makes an effort if it can serve him."

"I don't care about that," she said without much conviction, before putting the computer down on the bedside table. "What did Pontus Bremer have to say?"

Once again, Rekke pictured Sandra's broken fingers and the beaten body.

"Sometimes there are simple explanations. Perhaps your Caspar is actually on this woman's side," he said.

Micaela glowered at him as if he'd said something indescribably stupid.

"What did Pontus Bremer have to say?" she repeated.

Rekke looked at Micaela and wondered whether to turn the conversation back to her. Suffering a miscarriage and finding out at the same time that the father of the child she had lost was potentially a supporter of a tyrannical regime was a bit too much for one day.

"Bremer mentioned a particular writer who ten years ago wove Sandra Ramirez's short story and her death into a feverish fairy tale one wet night. He says there was a peculiar authenticity to it."

"Surely he could have read about both of them?"

"Only fragments of the short story had been published at the time, and according to Bremer the author was absolutely terrified when reminded of the murder. They spoke last night."

"What's this author called?"

Rekke hesitated.

"Dag Wrangel," he said. "His wife Andrea runs the Five Stars hotel group."

"Never heard of him. And the hotels are too expensive for me, but I can check him out," Micaela said.

"*I'll* do it," Rekke said. "You need to rest."

"You've got to sell your case notes."

"I'm sure I can manage both."

She shook her head.

"I'll get help from Jonas Beijer and our databases. I need something to do," she said, and he thought there might be something in that after all, and he kissed her on the cheek and stood up to leave for his meeting with Oliver Popov at Riche.

SIXTY

Andrea Wrangel had already got through three meetings and thirty emails by the time she took a break ahead of an employee appraisal to look up the man who'd called her.

"Well, I'll be damned," she muttered.

That was quite a business he'd built, which made it even stranger that Dag hadn't mentioned him, since they'd been friends back in the day. How come he hadn't come up in conversation? They'd talked about everything else in their lives.

Granted, Dag would say he was ashamed of his life in the eighties. "I was a blockhead back then," he once said. "Who wasn't?" she'd replied, and they'd laughed. But he'd never mentioned a European road trip. All he'd said was that one summer he'd owned a red BMW which he'd sold afterward because he'd driven it much too fast on the Autobahn. But a guy named Pompe? Nope, she'd never heard of him. And that was strange. He and Dag had clearly been close, and not only because Pompe had said as much on the telephone. Dag's reaction had shown it clearly. He was obviously worried when she mentioned the name. Admittedly, that didn't necessarily mean much. Dag was of a nervous disposition, and more or less anything could cause him anguish, but maybe . . .

She looked at the oldest photo of Pompe she had been able to find online. There was something androgynously charming about him. The slim, graceful body and the plump lips, and the eyes which were at once proud and derisive. Had he and Dag . . . ? No, she didn't think so. But she definitely felt drawn to the lean figure in the picture, and she also felt increasingly curious. Pompe's tone on the phone had been so direct and refined, almost as if she were speaking to Dag himself. His use of language was as elegant, and as ironic, and there really was nothing amiss with his call. Apparently they were considering giving Dag the Stig Dagerman Prize, he said. Andrea had verified that Pompe was on the jury, and it would be incredible. It would really mean something to Dag if he were awarded it, and without much further thought she rang him up. Surely it couldn't hurt to have another chat.

"Yes?" said a voice so heated and angry that she wanted to hang up, but then Pompe realized who she was and changed tack in a second.

"Sorry, sorry. You caught me at my worst. So many idiots call just before lunch and I have to go out to an unexpected meeting. But I'm so pleased you called. It's strange we've never met; I can barely understand it."

She cut to the chase.

"Do you really want to give Dag the Stig Dagerman?"

"Well, assuming we decide in his favour," he said. "But I suppose I shouldn't be telling you about it. Jury deliberations are supposed to remain confidential, although I'm keen to pave the way. To cut to the chase, we have a couple of naysayers—not that anyone questions Dag's qualities as an author, but the Dagerman is more than simply a literary distinction. It's a political prize too, in the spirit of the man himself. There's some trepidation about what Dag might say if it were awarded to him."

Andrea considered this.

"I expect Dag would say exactly what it took for him to be given the prize," she said. "He loves Dagerman's work."

"You think I don't know that? I know all his favourites as a young man. I know him inside out."

"Really?" she said. "I'm curious about what you two got up to on your Euro trip."

"Me too," he said with a laugh. "I've repressed most of it."

"That bad?"

"I think so. It was interesting too, and we grew very close. It's been a source of great sorrow that we've fallen out of touch."

"And why did you?"

He fell silent as if it were something serious.

"I'm honestly not sure. Ask Dag. He hasn't replied to my messages. But my faint hope is that perhaps this prize could bring us together again. Perhaps we might meet briefly? We could devise a strategy to convince the jury—confidentially, of course."

She thought that sounded rather odd, but Dag had been having a difficult time of it lately and had felt forgotten and ignored. If she could help him to secure a prize it was worth trying anything.

"I don't know," she said.

"How about five o'clock at the Villa Godthem out in Djurgården? That's close to your work, isn't it?"

She wasn't quite sure which of the restaurants on the island of Djurgården was the Villa Godthem, but she could look it up online. She looked at the time and her calendar and was definitely going to say no, sorry, I can't make it today. But then she changed her mind for reasons she couldn't quite explain to herself.

"It'll have to be at a quarter past. That would be lovely."

"Most definitely," he said with enthusiasm. "But don't say a word to Dag. Let the prize we're arranging for him be a surprise."

She already knew she wasn't going to stick to that, but she lied and said, "Of course." After they'd hung up she rang Dag. His phone was switched off, so she went to send a text, but she felt embarrassed explaining it in writing, so all she wrote was: *Call me, sweetie.*

Dag never did call her back, and her day assumed the same hectic tempo they all did, and she had no idea that everything was heading for a full-blown disaster.

SIXTY-ONE

Gina Mo had held her press conference and Magnus Rekke was sitting at his desk at the Ministry in a hailstorm of phone calls and emails. What was more, Kleeberger wanted a word. Now. Damn it all to hell. Magnus straightened up. I'll sort this out, and who would believe that I groped her in prison in front of the guards and cameras? No-one, hopefully.

I have sympathy for her long incarceration, and I understand that she feels anger toward society, he wrote to *Svenska Dagbladet*, miming making himself vomit with his finger. *But obviously her claims are downright lies and a cheap attempt to seek revenge. There is photographic evidence to back this up*, he continued, quite certain the American authorities would never release CCTV footage from Guantánamo.

Beyond this, I am bound by the laws on state secrecy, he concluded, feeling a little enlivened by it all in spite of everything.

Discretion was his best friend. Seeking comfort, he logged on to Twitter. The platform was wonderful for its hounding of left-wingers and women, and he wasn't let down this time either.

Gina Mo was trending and her enemies were many: *How could they release that bitch*, said a poster named Bear, and—at this point Magnus perked up—a poster by the name of Truth-Teller said: *All credit to the undersecretary of state who tried to keep her locked up. Obviously he wouldn't have touched her with a barge pole.*

Rekke's just protecting national security, said one Martin Lindgren. Hear, hear, Magnus thought, but then, God in heaven, there were some other takes too. Legal scandal, disgusting man, pig, swine, he makes me sick—*If anyone should be locked up, it's Magnus Rekke*—and he took a deep breath.

A tidal wave of shit was washing over him. But what the hell—it would blow over, and it was damn lucky for him that Gina Mo was whining about all sorts of other stuff too. That would reduce her credibility. The entire press conference had been full of general accusations against the West, and there had been that sarcastic remark about the Iraq War being as good an investment as the Treaty of Versailles. Perhaps there was a little truth in that. Not that it was his problem; he was concerned with realpolitik and if the world got into any trouble then you had to use that to your advantage.

There was a tap on the door and Kleeberger entered, looking thoroughly upset. If the mountain won't come to Mohammed, then Mohammed has to come to the mountain, Magnus thought.

"Thank you for hosting yesterday. I'll get your trousers back to you," he said.

"I've just done interviews for both television and radio," Kleeberger said in an accusatory tone, and Magnus thought, you can forget about your trousers.

"How did you get along?"

Kleeberger sat down in the armchair opposite him.

"I said we'd been battling assiduously to free Gina Mo, and that you would never have behaved in an unbecoming way."

Magnus couldn't help but giggle, nerves presumably, but also because being *unbecoming* was one of his specialist subjects.

"Is this really so funny?" said Kleeberger.

"No, not really. Did they give you a hard time?"

"A very hard time. If this gets any bigger then you'll have to handle it yourself, but for the time being . . ."

Kleeberger fidgeted.

"Yes?"

". . . it seems manageable. There was no real emphasis in Gina Mo's accusations against you. It was as if she were holding back, and with a little luck people won't believe it. Even I don't, for once."

"That's kind of you, Mats."

"Very," Kleeberger said irritably. "I don't want to hear another word about it; the fact of the matter is that I'm more worried about the looming legal issue. The Left Party . . ."

"The Left Party," Magnus snorted. "Who cares about them?"

"It's not just the Left Party. All the opposition parties are all over us asking what we actually did to try and get her out sooner."

"Lots, you will have told them."

"Of course. Stubborn diplomatic efforts, conversations at a high level, all the usual stuff. But quite honestly, Magnus, this whole business of a Swedish citizen—and a journalist to boot—being imprisoned for years on end without charge or due process really does trouble me, and the feeling that we bowed down to the American administration pains me."

Pains him? What utter nonsense, Magnus thought. He was the one being tarred here.

"Bullshit," he said. "We'll be applauded for our actions in the long run. Nobody wants loudmouths like Gina Mo at large, and it's a damn stroke of luck that . . ." He might as well cheer him up a little, Magnus thought. ". . . that you're so good in front of the camera and able to say the right things, Mats."

"Thank you," said Kleeberger, immediately seeming more at ease. "But there's also something else."

Damn it, surely this is more than enough, Magnus thought, instantly regretting his compliment.

"What?" he said.

"Something we believe is related to the fact that you sent your brother to see Gina Mo."

"Hans can be an asset sometimes," he said.

"But not when he's manic."

"Hans isn't manic at present, is he?" said Magnus, picturing Hans at the reception at Kleeberger's.

"I wouldn't be so sure," the Foreign Minister said. "A number of guests in my own home yesterday said that, quite uninvited, he drew the most astonishing conclusions, most of them eerily accurate, others probably completely off the mark."

"Oh?" said Magnus, both amused and somewhat satisfied.

He loved it—provided he wasn't involved—when Hans made a fool of himself.

"And I've just received a telephone call from the Prime Minister."

"Oh?" he said again, now on his guard. "About what?"

Kleeberger fiddled with his wedding ring.

"He's proud of his book. Absurdly so, if I'm frank."

"He didn't even write it himself," said Magnus.

"He managed to suppress that fact long ago. He refers to himself as both a prime minister and a writer these days."

"Pathetic."

"And to top it all, he's now best buds with this agent guy, Oliver Popov. I think he makes him feel young," said Kleeberger.

"Sigh."

"And that's the problem, in short. Because even if Popov flirts with power very skilfully, he's got no shortage of enemies."

"That's true," said Magnus.

"And the most fervent among them is Gina Mo. She's apparently upset because Popov didn't want to represent her book on the Taliban. As such, she's been spreading the most dreadful stories about him, and now she's convinced your manic brother that Popov has committed violent crimes against women."

Magnus leaned forward, trying to understand what it was Kleeberger had just said.

"Hans isn't so easily convinced of such things," he said. "Not even when he's manic. He sees through it when people have their own agendas."

Alas, he thought.

"Well, not this time, it seems. His conversation with Gina Mo was bugged, and now—indeed, at this very moment—Hans is having lunch with Popov at Riche on the pretext that he wants to publish a book of his case notes."

A twisted smile appeared on Magnus's face.

"And perhaps he does."

"Seriously, Magnus?"

He paused for thought. No, Hans would never yield to such vanity.

"What do you want me to do? Rush to Riche and stop the lunch?"

Kleeberger grimaced.

"I just want you to know that if Hans finds anything—however small it may be—on this agent, it'll spill over to the Prime Minister, and we don't need that."

All of a sudden, Magnus felt exhilarated, envisioning the most wonderful crisis and the opportunity to advance his own interests while inducing everyone to forget all about that Gina Mo nonsense.

"So the Prime Minister is worried that Popov might have committed the odd minor crime against women after all," he said, beaming.

SIXTY-TWO

As Hans Rekke entered Riche, he was hit with so many impressions that he took a step back and closed his eyes. When he opened them again, he managed to keep his gaze steady and to disregard the question of why the young maître d's pupils were so unusually dilated.

He pushed aside all irrelevancies, at which point he spotted Oliver Popov on the right at the far end of the room, sitting at a window table. Popov wore a dark blue suit and was hunched over his mobile. When he saw Rekke he brightened and stood up with cold, enquiring eyes. His handshake was firm and two-handed.

"Do you know what I've spent all morning doing?" he said.

"Go on."

"I've been doing my research, and the more I hear the more fascinated I am. A modern-day Sherlock Holmes—is that how we should present you? The man who sees around corners."

Rekke sat down and did his best to conceal the degree of concentration with which he was scrutinising his lunch companion.

"I believe that last one is already attributed to another detective," he said. "But you're most kind. You too seem to have acquitted yourself well," he said. "What's your secret?"

Popov leaned forward.

"My ruthlessness," he said, fixing his gaze on Rekke while throwing his chest out and playing it ice-cold. Then came the expected metamorphosis: the face relaxed and Popov dazzled him with a big smile as if he had just cracked the world's funniest joke. It was doubtless a transformation he'd pulled off a thousand times before, and which might have been perfectly innocent had it not contained one point that didn't escape Rekke's notice.

"Ruthlessness—on behalf of my clients," the agent said. "I stand up for their interests, no matter what it costs, and I don't give up until I have the best terms the market can offer. Or often better than that. That's why authors and filmmakers love me, but it's also why I have so many enemies. Those I turn down know what they're missing out on, and they don't shy away from making the most shameless attacks."

Popov raised his face in an almost regal manner, and Rekke realized their encounter had been derailed from the very beginning.

"You know your value," he said. "Yet it must be reassuring when the envious attack."

"I don't care for petty people," Popov said, smiling again, this time not for Rekke but at a waiter who had appeared by their side with slicked-back blond hair and who seemed a little nervous. Perhaps he'd sensed the tension, but it was also without doubt because he regarded Popov as an important patron.

"Yo, Tobias," Popov said, turning to Rekke. "Tobias is Riche's star. He runs a marketing company on the side and he's godlike on the trumpet. Anyway, what do you say, Professor? I hear you're a pescatarian? I recommend the sole."

Rekke pulled an affirmative face.

"Very well. Two soles and a Perrier for me. I'm pretty much teetotal, despite my wine interests. I'm always tasting, but I rarely drink. Although perhaps I might offer you a better drink, Professor? A '98 Black Stallion. I'm the importer. It's exquisite."

"Sparkling water will be fine," said Rekke.

"Very well. Do say hello to your beautiful girlfriend from me, Tobias," Popov said imperiously, before returning his attention to Rekke. "I don't care about gossip or any of that bullshit—regardless of who it's from."

Rekke realized he was descending into a confrontation.

"I saw the episode of Beck you wrote the script for," he said. "It was a compelling, empathetic portrayal of the killer's obsession. Why did you stop writing?"

"I'm more of a man of action, and I don't regret it for one moment. I'm happy and proud of what I've created," he said. "Where do you stand on that point, Professor?"

Rekke shrugged.

"It varies," he said.

"What a pity. I could help build your self-confidence, if only you gave me the chance. But from what I hear . . ."

Popov smiled to himself and continued in a lower, flatter voice.

"From what I hear . . ." he began again.

"Yes, Oliver?" Rekke said, leaning forward with his most complaisant smile.

"You're not really here to discuss a book. You've come on other business."

"You have good sources."

"Very good ones," he said. "Which is also why I mentioned my ruthlessness. I'm not one to be threatened."

Rekke maintained his amiable smile.

"I'm merely seeking clarity," he said. "*Claritas*, as I'm wont to say. You've happened to be close to women who have fared badly, Oliver. And that worries me."

Popov's pupils contracted.

"I'm warning you, Professor."

"I'd noticed. Your teeth are unnaturally clenched together, and the veins at your temple are bulging."

"I'm calm. Ice-cold, in fact," said Popov, lowering his voice even more. "And do you know why, Professor?"

Rekke looked him in the eyes and got a hint of something unfathomably dark.

"I think so," he said.

"You think you're this sharp guy, don't you?"

"Well . . ."

Popov fell silent and his expression relaxed again. His eyes focused on Rekke, like a predator seeking out weaknesses in its prey.

"But do you know what, Professor? I have contacts, and I've made my enquiries. Time was, you had a reputation of sorts. But now . . ." Popov paused rhetorically. "Now you're despised. People have started laughing at you—most recently at Kleeberger's. What on earth were you playing at? I hear you were an utter embarrassment. But I'm sure you already know that. Because what exactly are you, Professor? A pianist who couldn't hack it when the pressure became too much, an academic who got the boot, a nervous wreck of an addict, a mentally unstable patient who plays the detective but who in reality can barely make it out of the house. It's been a long time since . . ." Another rhetorical pause.

"A long time since what?" Rekke said, still smiling.

"I heard about someone held in such low esteem by everyone who matters at all. Do you know what the Prime Minister said about you?" said Popov.

"Do you keep such esteemed company?"

"My good friend Sten the Prime Minister called you a little parasite. He said you're a cockroach who gets in everywhere and disgusts people."

"Only that? Do send him my best," said Rekke.

"But it's true. You're nothing anymore, Professor. Complete insignificance. You're someone people look down upon. You're a weak man," Popov said, emphasising the last part.

"Don't underestimate the weak," said Rekke. "They're often more perspicacious than those who rush forward headlong."

"But that's not true of you. You're . . ." Popov said, summoning up his next words with a reinvigorated flash of excitement in his gaze, "a wretch, a guttersnipe, a disgusting insect, a chewed-up piece of gum that people want to stamp into the sidewalk, a cockroach."

"I think you already said cockroach."

"People jeer at your observations; they consider you pathetic. You're an anachronistic buffoon who exhausts them with matters of course that you imagine to be unique. People think you're ridiculous and repulsive with your staring eyes and your long, spider hands. If you knew then you wouldn't be able to stand yourself."

Rekke shuddered, surprised by the impact of the words—it was like a poison seeping in, and for a moment, rather idiotically, he could tell that he was exhibiting signs of vulnerability.

"You're a master in the art of wounding," he said. "Shifting your guilt onto others. Is that a trick you use often?"

Popov smiled with even greater confidence.

"No-one would mourn your demise, Professor," he said, changing expression with astounding ease and beaming as the waiter returned with their order, as if he were able to shift from one mood to another at the drop of a hat. "Thank you Tobias, that looks wonderful," said Popov, gazing down greedily at his sole, and Rekke decided he might as well eat.

"I'm flattered by your enquiries," Rekke said.

"It's not hard to get people to say what they think about you. They spit it out like flies in their mouths."

"I'm glad to have saved you the work."

"I'm warning you," Popov said again, and Rekke was silent for a moment, still shaken in some absurd way, and not entirely certain how to interpret the attack.

There was an uncannily habituated air to it, as if this was the agent's customary approach to demonising his opponents, but there was also another element to it that intrigued Rekke. There was a streak of lust, he thought. Pure sadism. Best to strike back hard. I may need to.

"You use words as an alternative to violence, don't you?" he said.

"All I do is tell the truth."

Rekke permitted himself a laugh.

"With language that wouldn't look out of place in an issue of *Der Stürmer.* But so be it. The interesting thing is that you seem to find the same pleasure in the tangible too. My spider hands, for instance," he said, raising them in the air. "You don't feel like breaking a couple of fingers, do you?"

Oliver Popov narrowed his eyes, but otherwise maintained the same stony face and there was no real shift in the pupils either, no nervous movement of the hands.

"Do you know how many people have tried to take me down?" he said.

"Go on."

"Lots. And do you know how many have succeeded? Zero. They've all been crushed."

"Past performance is no guarantee of future results. What are you most afraid will come out?" Rekke said.

"I'm not afraid, and there's nothing to find. I've only ever done what I had to do," said Popov.

Rekke started on his sole.

"That sounds familiar," he said. "Inner compulsion drives us forward, but I would guess that my inclinations are rather different from yours."

"You're scum, Professor. You're the most disgusting person I've ever met."

Rekke thought it was time he tested the limits.

"Didn't you once pride yourself on your way with words, Oliver? Now all you do is repeat invective."

He felt a hand grab his own hand hard, like a bird's claw.

"Be careful," Oliver hissed.

"No, I don't think so," Rekke said, seizing Popov's other hand with the same strength, leaving them in a position that might almost have been interpreted as tender. "I'm not careful," he said. "And surely you must have taken that into account? I dare say that vile tirades are often effective, but sometimes they only strengthen the detective's resolve."

Popov freed himself from Rekke's grip and looked him straight in the eye.

"I can go further than that."

"Oliver, I know. By the by, when did you last see Dag Wrangel?" said Rekke.

"That piece of shit," Popov said, and Rekke was overcome by a sudden calm.

"Oh, him too?" he said, resolving not to say another word for at least a minute.

He knew how to play hardball too, no matter how frazzled his nerves were.

SIXTY-THREE

What didn't occur to Rekke in his feverish state was that a sequence of events with its own dynamics had already been triggered. Everywhere there were translocations and repositionings taking place, including in the Wrangel residence, even if the change in that particular case was that nothing was happening at all.

The son, Viktor, hadn't left for school because his father had not—to Viktor's surprise—hurried him along as usual, packing his bag and tying his shoelaces. Instead, he'd lain in the bedroom as if he were ill.

Consequently Viktor was sitting at his piano, working as meticulously as ever on his technique and his touch, oblivious to the fact that four hours had already elapsed. Then again, it was often like that. He forgot time and space. The keys were dead; that was what his piano teacher Boris had told him: "They're stone dead, lifeless pieces of plastic. Almost like rocks. But you, Viktor," he'd said, "can bring them to life—if you practice and practice and practice."

Those words had been etched into Viktor's mind and since

then he'd barely thought about anything else. That was why he'd ignored school and ignored all other distractions, instead devoting all his energy to his hands and arms. His back had to be straight and still, Boris said. Movement had to come from within. The arms and wrists, however, needed to be relaxed and mobile, while the fingers needed to be hard, hard and sensitive all at once, just like the keys. While to play a wrong note was insignificant, to play without passion was inexcusable, as Beethoven had once said. Inexcusable. The notes had to live and fly up from the heart, which was why Viktor closed his eyes and lost himself in the melody written in 1833 and which Chopin had said was his most beautiful, and he couldn't, shouldn't, do it an injustice. And that accounted for another hour, and not once did he think about the fact that his dad still hadn't emerged from the bedroom.

But Viktor probably would have cared had he divined the torment that had beset Dag. Dad was the only person he could talk to—he had no interest in his own peers, or anyone else for that matter. Only Dad understood him, and even though Dad sometimes got out of hand and became insanely angry as if he were losing himself, Dad and the piano were Viktor's whole world. Everything else came second, and he wouldn't have been able to stand it if he'd known Dad was thinking about taking his own life, or that he was thinking about a night long ago when a young woman had been murdered beside a big old tree.

Dag, on the other hand, was listening to his son play the piano. It was like a dirge for everything he was in the midst of losing, as he kept trying to repress the image he saw of Sandra in his mind's eye. He saw her and Pompe disappearing into the crowd in Santander and then heading out of the city, and he saw himself following—as if he were drawn toward what hurt too much to see.

He'd never been predisposed toward jealousy, and Andrea

sometimes lamented this teasingly. "I can never worry you, no matter how much I flirt and play around." But that evening, that night, when he followed Pompe and Sandra at a distance, a jealousy straight from hell had coursed through him. It was as if he were going insane, and when he saw them hold hands it was like a wedge being driven between his ribs. Yet he kept going, twenty or so metres behind them, feeling reckless, foolhardy. They might spot him at any moment. But perhaps that was just what he longed for? He wanted to destroy the closeness that had grown between them and force himself into that space. But Pompe and Sandra were far too preoccupied with each other to see him, and Pompe seemed to be neither drunk nor unkind, which was unfathomable given the hour.

He was gesticulating as if regaling her with an exciting account, and Sandra seemed to be taking an intense interest. A thought occurred to Dag: was she safe as long as she didn't reject Pompe's advances? In La Rochelle, Pompe had been chatting away with that sweet-looking short German girl. He'd been drunk, for sure, but he'd ably concealed this for some time and the girl had seemed interested, but then something had happened, Dag couldn't understand what, he'd been sitting nearby in the restaurant, but suddenly the girl had grimaced and taken a step back as if she'd realized who Pompe really was. And then it had kicked off with a bang. Pompe had headbutted her. Blood had been gushing from the girl's eyebrow, and it had been downright bad luck that the customers in the place hadn't killed Pompe on the spot. But he'd got out, and when they'd met up later that night there was no trace of remorse. On the contrary, he'd called the girl a bitch and a whore. Dag really should have left him then, but the paralysis he'd been suffering from throughout the trip meant he'd been unable to do it.

And that was why he followed them through the streets of Santander. It was past midnight. The stars and a crescent moon shone in the night sky, and Sandra laughed. It was a delightful laugh and it cut through Dag, and he was about to turn back. He settled for stopping and giving them a greater lead. Then he carried on, barely noticing that they had left the city and were climbing into the hills. He could barely see anything except his despair. He felt nothing except for his contradictory motivation: he wanted to protect Sandra and to punish Pompe; or to punish both of them. He didn't know, he simply carried on.

But eventually he raised his gaze and took in the sea visible below, and the waves rolling toward the beach. The pebble path crunched beneath his feet, and beside the path there was a branch, a crooked thing with two twigs at the top, and, without reflecting upon why, Dag picked it up and swung it at a bush. The foliage rustled and he worried he'd be discovered. But Pompe and Sandra didn't seem to notice anything. Instead, Dag became aware of something else. He heard footsteps behind him.

He thought he'd left the festivities and the city behind, but there, some fifty metres behind him, there was someone coming. A man with a ponytail and a backpack and clutching a guitar. He looked like a hippie, someone who had been on a long hike and still had a long way to go. He's got nothing to do with us, Dag thought. Nothing except he's following the same path, which is a bit weird, isn't it? But he didn't know what to do about it, and he looked up toward Pompe and Sandra.

Pompe's gait had altered. Dag assumed it was the intoxication setting in at last, and perhaps he was partly right. Pompe was taking side steps and his movements had become more angular, but he realized there was more to it than that. Pompe turned around. Dag was further away at that point and able to hide behind an abandoned stone cottage beside the path, which should have been alright. But then it finally dawned on him. Pompe had spotted him—maybe while he'd been eyeing up the hippie following—and he should turn back. Still, Dag stayed, as if hypnotized by the man behind and by the fact that Pompe wasn't reacting as he should. Pompe showed no signs of anger; he didn't shout "Get lost, leave us alone." Rather, he radiated a sense of understanding, amused, the embodiment of a wink, and that was weird. But doubtless Dag was affected by the fact that at that moment he saw the oak.

The tree was a hundred metres away on the hillside, slightly off the path, and it looked both majestic and ghostly in the darkness. It was clear even from a distance that it had seen better days. Its branches were diseased and the trunk cracked, and there weren't many leaves. But this only strengthened the immense impression the tree made, and Dag drew breath and moved forward as if there were no turning back now.

Behind him, the hippie carried on too. It was all so strange. Three men and a girl that Dag could have loved, and an old oak that had been struck by lightning. And that tree looked just like the one he and Sandra had talked about. It was impossible to grasp, and it must have confused him and made him lose track, and this point in the narrative was where Dag usually cut short his recollections. Remembering hurt too much. It was unfathomable.

He climbed out of bed, switched on his phone and saw he'd missed a call from Andrea, another from his mother and one from an unknown number. Dag didn't care. Instead, he stood there and felt his body begin to shake.

SIXTY-FOUR

Micaela put her phone down on the bedside table and hugged herself. Rekke had sounded annoyingly excited.

She remained sceptical, preferring to wait and find out more. They weren't in that much of a hurry. It had been twenty years since Sandra Ramirez's murder, and surely Micaela could at the very least take the time to recover from her operation. But Rekke had to run off and confront people; it was enough to drive her insane. One moment, he was unable to do a thing and could barely bring himself to take the trash cans out. The next, he was suddenly making calls and dashing about and drawing overly hasty conclusions. In fact, this was the point for taking a step back and trying to take a sober view of the material and making sure they mobilized her colleagues. They needed help running searches and questioning suspects.

They couldn't work alone if they were close to a solution, and help was on the way. Jonas Beijer had contacted his superior officer and the lead detective in Finland, and had tracked down Deputy Commissioner Corales at his conference. If they just waited a day or two, they might be in a position to launch an operation. They were already starting to bring in valuable information.

Jonas had found out that the author Dag Wrangel had bought a BMW 325 in May of 1988 and driven it south to Spain. Whether he'd made it to Santander was unknown, and whom he had travelled with they did not know yet, but that was only a matter of time. Micaela had telephoned Wrangel's mother and she'd remembered the travel companion well, even if she had forgotten his name. "Has that man done something? Dag never did want to talk about him afterward," she said. "I had misgivings."

Micaela assured her that it was just a routine enquiry, but obviously didn't fail to miss the anxiety in the woman's voice, and felt even more convinced that they couldn't muck this up. It had to be done properly. But it had been almost impossible to talk to Rekke, and Micaela felt abandoned. She wanted him here at the hospital. Her roommate's mother was visiting and was now perched on the edge of the girl's bed comforting her in Arabic, and on a whim Micaela called her own mother.

"Cariño," said Mamá. "I was just wondering why you never call anymore."

And I could ask you the same thing, Micaela thought.

"Something happened to me," she said, making an effort to sound pitiful.

"Only the one thing?" Mamá said without paying any heed to her tone. "All sorts has been going on here. Lucas—"

"I was pregnant," she interjected.

Mamá fell silent, which made for a change.

"*Was* pregnant?" she said. "If you've got rid of it then I'll throttle you. I've always hoped you two would start a family."

Micaela gulped.

"It wasn't Rekke's," she said. "We've never . . ."

"Well, it doesn't matter now. You don't do that—at least not without speaking to your mother first."

"Mamá, I lost it."

"What?"

"It was developing in the wrong place. I had an operation to remove it."

"Oh honey," Mamá exclaimed, but she had some difficulty transitioning from her aggrieved tone to one of genuine regret, and that was when Micaela lost interest and picked up her laptop. Calling had been a mistake.

"It's not that big a deal," she said. "It was for the best it happened."

"How can you say that?"

Micaela opened the laptop and looked again at the file that Jonas Beijer had sent her on the Finnish murder. Could the Popov guy that Rekke was so worked up about really be guilty after all?

"Hello? Are you still there?" Mamá said.

"Oh, I was just . . ."

She typed *Oliver Popov* into her search engine.

"Yes, sweetheart?"

"There's someone here. A knock on the door. Talk to you later, Mamá."

Micaela hung up, suddenly locked in as if she too had been struck down by some irrational sense of urgency. As she read the transcripts of Popov's interviews in the Finnish case file, she had the feeling he was lying. She sent a text to Rekke with a hint of irony:

You might be right about Popov. Watch your back, Professor.

SIXTY-FIVE

Easy now, Pontus Bremer thought. Don't get carried away. So far, he knew nothing and for want of anything else to do he Googled himself. It was an addiction of sorts; practically a tic. He was always running the search, and after recently reading an article that said it was impossible to cover your digital tracks, he'd been worried it might get out.

A man like him was supposed to be reading learned commentaries on the classics in German—not Googling himself two hundred and eighty times a day and ogling celebrity pictures. It could be perceived as anxious. The great Pontus Bremer should know his worth and not care which way the wind was blowing. He wrote for eternity, and was above the butterflies fluttering in the media limelight. But it wasn't easy. None of those fools knew what it was like being Pontus Bremer. People always had opinions on him, and he wanted to keep an eye on them, and frankly he wanted some validation too.

He needed it so that he could hold his head high like he deserved to, but right now he couldn't find anything new, just the same old articles and photos. His thoughts inevitably returned to Dag Wrangel. Surely he wasn't a murderer? It didn't make sense. But he needed to know, and he wanted to be one step ahead of that damn professor. Pontus wanted to show that he himself was the intellectual exception—the truly brilliant thinker. But who was he supposed to ring up for more clues? Then it came to him: Dag's mother.

Cultured ladies like her loved him. What was her name, again? Victoria. Or Elisabeth. Something exuding the air of the upper classes. It was Charlotte, he ascertained when searching online for her number. He rang her and to his surprise she picked up after one ring, sounding agitated.

"Good afternoon. This is Pontus Bremer speaking," he said. Usually he loved introducing himself to strangers on the phone. He'd often hear a "My God, is it really you?"

On this occasion, he could tell at once that something was amiss, even if Charlotte Wrangel kindly flattered him.

"Oh, how lovely. I've always been an admirer of yours, Pontus," she said, but before he'd had time to thank her she added nervously: "Do you know where Dag is?"

"No," he said, ill at ease. "Is he missing?"

"I can't reach him and a policewoman just rang me."

He swore to himself.

"A policewoman?" he said, feigning surprise. "What did she want?"

"She was asking about a trip Dag took to the north coast of Spain years and years ago."

With all the innocence he could muster, Pontus said:

"Where on the north coast?"

"I haven't a clue, but the police wanted to know who Dag went with and I couldn't remember. Do you have any idea why they're so interested in it?"

"None whatsoever," Pontus said blithely. "Dag's as gentle as a lamb."

"As a lamb," she repeated, before adding: "But his friend . . . I seem to recall Dag really did dislike him afterward. I don't think they saw each other again."

"Do you remember what the friend was called?" Pontus said.

"Pompe," she said.

"What?" he said.

"It was Pompe. I just remembered. He was the son of that poor tailor on Artillerigatan."

Pontus felt the room closing in, but he managed to stammer a few more words before hanging up and going into the kitchen, his chest tight with panic.

Dag didn't feel up to calling back either his mother or Andrea. It was five o'clock and he knew he should feed Viktor. He should get a grip and ponder a defence. But he got nowhere and instead he nervously switched on the television in the bedroom where he saw an image of Obama and his wife and their daughters on a dais. They looked so painfully happy. Dag couldn't fathom how that was even possible.

His world was on the brink, and it was no real consolation that he more than deserved it. He had blood on his hands, and he was going to take his family down with him. He couldn't think about it. Now the phone was ringing again, and so was the doorbell. Ringing and ringing all at once, and then he shifted his feet, in spite of it all, and went into the kitchen.

There he stood still and took a deep breath and remembered the oak on the hillside and the night and the stars and the birds that had flown into the sky in fright. Then he went into the hall and noted that Viktor was still playing the same piece, albeit with even more melancholy and clarity than before, and he thought, I'm going to open the door—even if it's Pompe himself come to spit his poison at me. *Cockroach, wretch, feeble creep, you disgusting murderer.*

Bring it on. Bring on the fall. He opened the door and stood there dumbfounded. Standing outside was a completely different person from the one he'd been expecting—a tall, hawkish man in an elegant, somewhat crumpled jacket who proffered his hand, but about whom nothing was offensive or suspicious. Instead, he seemed touched and a little surprised. There were tears in his eyes and his gaze wandered into the apartment.

"Who's playing?" he said, looking as if he were either in the midst of a personal crisis or had just become unexpectedly happy.

SIXTY-SIX

Micaela was lying down and reading the old police transcripts concerning Popov. He'd been questioned in Swedish in Helsinki during the investigation into the murder of Jenni Järvinen in Espoo. She was taken aback.

She couldn't think of anyone she'd heard about or come across who treated a police interviewer with such arrogance. Not even the hardened gangsters in Solna. The crooks she met in the line of duty could be contemptuous, rancorous or ice-cold, or even eerily unaffected, but they didn't lecture you and they didn't threaten to sue you for every penny you had or name-drop you to death. Granted, Popov had started out by flattering his interviewers, telling them they looked fit or that they were handsome specimens. But when subjected to questioning, he had launched a counterattack, creating the sense that it was the police who were hiding something, rather than himself.

"I'm not going to answer your questions. You have no right to ask them. I have nothing to do with this and you know it. But you're obviously bitter and incompetent, and the idea of taking down a guy who's actually achieved something has clearly got you all hard," he had said, and while it wasn't always apparent in the transcripts how the detectives had reacted, they hadn't been as fired up as she might have been. They had allowed themselves to be belittled, and perhaps they'd had no choice in the matter.

Oliver Popov had an alibi. A whole host of people who were at the party thrown by the Dutch businessman Klaas Martens in Helsinki had initially sworn blind that Popov was there all night. Yet when the Finnish detectives had drilled deeper, the only people able to confirm his later presence as the soirée extended into the small hours had been the film producer Per Morton and his associate Lene, a former employee of Popov's. This account of Popov's movements was seemingly borne out by the available CCTV footage and other witness statements also seemed to confirm this.

The unequivocal conclusion was that Popov couldn't have had time to make it to Espoo and murder a woman. Yet something was up. Morton and Popov were a little too concordant under questioning, while the producer Askvall was vague and uncertain, and said she'd been inebriated toward the end. There was nothing discernibly the matter with the statement, and she had been questioned several times, but Micaela still suspected that Askvall had been holding something back. She got the feeling there were ties of loyalty between the men, and she was increasingly persuaded that Popov had been ruled out too easily. It wasn't a stretch to imagine that Per Morton might be protecting him. They were obviously close. Almost every single film adaptation of a Popov client had been produced by Morton's company, and they were apparently often seen out and about together and were a regular fixture at premieres.

"I wonder," Micaela muttered, looking up the phone number for Lene Askvall.

Askvall picked up after two rings and sounded busy and distracted, but "police" was very much the magic word and the producer snapped to attention. Her voice was soft and slightly muffled. The online photos showed someone good-looking and fair-haired, and still young. But she was rather worryingly skinny and she had vulnerable eyes. She was one of three producers attached to the adaptation of Pontus Bremer's novel *The Wrath of Illusion*, which seemed like an odd coincidence, although perhaps it wasn't. It was a small world, Micaela had learned.

"I'd like to run through your statement from the night of Jenni Järvinen's murder in Helsinki."

"They questioned me about that multiple times," Askvall said defensively.

"I know," Micaela said, "and I'm sorry to bother you about it again. But you were there until almost the end of the party, right?"

"That's how it worked out."

"What's your relationship to Popov?"

"I used to work for him, and we've stayed in fairly close touch."

"What's your perception of him?"

Lene fell silent.

"That's a big question," she said. "But he's definitely a better man than his reputation would suggest."

"What would his reputation suggest?"

Lene Askvall hesitated again.

"That he's merciless and threatening. But if you're loyal to him then he's fantastic."

"And you're loyal?"

Lene made a sound that implied she regretted her choice of words.

"Not in that way," she said.

"Not in the way that you'd lie on his behalf in a murder investigation?"

"Jesus! No."

"If I've understood correctly, you didn't meet Järvinen at the party?" Micaela said, a little more gently.

"I recognized her after the fact when I saw the photos in the papers. But I didn't speak to her. I think she only stayed for a short while."

"Did Popov speak to her?"

"He spoke to everybody. He's like that. He wanders around and spots people and pays them compliments."

Micaela skimmed the transcript again.

"You said previously that he'd behaved differently that night."

"Only toward the end. But that wasn't so strange, really."

"No?"

"No, at least I don't think so."

Micaela could hear the hesitation in Askvall's voice.

"Was he there for the full evening until midnight?"

"Popov was definitely there."

Definitely, she thought. That was an upgrade on the last time.

"But he was behaving differently?"

"Like I said, he's amazing toward the people he likes. There's no-one who fights for their authors like he does."

Blah, blah, blah, Micaela thought.

"But . . ."

"Well, it's all a bit risky with all those expensive wines lying around, isn't it? Sometimes he trips up a little bit."

"Did he trip up on this particular night?"

"He got drunk and a little, how should I put this . . . ? But it doesn't have anything to do with the murder."

Askvall hesitated before continuing:

"He would never hurt anyone like that. Never. And I don't want to add to the bullshit out there about him. He really is the sweetest guy," she said, and Micaela wondered how on earth the detectives in Helsinki had managed to miss that this girl was so obviously under Popov's influence.

"How about *I* tell you a secret?" she said.

Lene Askvall was surprised.

"Sure."

"I'm not really working on the murder investigation. I'm in hospital after having a miscarriage and I'm only doing this because I feel miserable and don't think that women should get murdered without their killers going down for it."

"I can subscribe to that."

"So whatever you say won't end up in any file, or leak out. You're only telling me, and you don't need to be afraid that Popov will find out."

"I'm not afraid."

You damn well are, Micaela thought.

"And if Popov has an alibi, which he seems to have, then he's in the clear. But I'm trying to see the whole picture and any detail, no matter how insignificant it may seem, might lead somewhere. What did Popov do that night that seemed different to you—apart from being drunk?"

"He just said some dark stuff."

"Like what?"

Lene mumbled something inaudible.

"What?"

"He said he was above everyone else."

Micaela considered this.

"In what context did he say that?"

"I think we were talking about people who had attacked him, and how it hadn't worked out for them. He was proud of breaking them. He said he could do anything. I mean . . . He can be a bit like that sometimes. But this time it felt more like the booze doing the talking, rather than him."

Interesting, Micaela thought.

"Do you know Dag Wrangel?"

"Yes, of course," the producer said.

"What does Popov think of him?"

Lene Askvall hesitated again.

"He doesn't like him, and in cases like that he can be pretty harsh, like I said."

"Did he want to break Wrangel too?"

"Not really. But when I worked for Popov, none of the staff were even allowed to give Dag the time of day. He said Dag didn't deserve it."

"Not the nicest guy then."

Lene was silent for a while.

"No, I suppose not."

"Why does he hate Wrangel?"

"I don't know."

"But if you put your mind to it?"

"All I remember is that Popov once said Dag was a weak little wretch. It was very harsh, and frankly a little strange. Dag seems so friendly."

"But Popov's a nice guy, you say?" Micaela was provoked to say.

"Fundamentally, yes," Askvall said, as if trying to convince herself too, but she didn't have time to say any more.

A young doctor entered the room and Micaela had to interrupt the call and listen to the medic's exposition and fake pity. But before long, her concentration failed her. A worrying thought occurred to her and she realized that she too had been an idiot.

SIXTY-SEVEN

"Who are you?" said Dag.

The man who had rung the doorbell gazed back at him with piercing blue eyes.

"My name is Hans Rekke and I'm very sorry to disturb you," he said.

Dag wanted to slam the door in his face.

It was the Professor who'd started this whole nightmare. Yet Dag remained still and passive, perhaps falling under the spell of the man's strange charisma.

Nothing about him looked hostile. He raised a hand to his ear.

"I have nothing to say," said Dag.

"Who's playing?" Rekke said again, peering over his shoulder into the apartment. Dag didn't want to answer the question.

The last thing he wanted was to drag Viktor into this.

"My son," he said reluctantly. "He's playing some Chopin at a rather low level."

"A low level?" Rekke said as if completely dumbfounded. "A low level? No, no. It all comes down to touch, and this performance is nothing short of outstanding. He must have played it a thousand times."

"Huh? Well, yes, he's always at the piano," Dag mumbled, without quite knowing what he was saying. "But I'm in the middle of . . ."

"Then again, a thousand times isn't enough," the Professor said, interrupting him. "He must have understood it in his heart too." He craned his neck to see inside the apartment again. "Twelve years old?"

"Eleven," Dag muttered.

"Eleven—but he plays as if he's had a long life. Centuries almost. Listen. It might alleviate your anxiety, Dag."

"I'm not anxious," Dag stammered.

The Professor shot him a brief glance.

"No? You're mistaken. You see, I was like that myself—constantly playing Chopin's études, and I loved this one, Opus 10, number three. *Tristesse* as it's sometimes named. E major, as I'm sure you can tell. But your son is making it sound like a minor-key requiem. He's playing as if it were life and death. He's exceptionally gifted."

"That's nice of you to say. But like I said, I really must . . ." Dag said, beginning to close the door.

"No!" Rekke said, inserting his foot in the gap. "You'll forgive me, but I really must come in and listen to this some more. It's as if my entire childhood has been returned to me."

Then he simply stepped into the hall and moved toward the grand piano in the living room where Viktor immediately stopped playing, and Dag wanted to hurl himself at the Professor, saying, Don't frighten the boy. Yet something made him hesitate, and perhaps he felt a little pride too—although he was too worked up to think lucidly. Viktor was peering anxiously down at the keys.

"For goodness sake, continue!" the Professor said.

Viktor shook his head, so Rekke bent down and played the same piece himself, standing there with a crooked back, and it was immediately obvious that Viktor was moved.

"Wow," he managed to say.

"It took me years, decades, to acquire a touch like that. I played until my fingers bled. But you, my friend . . . what's your name?"

"Viktor."

The boy looked up.

"You already have it. Who is your teacher?"

"Boris," said Viktor.

Rekke beamed.

"Krasnov?"

The boy nodded.

"My God," said the Professor. "How did you find him?"

"He was recommended . . ."

Dag didn't manage to say any more.

"Well, I don't suppose it matters. What a stroke of luck though! Boris and I were friends once upon a time—"

"Are you Hans Rekke?" Viktor said, interjecting as if he'd suddenly realized something astonishing.

"Indeed I am. But what I was about to say was that Boris understands the value of slowness. He—of all people—knows that fast-playing virtuosos who can hammer out Rachmaninoff's second are a dime a dozen. The real art is in feeling the notes; making them cry like you do. Now, what is it that Boris always says about the keys?"

"That they're dead."

"Exactly. But you, Viktor, bring them to life. It seems to me that you must spend all day playing and then dream about it at night."

Viktor didn't reply. His body became strangely tense and Dag couldn't quite fathom what the boy was going through. His hunch was that while he himself was crashing, his son was experiencing something at the opposite end of the emotional spectrum, and perhaps the Professor realized that too. He turned to Dag and smiled wistfully.

"Do you know who Viktor reminds me of?"

Dag shook his head.

"He reminds me of you, Dag—of your way of writing. There's the same attention to the melody. You're alike, aren't you? Obsessed with making it sing, which is why you also both create a soundboard that stands out. You too have sat with your words until you were on the brink of madness, haven't you?"

"I suppose it's possible," Dag said, struck by the thought for the first time, though he was in no state to appreciate it, and he didn't manage to think about it for very long either.

A text message arrived and he nervously touched the phone in his pocket, not daring to pull it out. He could tell that Rekke had noticed. Yet the Professor didn't make a big deal out of it. Instead, he went to get a chair from the hall and then sat down next to the piano as if he'd actually come to see Viktor, and Dag had no idea what he should do except that he felt a compulsion to flee. But that was hardly an option, was it? I'm guilty, he thought. And the guilty have nowhere to go. Far away, as if in a fog, he heard Rekke say to Viktor:

"Play it again. *Lento ma non troppo*, softly and with feeling. But importantly, stay restrained; maintain your emphasis. Just like that, angle your hand a little . . ."

Dag went into the kitchen and was about to read the text message when his phone rang and he checked who it was. Andrea, for the tenth time. But he didn't answer it this time either. He stood motionless by the kitchen table, trying to think. What was he to do? He didn't know. Instead, he slumped onto one of the kitchen chairs and read the message that had arrived:

Meeting your friend Pompe for a quick chat. He has something exciting to tell me. Love you.

Just seconds ago, Dag couldn't have comprehended, or even imagined, that things could get any worse than they already were. But of course there was always a deeper shaft to fall down. No, Andrea could not meet Pompe. But he couldn't bring himself to reply. Paralysed, he listened to the Chopin étude which had now become wild and cacophonous, as if it were a reflection of his inner self, and seconds and minutes slid by. At last, Dag was wrenched out of his paralysis. There were footsteps and the scrape of a chair being pulled out and then pulled forward. Viktor continued to play alone at the piano.

"That bad?" said a voice.

He looked up.

Rekke was sitting opposite him, leaning forward.

"I'm fine," he said.

"Your arms are folded across your chest. Your pulse is rapid and your pupils are so dilated and glassy that I can't help wondering whether your vision is a little blurry."

Dag could find no reason to reply.

"Is there anything pressing we should address?" said the Professor.

"No," he lied.

"Are you sure?"

Dag shifted his head irresolutely.

"If I had authority and wasn't merely here as an uninvited guest, I would ask to examine your telephone. It seems to be positively aglow," the Professor said.

"It's not that bad," Dag muttered, thinking about Andrea and Pompe.

Surely Pompe wouldn't dare do anything to her? Or would he? The anxiety contorted itself in his chest like a knot tightening, and he nervously put a hand to his pocket.

"You're left-handed?" said the Professor.

"Huh? Yes."

"Left-footed too?"

He nodded, feeling intensely uncomfortable.

"You liked her, didn't you?" Rekke said.

Dag looked up and it really did feel as if his vision was blurred, like the Professor had said.

"Who?"

"Sandra Ramirez—the girl in Santander."

Dag pictured the old oak tree and Sandra turning toward him, pleading.

"I . . ." he said, unable to get any further.

The Professor sat still—he was almost completely motionless and his gaze was fixed on Dag.

"Did you know that I was once regarded as a world-leading expert in interrogation techniques?" he said.

"I'd heard something to that effect," Dag muttered.

"A rank exaggeration—I have my weaknesses. When interrogating men whose sons play Chopin with that degree of sensitivity, I tend to become gentler and risk losing my edge."

"That can't be a particularly common occurrence."

The Professor laughed.

"That's true. It doesn't happen on a regular basis. But when it does, I'm affected."

Dag attempted a smile too.

"And I suppose that's good for me."

"Yes Dag, it's good for you. I become more forgiving—even though I can presently see Sandra Ramirez's beaten and bruised body in my mind's eye."

Dag grimaced briefly.

Rekke continued to smile, ostensibly still just as friendly.

"I don't know what you've done," said the Professor. "But I believe there are extenuating circumstances. I believe that I would actually understand."

"I doubt that," said Dag.

"Don't underestimate me," said Rekke.

"I'm not."

"But perhaps it's hard to explain it to yourself?"

"It is," Dag said, realising that he was about to confess and that there was presumably no other way out.

"*Rem tene, verba sequentur.* Grasp the subject, the words will follow," said the Professor.

"It's not that easy."

"No," said Rekke. "It's certainly not easy."

He leaned forward, his elbows on the kitchen table.

"But this trip in your BMW in the summer of 1988 got off to a fine start, didn't it?" the Professor said.

Dag nodded, unable to utter a word. He was thinking of his wife and Pompe and could feel the dread cutting into him. I have to do something, he thought. That was why he pulled out his phone and showed Andrea's text message to Rekke.

The Professor read it and then looked at him quizzically.

"Who is Pompe?"

Dag took a deep breath.

"My traveling companion in 1988."

"Does your wife make a habit of seeing him?" Rekke said.

"She didn't even know of his existence until today."

Rekke became completely silent.

"And you think Pompe may harbour malicious intent?"

"He always harbours malicious intent. He's the devil incarnate."

Rekke looked down at the table.

"Ring your wife and tell her to take a rain check on Pompe," he said, so Dag did, almost relieved to obey, but Andrea didn't pick up, even though he kept on trying over and over again. He glanced nervously at Rekke.

"She's not answering," he said.

Rekke looked intently at him.

"Does your wife have a secretary? Someone who keeps track of her meetings?"

"Yes."

"Can I have her number and Andrea's too?"

Dag nodded and supplied the details to the Professor, and he thought Rekke was going to try them right away, but he remained seated and motionless.

"Is Pompe Oliver Popov?" he said.

Dag stiffened and felt a thousand conflicting impulses tugging at his insides, but he never managed to answer. Rekke had already stood up and exited the kitchen in a fluttering, nervous movement before hurrying through the front door.

SIXTY-EIGHT

Could it be possible?

Muttering to herself, Micaela grabbed her phone from her hospital bedside table and rang Rekke, who was breathing hard and seemed even more worked up than she was.

"What's going on?" she said.

"I've got to rush," he said. "I need to get hold of Andrea Wrangel."

"Why?"

"I believe her life may be in danger. Could you help me track her down? She's going to see Popov."

Popov, she thought. It was about Popov that she was calling.

"It's not him," she said. "He's not our guy."

Rekke fell silent.

She could still hear him breathing down the line.

"No," he said. "It's him. I've just had it confirmed."

"You have?"

She was at a loss.

"But . . ." she managed to say.

"Must dash," Rekke said as if he hadn't heard her. "Can you help me to find her?"

"Sure," she said, and then he was gone and she sat up in bed and wondered what she was supposed to do.

Find Andrea Wrangel, apparently. But if she was going to see Popov then there was probably no immediate danger. Popov might be a bastard, but she didn't think he was a killer. Perhaps he'd protected a killer, but it wasn't at all certain that he'd done so deliberately. Or was she the one who was wide of the mark?

Uncertainty consumed Micaela and she switched on the computer that had been on her lap in bed and went online to run a series of searches while biting her lip and muttering. For a while she was inclined to agree with Rekke. But then she changed her mind again and her doubts dissolved—most of them anyway—the manic idiot here was Rekke, not her. She texted him and Jonas Beijer to tell them what she thought. Then Micaela did something drastic.

She yanked the drip out of her arm and stood up. Thc swiftness of the movement made her blood pressure drop and she stumbled, but supported herself on the bed and regained her strength. "Pull yourself together," she muttered, pulling on her clothes which had been draped over the chair next to her bed and then going out into the hallway. When she heard the sound of running feet heading toward her room, she picked up the pace and found herself overcome by another attack of dizziness, but she hurried on. She'd just have to sink or swim, and it wasn't as if she had to worry about a foetus in her belly.

The journalists continued to call, but Magnus could already sense the end was in sight, and he'd begun to meditate upon new, more entertaining conflicts. He was pondering Popov and the Prime Minister. If his manic brother suspected Popov was guilty of violent crimes then surely he himself should shake a few trees as well. For instance, he might speak with a like-minded individual. Why not that guy at the Security Service, Erik Kvarnström?

Erik bore a passing resemblance to Magnus. Übercompetent, quick-witted, and loved a good intrigue. Especially if it could benefit him. There was something here, irresistible and downright explosive, and surely they could exploit it somehow. He dialled Erik's number on a secure line.

"Gosh, you seem to be in high spirits," said Erik. "I thought they were out to get you."

"Piffle," Magnus said. "It'll blow over. I'll come out of it stronger than ever. I'm calling about an altogether different matter that I think might amuse you."

"In that case I'm interested," Erik said.

"Oliver Popov," Magnus said. "What are we going to say about Mr. Popov's friendship with the Prime Minister?"

"Problematic," Erik said, and Magnus smiled to himself.

"Go on," he said.

Erik fell silent as if trying to put up some resistance after all.

"Has something happened that I should know about?" he said in the end.

Magnus considered this.

"My brother, Hans," he said.

"The master detective?"

"Precisely. He seems to suspect Popov may be guilty of violent criminal acts, and we're all a little worried there might be blowback on the government."

"Interesting," said Erik. "We have warned the PM on several occasions about being seen with Popov."

"And what's his answer been?"

"That he needs something concrete. He doesn't want to ditch a friend over a rumour, and he says that Popov is an important contact. He's a tie to the cultural sphere that he wants to stay on the right side of."

"Blah, blah, blah," said Magnus.

"But I think it's mostly that Popov makes him feel cool. He's a bit too proper for his own good, isn't he? There's something of the eternal student council president about him," Erik said.

Magnus laughed.

"What sort of rumours are we talking about?" he said.

"Mr. Popov is said to sometimes be violent toward women, to threaten his colleagues and be a nightmare to deal with. Then there's the business of this murder in Finland. He has an alibi, but those of us who have taken a look at the files and know a thing or two about murder investigations feel there's something amiss. Is that what your brother is looking into?"

"That and something even more antiquated, I believe."

Silence on the other end. This felt serious.

"And your brother is usually right, isn't he?" he said.

Magnus chose not to answer.

"This Popov guy . . ." he said tentatively, ". . . he must be a bit of a psychopath? Otherwise he'd never be able to run rings around the PM like this."

"Of course," Erik said. "I gather he's damn good at scaring people, and it wouldn't surprise me . . ." He paused for effect.

"What?"

"If he's got something on the Prime Minister. Mr. Popov loves to have a hold over people."

Well, that would be a happy surprise.

"So naturally I'm curious as to what your intentions are," Erik added with unnecessary irony. "Are you seeking to be a help or a hindrance to your head of government?"

Both, Magnus thought.

"Help, of course," he said, pretending to sound hurt. "It wouldn't do for us to hit something difficult head on right now."

"Is your brother running this solo, or has he got the police on board?"

Magnus pondered which answer would serve him best.

"I think he's working solo."

Erik seemed to be thinking through various options.

"Do you want to stop Hans?" he said. "I mean, if he's engaged in his own ferreting about then that might be considered arbitrary conduct exposing the Prime Minister to risk."

Magnus paused for thought. What did he want? To stop his manic brother? Not necessarily. The important thing was—as ever—to make the ultimate powers that be more dependent on him.

"I think that's for the Prime Minister to decide," he said sternly. In a more lighthearted tone he added: "Although it would obviously be good for you to mention that it was me who provided the information."

Erik laughed.

"Naturally."

Magnus became roguish.

"And tell him that my brother is manic and might do anything."

"Are you serious?"

"Unfortunately, yes," Magnus said, remembering the last time Hans had had a manic episode, when he'd started shorting the markets and set himself on the path to ruin while also trying to solve every single murder he could find.

Magnus said a couple of words in parting to Erik and hung up, feeling very pleased with himself.

SIXTY-NINE

After Rekke had ended his call to Micaela, he rang Andrea Wrangel over and over without getting any answer. Then he hurried onto Östermalmsgatan, and as he went he looked at his wristwatch, although rather oddly without noting the time. He became wrapped up in the observation that the minute hand was slightly bent and that led his thoughts into a loop he could never have explained. “Osama bin Laden,” he muttered, “hidden by Pakistani intelligence.”

It was as if he were seeing a pattern that was connected to the minute hand and the length of time since new traces of the terrorist leader had emerged. But then he shook this off, moving so quickly that he didn’t notice his Borsalino hat flying off his head and then blowing along the sidewalk in the gusting wind. He was fully concentrated on other strands unraveling in his head.

Once again, he saw Sandra Ramirez’s body in his mind’s eye and he returned to his very first thought: there was something disparate about her bruises and wounds, and that might indicate two attackers. But was that possible? The person who had killed women and marked them with archaic numerical symbols was undoubtedly suffering from severe psychopathy. In one look Rekke had determined that the man was grandiose and misogynistic, and his empathy was most definitely impaired. Dag Wrangel was none of those things. Yet his face had shone with such hellish guilt that it had almost felt like a confession.

Dag was mixed up in this somehow. Otherwise it didn't add up. There had to be several possibilities. Dag could have lost it in a moment of jealousy, or been manipulated into doing something that would ordinarily have been completely alien to him. Rekke knew all too well that it was natural for psychopaths to seek out fragile people whom they could control, people who were their opposites. What was more, he knew that psychopaths were capable of getting completely normal people to commit atrocities. All it took was a slow and incremental normalisation process—like in a cult, or perhaps a road trip across Europe? But it still seemed difficult to grasp.

It felt inexplicable that a man like Dag Wrangel could have ended up involved in this and not have said a word about it for twenty years. It must be because of fear, Rekke decided, and threats—threats to him and his family, which meant it couldn't be anything other than ominous that Popov was on the way to meet Dag's wife. There were no limits to how badly it might go, especially if Popov knew that the net was tightening around him and he had nothing left to lose—and if he was compulsive in his actions.

Rekke reduced his tempo and stopped running. Above him, dark clouds were rushing across the sky. The wind had picked up—perhaps another storm was brewing—and he pulled out his phone once again. He had the impression it had buzzed or beeped. He was by then at the intersection of Narvavägen and Strandvägen, only two hundred metres from Andrea Wrangel's office, and he saw that Micaela had sent a long text message. He recalled what she'd just said on the phone. Popov wasn't their man, she'd said. But he hadn't cared. He'd seen Popov's eyes and sensed the abyss that lay within. But Micaela's text said it couldn't be him. Rekke pondered this for a few seconds and he read everything she had said once more. Micaela, who was usually so wise, was, in his view, wrong on this count. At any rate, his foremost priority was to find and protect Andrea Wrangel. Rekke began frantically calling again, finally managing to reach Andrea's secretary and hearing how frantic and unstructured his own voice sounded.

"Where's Andrea?" he said.

"I'm sorry, who's calling?" said the secretary, who had introduced herself as Hedvig.

"You're from Saxony—near the Bavarian border," he said.

"What? Yes. How do you know that?"

"I can hear it. My name is Hans Rekke and I believe it's of the utmost importance that we reach Andrea. Do you know where she is?"

"No, she just left. She was in a hurry, but there's nothing in the diary."

"Do you know which way she went?" he said.

"Toward town, I think. But I'm not sure."

He hung up and hared along Strandvägen toward the city centre while dialing Popov's number. Popov's phone was switched off and at his office on Birger Jarlsgatan the receptionist said that he'd also just gone out, and that only enhanced Rekke's perception that he needed to get hold of Andrea Wrangel and Popov—right now.

SEVENTY

Andrea had crossed Strandvägen and was walking along the waterside past the boats, heading for Djurgården and the Villa Godthem restaurant.

She was both in high spirits and uneasy, as if she were doing something forbidden. But surely it wasn't that bad, she thought.

It was for Dag's sake—with a little luck, he'd get a prize and she really had tried to reach him every way she could. But he hadn't picked up; they'd kept missing each other. Hopefully he'd had a good writing day and was now looking after Viktor, who would surely be back from school again. On the other hand, there was a hell of a lot of calls and texts from other people—the usual, or possibly even worse—and she would have to deal with those once she was in the warm and could see what they were all about.

She tugged her coat closer. It was bitingly cold, but better than the day before—at least so far. Gone was the blizzard—now it was just trickily windy as the sky darkened. Nevertheless, the streets were full of people hurrying home from work, hunched over like she was.

This would be exciting, Andrea told herself, sending up a silent prayer, but the feeling of unease returned and she quickly looked over her shoulder. Was someone following her? The only thing out of the ordinary that she could see was a tall man on the other side of the street who was running in the opposite direction with jerky, fluttering movements. He seemed somehow anachronistic to her, like a figure from the nineteenth century. But she forgot about him immediately. Her unease intensified and she supposed it had been there since that morning when Dag had looked so afraid, and Andrea realized with a sudden rancour that no, this was not going to be fun. The meeting was a mistake.

Something was the matter, she thought. She should go straight home, or at least try to reach Dag. Perhaps he'd called or texted while she was walking? Her phone was in her handbag, but as she went to check it a brown Porsche squealed to a halt and honked its horn at her. Andrea jumped—what was the driver playing at? She hated those flash cars—what sort of person needed that kind of nonsense to feel validated? She glowered at the car. But she never did spot who was behind the wheel. The Porsche pulled away with a testosterone-fuelled lurch and she glanced around anxiously before picking up the pace. The wind lashed Andrea as she crossed the Djurgårdsbron bridge, and she glanced down at the black water as she approached the Villa Godthem restaurant. Although a couple of minutes earlier there had been lots of people on Strandvägen, this spot was deserted. She couldn't see a single person, although that wasn't so strange. Ahead of her were the woods and the walking trails. On a sunny Sunday, this area was crammed with people but right now a storm was brewing and very few people lived here—only the very wealthiest in their solitary houses by the water's edge. But then . . . Andrea started. She could see the Porsche that had honked at her, arrogantly and carelessly parked on the gravel path where cars weren't allowed, and she swore and hoped that a fastidious meter maid would come along and apply parking tickets to it. But the Porsche wasn't the only odd thing she noticed.

The restaurant was closed for refurbishments. Surely Pompe would have known that. Hadn't he said he would book a table?

Andrea spun around and looked toward the shoreline where a waddling of ducks was nervously emerging from the water, and as snowflakes landed on her coat and her skin she shivered with cold. Her hair fluttered about in a sudden squall. This whole thing had been a mistake.

She made up her mind to go home and look after her family, and pulled out her phone to text Dag.

Viktor was standing in front of Dag in the kitchen, his eyes wide as he showed him a YouTube video in which Hans Rekke was performing on a concert stage.

"Can you believe that he was here?" the boy said. "Can you hear the way he plays? His touch is awesome."

Dag said he could believe it; that it was incredible.

"He thought you were amazing, Viktor," he said, seeing the boy's face light up in a smile as he held the computer screen up in front of himself.

He ruffled his son's hair and said he had to do something. He went into the bedroom to text Andrea and tell her that she absolutely must not meet Pompe, and at that moment he heaved a sigh of relief as he saw her message to him. Andrea was on her way home; Pompe had no-showed.

Great. Hurry. He's dangerous, he replied, feeling a sense of hope as if he'd been pulled from a well.

That didn't last long. It's all going to hell soon, anyway, he thought, wondering whether to go to his computer and open the confession he'd written so many years ago and hidden away in his files disguised as a short story. But he wasn't sure he could cope with reading it. Composing it had plunged Dag into a black hole, and somewhere there was a strange comfort in that. Or perhaps it wasn't so strange.

His writing was often more important than life itself, and perhaps it would sustain him even as everything fell apart if he could only make literature from his horror. The idea attracted him with unexpected force: writing about the hideous with such pain that it seared straight into people's hearts: *I'm a murderer. I've seen the very bottom of it all.* But he was immediately ashamed. Was he prepared to leave his whole life in ruins and shame his family just to write something of true significance? Perhaps. "To write is to preside at Judgement Day over one's self." The solemn words from his youth returned to him.

He was an eminent writer. Somewhere deep down, he knew that, in spite of it all. But perhaps he could advance even further if only he were to uncover the darkest places and dare to return to the old oak, the tree that had shone faintly in the moonlight and had shaken itself as if it were a living being waking in the middle of the night. Dag's body tensed, almost spasming at the memory, just like it always did.

The memory was at once distinct and unclear. There were scenes he remembered as if they had happened yesterday, or as if they were happening in real time, while others were strangely blurry and mixed up. The oak was one of those, all the more so since he'd bought the *London Review of Books* a couple of months ago and secretly read the short story over and over again. After that, he wasn't always sure what he'd seen that night and what stemmed from Sandra's story. The branches extended upward as if the oak were praying to the sky with thirty arms, she'd written, and that was now how he remembered it.

But was that possible? It was an old tree with almost no leaves on its branches and a split trunk. It could hardly have reached into the sky like that, could it? But that was how he remembered it, at once dying and majestic, like a wicked mythological being connecting the heavens and the underworld. He'd walked toward it as if propelled forward by an inner gravity, and he'd been certain that Sandra had seen him too, but he couldn't interpret her reaction. He wasn't close enough, and it felt so strange. The sky was starlit and it was still hot, and the closer he got to the tree, the more flies and mosquitoes were buzzing about. Besides, Pompe was moving differently.

The nonchalance in his gait was gone, replaced by an eerie sense of purpose, and then something happened that Dag wished he'd never seen. Pompe turned around and beckoned discreetly. There was nothing friendly in that gesture, nothing inviting. Come, come, he seemed to say. I'm going to mock you some more. Dag should have turned around at once—well, he probably would have done had he not seen Sandra's eyes.

She looked scared, not only of Pompe but also of him, and naturally he should have realized that this was perfectly natural. She was alone on the hillside with two men—three if you counted the man with the guitar bringing up the rear. It was quite obvious that she would be afraid.

He should have understood that sooner, but he'd been so heartbroken that he hadn't been thinking clearly. All he had was the thick branch he'd picked up from beside the path earlier, and he approached the old oak as if propelled forward by a dark, inexorable force.

SEVENTY-ONE

The Stockholm streets were jumbled together in Rekke's head and suddenly he wasn't sure where Birger Jarlsgatan ended or how it joined to Hamngatan on the final stretch. It was as if he could see multiple realities before him—multiple Stockholms—and he felt the sudden urge to run around in circles to orient himself. But then he stopped outside the Hotel Diplomat, troubled by something as he gazed across the water.

It was snowing now and there were white waves on the water. It was dark and cold—icy cold. A good thing, surely. The cold makes us less prone to violence. Then again, what did he know? Nothing! He had to get hold of them, and it occurred to him that he might be rushing in the wrong direction. If Popov really did harbour malicious intent then he wouldn't have agreed on a meeting place in the city—he would have picked a more secluded spot. Rekke envisioned the old oak in Santander and in that moment he was able to add another piece to the jigsaw. He understood Dag Wrangel's role in the drama. The truth came to him almost as a vision, and he froze for a moment before looking up again. In the distance on the other side of Strandvägen, he could see a man and there was something unsettlingly familiar about his body language . . . Could it be? Surely this was just his brain conjuring up what he wanted to see.

The man wore a big blue padded coat with a hood pulled up over his head, and he was walking quickly as if he were late and in a hurry, and while Rekke doubted himself for another couple of seconds and thought of Micaela and her long text message, it was then that he knew for sure. It really was Popov.

The blood rushed to his chest and he ran straight across the street, so carelessly that cars had to floor their brakes and an old man he must have bumped into swore at him. But Rekke ploughed on, and it didn't take long for Popov to react. He turned and looked at him, not afraid for even a second as far as Rekke could tell, merely still and hostile as he hissed threateningly: "What do you want now, you wretched piece of shit?" And in that moment Rekke lost it, perhaps because he could once again picture Sandra Ramirez's beaten body, or perhaps—which would be less honourable—because the words Popov had spat out with such icy contempt had once again got under his skin.

He grabbed the expensive coat and flung Popov against the wall of the adjacent building, not caring one bit that people were staring at him and that a woman had pulled out her phone to call the police. Rekke hurled Popov down onto the sidewalk and said in a voice trembling with fury:

"Don't touch Andrea Wrangel—this ends now!"

Popov spat at him and tried to pry himself free, but Rekke continued to hold him fast with all his might, convinced that he had prevented something terrible from happening.

SEVENTY-TWO

Dag was sitting at the computer reading his old confession, part of him proud of the power and strength of his own words. Nothing else I've written is this strong, he thought. Never before had he expressed himself so authentically and so chillingly. But the pride didn't last for long. He was even more violently overcome by anxiety, and at first he didn't react to the beeping of his phone, instead staring at the screen and muttering his old sentences as if entranced. Then he looked, noting that it was 5:23 p.m. Outside, the thick November darkness had descended and he was breathing heavily, filled with misgivings. He pulled up the text message.

My God. Sorry. Dangerous?! What's he done? Hurrying back. Be home in 15–20 minutes.

Dag closed his document and stood up and went over to Viktor, who was still hunched over his YouTube clips in the kitchen. Impulsively he hugged him—a little too tightly—said everything would be alright. Viktor gazed back at him uncomprehendingly and then Dag left him alone. Instead, he began to tidy the kitchen. He wanted to get everything shipshape before Andrea's return home. But the optimism didn't last, and once again the memories welled up, now influenced by his own words, words that he had written so long ago, and which once again shattered the illusion that it was all just a bad dream.

Standing there, dishcloth in hand, he remembered how afterward he'd staggered down the hill toward Santander, away from the old oak, and on his way he'd bumped into the weird man with the guitar. Where had he gone? That was one of the mysteries in this story, and it was a strange encounter. He'd had a weather-beaten, tanned face, and his salt-and-pepper hair had been tied in a ponytail. He'd been perhaps forty years old and wearing a simple pair of plastic sandals, and his battered guitar was covered in exotic stickers. But the truly perplexing thing about him had been his expression. He hadn't looked afraid or shocked—rather, he had appeared surprised and thoughtful, and had then uttered a couple of sentences in Spanish before switching to English. But Dag hadn't had time to catch what he said—something about Sandra, or the young woman as he called her, and an amulet that he'd given her. Dag had rushed on past the man, and had soon begun to sob.

Tears ran down his cheeks as he approached the city and its fiesta, and he probably hadn't yet understood what had happened. It wasn't as bad as it would become. Life was still there, somewhere around him. He remembered a dragon puppet moving along the street, a man breathing fire and juggling, two boys screaming. Everything imaginable at once close and distant, and he staggered on through the city toward the harbour, eventually finding a taxi that agreed to take him to his digs in Laredo for a rip-off fare. And perhaps it was there, on the way back to their digs, or perhaps later when Pompe returned at dawn, that Dag understood properly:

I'm a wretch, a repulsive creep, a cockroach. A murderer.

SEVENTY-THREE

Andrea shivered and pulled the coat tighter around her body.

Never again would she go behind Dag's back, she resolved—not even with the best of intentions. Not even for a wonderful prize. *Dangerous.* That was how Dag had described Pompe in his message, which had sounded crazy. But he hadn't said in what way he was dangerous or what exactly he had done, and she supposed that could wait.

Right now, she needed to get home at once. She wondered which way to go. It was definitely quickest to retrace her steps across the Djurgårdsbron bridge and then walk up Narvavägen. But she risked crossing paths with Pompe if he should arrive a little late. So she took a left and continued eastward along Djurgården on the shoreline footpath, thinking that she'd take the next bridge, before doubling back and going along Nobelgatan instead. Not that it seemed much of an improvement.

There wasn't a soul in sight, and she felt unsafe and cold. Fear crept under her skin along with the wind and the cold, and she recalled the brown Porsche that had startled her on Strandvägen and that she'd seen parked outside the shuttered restaurant.

Why was it there if the place wasn't open for business? Wasn't that rather strange? Whatever, she thought. Keep going; pick up the pace. The weather continued to deteriorate. The snow was falling hard and the wind was whistling through the trees, but she thought she could hear other things too—were those footsteps behind her? She hoped to God they weren't. It was probably just the creaking of her own shoes on the snowy ground. There was a house in the distance right by the water's edge; the windows were glowing and she could even make out the contours of a child inside, and she felt a sudden urge to go and ring the doorbell. But she never got that far. Now there really were footsteps behind her and her chest tightened with panic.

"Hey, what's the rush? I'm so sorry," a male voice called out. The same voice she'd spoken to on the phone. And although her heart was pounding and Andrea's mouth had gone dry, she saw no option but to turn around and smile.

Just don't provoke him, she told herself. Remain kind and calm. There he was, just ten metres behind her. Surely he couldn't be dangerous? He was smiling broadly at her and he looked pretty cool with his bright blue hat. He wore boots and a quilted jacket and he had twinkling blue eyes. He was better dressed for the cold than she was, and even as she scrutinized him suspiciously and with a ticking fear in her body, she found his smile almost enchanting. His eyes sparkled with curiosity and warmth, and his teeth shone white. It'll be fine, she thought. I can do this.

"I'm so sorry," he said again. "I really should have checked they were open."

Andrea stayed put, waiting for him to catch up, afraid but cautiously optimistic. Perhaps he is dangerous, she thought, but surely not out here in the cold, and not to me. I've done nothing to him.

"I suppose we both should have," she said.

"How dare they be remodeling when we're supposed to be meeting for the first time ever?"

He laughed and began to move slowly toward her.

"Unforgivable," she said with a strained smile, approaching him and wondering when to say she needed to go home. She decided to hold off so as not to provoke him, and she looked down and saw he was wearing black gloves and that just like in the photos of him online there was something a little feminine about his form. He moved with unusual grace.

"I really can't believe that we haven't ever met before," he said in the same light tone of voice.

She didn't reply.

"Tabbouli's are only up the hill and they're open. I just rang them to check," he said. "Why don't we go there instead?"

She didn't know how to answer, and she didn't believe him either. Wasn't Tabbouli only open for the summer season, given its large outdoor seating area which was hardly useable right now? But she decided to prevaricate on that point too, and instead tried to bag herself some life insurance by mumbling:

"I told Dag and my secretary that I was seeing you."

His eyes darkened.

"So you ruined the surprise."

Her chest tightened with fear.

"Dag seems scared of you," she stammered.

Pompe looked at her in concern, or perhaps it wasn't so much concern as disappointment, as if he felt both she and Dag had failed to live up to his expectations.

"Perhaps he's running away from himself," he said.

She regretted mentioning it.

"How did you meet?" she said.

"At high school. We both went to Östra Real," he said, looking around. She noted that there was still no-one in sight, apart from that house where she'd seen the outline of a child. "But we grew very close on a road trip across Europe."

"And what did you get up to?" she said, immediately regretting the question. She really should leave, but fear was making her ramble on—perhaps the cold too. She was suddenly feeling even colder than before, and she noticed that Pompe kept surveying their surroundings.

"We drank and read books," he said. "But something happened, and that was what I was going to tell you about."

She'd spent the whole day wondering whether something had happened on that trip, but now she no longer wanted to know. She wanted to go home to Dag and Viktor. She didn't like the fact that Pompe was walking so close to the ditch and the woods beyond. It felt unnatural somehow, and up there on the nearby slope was Tabbouli's, dark and very much closed for the season as she had suspected, and then she was gripped by terror, which he noticed.

"Give me your phone," he said.

"What?"

With a jerk, Andrea tried to run. But Pompe caught up and grabbed her arm and her waist with a sudden violence, whispering flatly into her ear, "Give me your phone and your PIN, or I'll hurt you," and she saw no way out except to do as he asked.

She handed over the phone, and after he took it, his face changed and his eyes darkened. In a swift and brutal movement, he did something to her hand. Her fingers flared with fiery pain and she sank to the ground in agony.

"What are you doing?" she shrieked.

He didn't reply. He kicked her once or twice, looming above her with a ghastly smile playing across his lips as he examined her phone. Then his face lit up.

"Well, this is splendid," he said. "I never showed."

"What?" she stuttered.

"You say so in as many words. *Pompe never showed.*"

He waved her phone at her as if it were proof. Then he hurled it away—she didn't see where; all she heard was a splash and she tried desperately to get to her feet. But that too was a mistake. Standing was how he wanted her, she realized. He grabbed her arms again and shoved her aggressively toward the woods, and at that moment she realized exactly what Dag had meant. Pompe wasn't dangerous in the sense that he was rather violent and uninhibited. No, he was dangerous in the sense that he was the most evil bastard on the planet.

He was a beast, a monster, and nothing else. Instinctively, as if she too had been transformed into an animal in a split second, she tried to bite his throat when he bent down to drag her further into the trees. But he jerked his head away and grabbed her. A branch slashed at her cheek, and she screamed even more and kept on kicking. He simply pulled her along with furious force, and eventually, some twenty or thirty metres further on, he hurled her to the ground. She hit her head on a rock or a stump and felt him land on top of her with a thud, a blow. He smelled of alcohol, and his eyes were black, and empty of all mercy. He slowly tore open her blouse, smiling at her with icy contempt.

"How much loneliness can you take?" he hissed.

Terrified, she shook her head.

"As much as you like," he said, striking her face. "It doesn't bottom out."

SEVENTY-FOUR

"As much as you like," he hissed. "You said as much yourself."

Sandra could no longer see anything. Her eyes were swollen, her face beaten to a pulp, and there was so much pain radiating from her fingers that she could barely think. But she knew she was lying right beside the oak. She could touch the trunk. She could feel sticks underneath her back, and before she'd been struck in the face she'd seen the moonlight above.

It seemed to her that the branches weren't reaching up as if praying to the sky with thirty arms; instead they were drooping, brittle and dry, as if all it would take to snap them off was a single twist. The oak wasn't how she remembered it from childhood or how she had described it in the story. It was decaying, smaller, mundane in a way, but also more ghostly. And that was why poetry and reality still merged into one for her, and briefly she thought the evil was emanating from the tree itself rather than from Pompe standing above her. Or was Dag there too?

They'd both been up here, and there was such a strange atmosphere between them. Sandra had expected Pompe to be angry that Dag was following them and interfering, but instead it had excited him. His eyes were terrifying, and that was when she really felt afraid. She told Dag to head back to the city—everything would be calmer then. She told him very kindly to leave them alone, and she watched him recede into the distance. But had he come back? She didn't understand, and she couldn't see, but she was consumed by the feeling that there were two people standing over her. In any case, she was now taking kicks to both sides of her body and those striking her right side were looser and more half-hearted. Often, the panting and spitting seemed to be so heavy that it must have been coming from two people. Yet the only voice she heard was Pompe's, and it was only Pompe who ripped off her dress and tore off her tights.

"You're going to suffer like no other woman," he said.

There was a sudden pause in the assault, a respite of sorts, but it felt worse than the kicks and blows, and she got the impression he was looking at her bare legs.

"Please," she begged.

"I like the scars," he said.

"They're from when I was little," she stammered, hoping to summon up a shred of humanity in him. "A dog attacked me—I almost died."

"You'll have new ones. You'll be nothing but a scar."

She screamed, or so she thought. He—they?—hissed in reply, but she couldn't understand a word of it. It was in their language, Swedish, and it sounded like curses and evil spells rising from the underworld, and before long she didn't even have it in her to writhe or try and escape. She just lay there, at the mercy of the violence and loneliness, thinking about her stray.

Rekke gazed at Popov, who was lying beneath him on the street and had just spat in his face, and something about the sight made him feel ill at ease, which was hardly a surprise. The whole thing was distinctly unpleasant. There were people surrounding them and a man had tried to pull him off as if he were a delinquent schoolboy, and people were speaking in indignant tones.

Still, it wasn't the situation itself that bothered Rekke. It was the look in Popov's eye when he'd mentioned Andrea Wrangel's name. There had been a hint of confusion. Popov hadn't looked like a guilty man caught red-handed but like someone who didn't fully understand, and that insight began to spread through Rekke's mind, merging with Dag Wrangel's expression when he'd asked him who Pompe was, and above all it blended into Micaela's call and message.

"I'm sorry," Rekke mumbled, letting Popov go, getting to his feet and not much caring about the commotion around him.

He was fully concentrated on feeling ashamed. He'd been indescribably moronic, and when Popov also got to his feet and shoved Rekke and bellowed invective at him, Rekke had to admit that it was justified. He'd been an unparalleled idiot.

"I apologize," he muttered, which elicited another shove that sent him crashing into the wall of the building, but Rekke didn't care about responding to the attack.

All he was focused on was trying to understand, taking in everything he had read in the case files, and he realized with even greater shame that Micaela was right. But there was another thing, he realized. Something that didn't excuse his idiocy, but at least explained it. There was a troubling pattern around Popov, and that pattern had come about because he was close to a man whom he admired and had learned from, and that man was without doubt Per Morton, even if that didn't matter very much right now. Rekke had been as blind as a bat, and now he firmly pushed Popov aside.

"I apologize, but I really must go," he said, freeing himself and pulling out his phone. He saw that Micaela had called him again.

Then he began to run, but he didn't get far. A car skidded to a halt nearby and then rapid footsteps approached, and he was once again shoved against a wall, but this time it wasn't Popov.

It was two stiff-necked young men, with bulging muscles and buzz-cut blond hair, both with confident and rehearsed body language, and it took a moment for Rekke to understand. This didn't feel like resourceful private citizens intervening, nor plainclothes police either. This was something else—something bigger—a new drama that extended beyond his attack on Popov.

"Let me go," he said mustering all his authority. "My name is Hans Rekke and I'm in a hurry."

There was no suggestion the men were going to release him. Instead, they waited for Popov to catch up and when he did and began to mete out his accusations it hardly strengthened Rekke's case.

"You're staying here. We have just cause to hold you," said one of the men, at which point Rekke realized they were Security Service spooks and he stood still, paralysed for a moment, wondering what to do. Fight his way out or explain that they couldn't hold him?

But all he did was curse himself even more.

SEVENTY-FIVE

Dag Wrangel still didn't quite understand what had happened in Santander. His memory was envenomed—or even sabotaged, one might say—and now as he stood nervously in the kitchen waiting for Andrea, he unconsciously began to produce a hissing sound of anxiety through his lips.

"Dad, are you okay?" Viktor said from right behind him.

"I'm fine," he said.

"Where's Mum?"

"She'll be home soon," he said. "She was going to see someone. His name's Pompe," he added, almost for his own benefit.

But he never did turn around, which was why he didn't notice the change to Viktor's face. His son, who was ordinarily absorbed in his own world, felt the tension in the air and was afraid. Oblivious, Dag absented himself, going back to the bedroom, where he locked the door as the sequence of events in Spain replayed in his mind's eye, mercilessly and without pause.

He remembered lying there in the attic room in Laredo, waiting for Pompe. Dag remembered the faint glow of a streetlight seeping through the crack in the curtains. It was otherwise dark and oppressive, and he'd tossed and turned in his bed. It felt like an eternity had passed: not just one night but many. But then at last he heard footsteps and he could already tell from a distance that the shoes were battered and covered in dirt. They were clattering up the stairs, and he could smell the stench: the scent of tobacco and drunkenness, and something worse that he couldn't identify, but which he still instinctively realized was alarming.

A second later, Pompe was standing in the doorway, unsteady and panting, his trousers filthy and his pale face barely visible in the darkness. But what was clear was that Pompe must have driven Dag's car while hammered. Afterward—when time and space began to merge into one—Dag felt he already knew everything. After all, he was *a wretch, a cockroach, a creep, a murderer.* But in fact it took a while for him to understand. To begin with, he squinted into the darkness while Pompe removed the clothes from his upper body, huffing and puffing and swearing, the unpleasant smile still on his lips occasionally visible in the glow of the streetlights.

Go to bed, Dag silently urged him. Go to sleep, you shit. But Pompe was rummaging about—presumably on the hunt for booze—and Dag could no longer contain himself.

"How did it go with the waitress?" he said in an almost neutral voice, as if it were a question from one guy to another.

"What?"

Dag could tell from the tone of voice that Pompe was not only drunk, he was completely out of it, and when Dag repeated the question in the same neutral tone, Pompe staggered toward the window and nudged the curtains apart, as if worried there were people watching him from outside.

"She was a bitch," he said.

Dag swallowed.

"Okay," he said. "But what happened? Did she go home or what?"

Pompe stood still, thoughtful, with that eerie smile on his face.

"You know exactly what happened. You were there too," Pompe said, and Dag should have sensed the danger at that moment.

"What do you mean?" he said, because he hadn't been there.

He'd left the oak long before Pompe had set on Sandra.

But Pompe ignored that. He carried on muttering the same words over and over until he managed to extract a bottle of whisky from his suitcase and began to drink. The gulping sounds made Dag feel nauseous. Afterward, Pompe moved closer to the window again. In the dim light seeping through the crack between the curtains, Dag could see him more clearly. His jaw looked distorted, and there were stains on his trousers. The seams on one shoe had split and there were scratches visible on his slim chest.

"You liked it, didn't you? Turned you on, didn't it?" Pompe muttered, taking another swig before kicking off his shoes, pulling off his trousers and collapsing into bed.

He fell asleep at once, as he always did when he'd been boozing, and as always he began to snore, although the snoring was occasionally interrupted by his smoker's cough. It was the same sound that had kept Dag awake the whole trip. But now there was something new there—a grunt that was both tormented and lust-filled, as if whatever Pompe were reliving in his dream were giving him an ugly satisfaction. Dag could no longer listen to it—he could feel it in his bones.

He needed to leave and never see Pompe again, which was why he got up and dressed, and he then peered out of the window and spotted the BMW carelessly parked in the street, seemingly undamaged. Crouching on the floor by the chest of drawers, he packed his things and then crept back to the bed to retrieve the car key that was doubtless in Pompe's pockets. But when he found the trousers in the jumble on the floor, he was paralysed with shock.

The trousers were a damp mess, and perhaps he screamed. Pompe stopped grunting and whispered a couple of inaudible words before rolling over. Then he fell asleep again, and Dag dared to breathe anew, and he stared at the trousers in the faint light from the curtains. The cuffs were a sticky mess, and that mess, he realized, was part of the stench that Pompe had brought into the room, and it was only with an effort that he brought himself to search the pockets, but no key was forthcoming. Dag stood up in the semidarkness and looked down at his hands. His fingers were now stained too. With blood. It's *blood.* Blood on my hands. Then he picked up his bag and stepped out of the attic room with one single thought in his head that was probably more a case of wishful thinking than levelheaded belief: the keys had to be in the car.

The drunken fool had probably left them there. He remembered descending the stairs, passing the door to the room where the landlady lived. He remembered the coolness of the air outside, the feeling of liberation as if he had escaped suffocation, and he remembered even more vividly that the driver's side door to the BMW was open. The seat belt had gotten caught in it, and that gave him hope, or more than that—he suddenly knew that he'd been right and the key had to be inside.

Soon, very soon, he'd be able to drive away and he'd never see Pompe again for the rest of his life. But when he got into the car, he couldn't find it. He rooted frantically around the driver's seat, but the keys weren't there and he cried out and eventually shut the door and began to walk—where to, he didn't know, but he had to keep moving. The only thing about that, he realized reluctantly, was that he could see no taxis and there were no trains at this hour. He could find somewhere to sleep and leave in the morning, but no, he needed his car, so he turned around, thinking that if he searched more methodically he would be able to find the key. It had to be there somewhere, and Pompe was sleeping like a dead man.

He went back in through the main door and climbed the stairs. He wasn't exactly sure when he realized it had all gone south. But it was before he opened the door. Nevertheless, he stepped inside to find Pompe sitting on the bed, and in that moment Dag knew exactly what was going to happen. Pompe could see him clutching his bag. He must have understood that Dag was trying to do a runner, and Dag was fully expecting the usual senseless cruel gibes. But what followed was even more diabolical. Pompe must have been planning it ever since he saw Dag up by the old oak, and without Dag realising it, a toxic nerve agent was injected straight into his mind, ready to slowly take over his body.

SEVENTY-SIX

Micaela tilted her head back as the taxi pulled away from the hospital.

She felt awful, and judging by her reflection in the rearview mirror in front of her, she looked it too. But she'd been overcome by a tremendous sense of urgency, which had descended upon her after her call to Lene Askvall, the producer, to verify Oliver Popov's alibi, at which point she had uncovered traces of an altogether different story. Now, as she was sitting in the taxi reading on her phone, more troubling details were falling into place. But progress in the taxi was painfully slow. It was rush hour in the city centre and she felt sick. First, she nervously tried calling Rekke, and then Andrea Wrangel, who didn't pick up either, and then at last she tried Dag Wrangel's home number which she had found via directory enquiries. A breathless female voice picked up with a "Hello? Hello?"

"My name is Micaela Vargas and I'm calling from the police," she said.

"You again? What's going on?"

"Sorry, who am I speaking to?" Micaela said.

"This is Charlotte, Dag's mother. We spoke earlier, and I've just arrived here quite out of breath. My grandson Viktor rang me to say that Dag was behaving strangely and had locked himself in the bedroom. Apparently Andrea has gone to see that Pompe man."

"Pompe?"

"Yes, you know, the tailor's son. Charles's boy."

"You've lost me," Micaela said.

"That was how I felt at first," Charlotte Wrangel said. "But then I understood the connection. My husband had some suits made by Charles back in the day, and he always took his dry cleaning there. It was a very nice, if rather ordinary place on Artillerigatan. Charles worked on Savile Row in his younger years—there was a photo on the wall of him pinning Sean Connery's trousers. If he's good enough to pin James Bond's trousers, he can pin mine too, as my husband put it."

Micaela drummed her fingers impatiently against her thigh.

"And Charles had a son?" she interjected.

"Yes, an only child. A kind, sweet boy, or so we thought at the time. He was a pupil at the Royal Swedish Ballet School for many years."

"And he was the one who befriended your son?"

"They were at Östra Real together for their senior high years, but Dag was so shy and withdrawn while Pompe was apparently popular, or perhaps I'm mistaken, but then . . ."

"Something happened?"

"Yes, after Dag had been to journalism college in New York, they went on that trip that Dag never wanted to talk about afterward. I suppose that's why I forgot about it. We never mentioned his name again."

"You're referring to Per Morton?" Micaela said.

"Exactly. The son of Charles Morton."

"And Andrea has gone to see him?"

"Yes, but apparently Andrea is on her way home. Although . . ."

"Yes?"

"She seems to be taking her time," Charlotte Wrangel said.

Micaela took a deep breath.

"Do you know where Andrea was supposed to be meeting him?"

Charlotte Wrangel fell silent.

"No," she said. "But call Hedvig—Andrea's secretary. I've got her number here."

Micaela jotted the number down and hung up, surveying the city. She was in pain and felt dizzy, but she pulled herself together and rang the secretary. This woman also sounded nervous.

"I don't know—Andrea simply went out. She told me it was a personal matter. Has something happened? You're not the only one to have called," she said.

"Could you check Andrea's search history on her computer?" Micaela said.

"Just a second," the secretary said, and Micaela sat there in the taxi with a hand on the fresh wound on her stomach while drumming her fingers against her thigh and wondering what was taking so long. Perhaps the secretary had had to go to another room and enter a password and so on and so forth. Then she came back.

"Mostly a lot of stuff to do with her job," she said.

"Is there anything that stands out?"

"Yes, actually," the secretary said slowly. "She did a search for Per Morton, the film producer. And she looked up the Villa Godthem restaurant."

"On Djurgården?"

"That's the one."

Micaela hung up and told the driver her destination and tried to use the sheer willpower to shift the lines of traffic, and once they were on Strandvägen they picked up the pace a little, although it was still much too slow, and without realising it she passed Rekke. He was standing on the other side of the street embroiled in an agitated scene with Popov and two other men, but despite the fact that she didn't notice this, he appeared in her thoughts and she sent him a text and told him where she was going.

Moments later, Micaela got out of her taxi having crossed the Djurgårdsbron bridge, and took a left off the road, noticing a change in the weather. The sky had darkened, the wind was blowing hard, and she was cold and feeling worse than before, nauseous, as if she were about to throw up, and there wasn't a soul in sight—all she could see was a brown Porsche parked ahead of her. She could already tell from a distance that the Villa Godthem restaurant was shut, and she began to run. As she passed one of the benches, she had to stop and sit down, struggling for breath, and for a brief while she sat there bent double. Then she stood up and called Rekke. He didn't answer and she cursed him, and not only because he wasn't available when she needed him most. How could that confounded genius have missed the truth? It had been right there in front of him all along. It was Per Morton's alibi in Helsinki, rather than Popov's, that had been leaky. But Micaela pushed aside the anger and walked more quickly despite her abdominal pain. She had no idea where she was going, and it occurred to her that the island of Djurgården was far too big for her to search aimlessly by herself. She needed help. She called the duty officer and explained where she was and that she needed a squad car sent right away. Then she staggered on, but without hearing the wind blowing and shivering through the trees.

Popov was croaking out all manner of dreadful things he thought Rekke had done—falsely accusing him and generally setting about him. But Rekke was barely listening. He was standing there with a blank expression, thinking about what he had read the night before about the Finnish murder investigation, and of all the details racing through his mind, there was a literary quotation that was at the front and centre of it all. It had come out of nowhere and it hadn't seemed significant. It had simply been an odd choice of words in the context, a dandyism perhaps, and not altogether typical of the man being questioned, who was otherwise unassuming and friendly and ostensibly aware of his complicity: "How terrible. I liked her. I'm absolutely devastated. If only I could have done more," he'd said, and it was obvious that no-one had suspected him, then or later on. He was liked by everyone and had gone on to make a donation to a Finnish foundation supporting investigative journalism in memory of the victim, but in those first interviews after Järvinen had been found, he'd said, *the dawn is an eternal road of thorns and roses*, which had been unnecessary and sounded pretentious, albeit still in keeping with his somewhat formal demeanour. But now, as Rekke stood there on the sidewalk while Popov was bellowing at him and the Security Service suits were holding him by the arms, he realized why the words had struck a chord. It was a quotation from Lorca, which wasn't a big deal per se. It was hardly strange for people working in entertainment to quote famous Spanish poets, but it should have garnered a reaction from Rekke. There was a connection to the Swede in Santander, and perhaps—Rekke had briefly looked him up—it was possible to see a resemblance to Jagger, if you were charitable, but above all . . . He gazed at Popov, at his eyes and his entire countenance, which seemed to will destruction on him. There was a connection between the men—a mentorship of sorts. One had taught the other how to destroy people with words. They had both mastered the same kinds of oppressive arts, and who knew—perhaps it hadn't been Popov who had broken that crime writer's fingers. Perhaps it had been his friend, the film producer.

"You provided an alibi for Per Morton in the Järvinen murder," he said, as if thinking aloud.

"What?"

Popov cut short his rant and stared at Rekke, and perhaps he too realized something was afoot in that moment. It was difficult to tell. But Rekke immediately recognized this as an opportunity he could turn to his advantage, and he looked at the men who were holding him in place and said with all his authority:

"I daresay this is to do with the Prime Minister and it's highly gratifying to see you taking your jobs so seriously, but it's also increasing the risks. You're on the brink of following the inappropriate directions of a government minister, and more than that, you're about to make a big mistake. There's a woman in serious danger," he said, feeling that the last part sounded dreadful, as if it were a line from some old slapstick comedy, but hopefully he'd delivered it with such conviction that it still did the trick.

"Who's in danger?" said the older of the two spooks, and Rekke should probably have taken them with him.

But he didn't trust them, let alone Popov, so instead he set off alone and they let him go, and Rekke looked down at his phone and saw Micaela's text and felt a dash of hope. He was going to do this. He rushed toward Djurgården. But unbeknownst to him, he was already far behind. Time was ticking, just as it had once ticked for Sandra Ramirez.

SEVENTY-SEVEN

"No, Mama, I don't want to talk. Look after Viktor instead," Dag called out from the bedroom.

"But my dear, what's going on?" Charlotte said anxiously.

"Viktor, play your Chopin étude for Grandma," he called out, and then he heard the sound of her retreating and leaving him alone with his thoughts, which was no improvement.

He remembered it all with such crushing clarity. What time must it have been when he returned to the room in Laredo? Four o'clock? Five? It was definitely dawn, and Pompe was perched on the edge of the bed, his chest bare and a whisky bottle in his hand. His bloodshot eyes were devoid of any emotion, but the thing that Dag noticed most were Pompe's feet. They were bruised and wounded.

Dag put down his bag and wondered what excuse he was going to make, but then he looked at Pompe's feet again, and decided to stand up for himself.

"I'm leaving. I've just come to get the car key," he said, expecting an eruption, but Pompe merely responded with an icy cold, "Oh you are, are you?"

"Yes, I can't hack this anymore."

"Then what am I going to tell the police?" Pompe said.

"The police?" Dag muttered.

"You kicked her."

"What?" Dag said, looking down again at Pompe's feet, which barely seemed to belong to his body. They looked more like bloodied slabs of clay attached to his legs.

"I saw you by the tree; you were completely crazed. But you were enjoying it, that much was immediately clear to me."

Pompe stared at him with vacant, reptilian eyes.

"Enjoying what?" Dag stammered.

"Your punches and kicks. I've never seen anything like it. You were standing there kicking away with your left foot. It was the worst thing I've ever seen. You were slavering away and muttering. You were really into it."

Dag continued to stare at Pompe's feet and could already sense a truth that was unbearable, and he lunged at him. It was the only reaction he could think of, and it immediately gave Dag the upper hand. He was stronger and more sober, but it didn't help much. While Pompe was beneath him on the floor, he continued to hiss and spit out his bile.

"Admit it: you enjoyed it. You broke her fingers and kicked away like an idiot and whispered things to her. What was it you said? Do you remember? You said loneliness doesn't bottom out, and that she was going to suffer. And you loved it."

Dag stood up, half-crazed already, but the torrent of words didn't stop: *You loved it, you wretch, you odious piece of shit, you cockroach.* It was unbearable, and although it would take a while for him to discern the purpose of those words, they felt like an act of rough violence even then, and violence was of course what it was—violence toward memory and self-perception, and Dag shouted back at him, "It was you, you beast! You hurt her. Look at your feet." But Pompe wouldn't allow himself to be swayed, and continued, providing more and more details so that eventually Dag could picture it and almost began to believe that he had done it. In any case, by the next day he was already dreaming that he really had kicked Sandra in the face, but that was still not as bad as the horror that was to follow. He still thought all Pompe had done was beat Sandra, like the girl in La Rochelle, and on the journey home Dag asked over and over how Sandra was.

Pompe didn't answer. He just kept describing the assault, and sometimes Dag shouted and cried and pounded his head against the car window, but he couldn't get away from it. It felt as if he had to try and understand, and sometimes things went so far that Pompe comforted him. "It's okay," he would say. "I understand—she was a bitch. You got sick of her; you snapped. I won't say a word. I'm your friend."

One day, as Pompe returned from the toilets inside a gas station, he said: "I really do feel for you—but your mum and I are going to be there for you."

"My mum?"

"I rang her," Pompe said. "I had to tell her. She had to know. But she'll keep her mouth shut."

Obviously it was a lie, and perhaps Dag realized that at once, but those kinds of statements kept him in a state of paralysis and uncertainty. "I'm calling the police tomorrow," Pompe would say. "Society needs to be protected from you, Dag. You're such a disgusting monster."

It was constant, and he was being broken down piece by piece. He was already debilitated—and then it got even worse. Dag saw Sandra's photo in a German tabloid. They'd just left France and he was waiting to pay for his lunch of bratwurst and mashed potatoes while leafing through a copy of *Bild-Zeitung*. Suddenly, he spotted a photo of Sandra. As he recalled later, he couldn't read the article. The text swam before his eyes; the whole world was swimming. Dag put down his plate and picked up the paper and showed it to Pompe.

"Was it you?" he said.

Pompe smiled. Dag was pretty sure he smiled, and he should have headed for the nearest police station there and then to report him. He shouldn't have hesitated for a second. But there was something about that smile. There was something about Pompe's expression that left Dag paralysed.

"You know who did it," Pompe said. "It was you." And then came the words again—*wretch, creep, cockroach*—and now there were more—*killer, you loathsome murderer*—and shortly after that Dag got back into the car.

He barely knew what was happening. He just sat there while Pompe continued to harangue him, describing in precise and extensive detail how Dag had murdered Sandra, and even then it was clear that Pompe was telling the truth—albeit with the perpetrator replaced and himself cast as Dag. That was why his words, dripping with poison and filth, seemed so incredibly authentic, and when Dag occasionally went crazy and shouted and threatened to hurl himself onto the Autobahn, Pompe became as smooth as honey and comforted him. He told him he understood; he'd thought she was a bitch too. Then their hours together became brighter. They travelled north, the landscape becoming more familiar. They took the ferry to Helsingborg and headed for Stockholm, while Dag eventually ceased to understand what had actually happened—or even who he was. Was he a person who wanted to write and live, or a terrible, disgusting murderer? A cockroach?

He verged on—or crossed the line into—the psychotic, and that had naturally been Pompe's intention from the very start. Everything that he was, he laid upon Dag. Everything that he had done, he blamed Dag for. But the real purpose was without doubt to relieve himself of the burden of guilt—the guilt that

Pompe was himself incapable of feeling due to his own shortcomings, but that Dag was much too receptive to, and that was the stroke of genius in the whole thing.

Pompe had committed the crime, but he made sure that it was Dag who bore the shame. It was Dag who shouldered the suffering while Pompe continued to grow, to validate his self-image, and the stronger he became, the weaker Dag got and the worse a person he thought himself to be. The words burrowed into his subconscious and became a truth that distorted his entire perspective. Nothing improved upon their return home. Pompe continued to hiss at him over the telephone, and while Dag resolved to go to the police a thousand times, he never pulled it off. He was convinced that Pompe would crush him, and he increasingly found himself dreaming of Sandra.

In his dreams, Dag loved her more than life itself—but for some reason, he still attacked her. Perhaps it was because she didn't want him. He dreamed he was towering above her by the old oak and kicking her face until it was beyond recognition. In his dreams, he killed what he couldn't have. He also killed because he was jealous. He killed her for writing so well even though she was only twenty. He killed her because she made him feel small and confined. In his obsessive thoughts, he was no better than Pompe. Still, of course, he knew that was no excuse for failing to report him to the police. There were no excuses, not one—except that for a long time he couldn't conceive of the idea that Pompe would do it again.

It was a thought too incomprehensible for him to take in. Surely there had to be bounds to Pompe's evil. But there were none—it was a force as never-ending as Dag's own paralysis and cowardice.

SEVENTY-EIGHT

Before Andrea lost consciousness as the blows and kicks rained down on her, she found herself thinking that this wasn't the first time Pompe had beaten a woman. She sensed something excited and greedy in his dark gaze, but also something blasé. He was striking her like someone who was enjoying himself, but not as much as he would have liked. He'd been afflicted by the addict's inevitable ennui, and his lips, moist and open, bore a bitter and dissatisfied grimace.

He looked like a beast weary of its nature, and immediately above them in the biting cold that Andrea could no longer feel, there were twigs and branches moving as if in a dance with Pompe's pounding body, as if they too were attacking her, and she thought about Dag and Viktor and realized she was going to die soon.

No-one spared someone if they were this unhinged, but at least the pain was gone. She was numb and ruined, and in the distance, as if in a dream, she heard him say: "Can you tell how alone you are? No-one cares about you anymore. Everything that people loved about you is gone; I've smashed it all to pieces and I despise you. You're nothing; I'm everything."

It was 5:42 p.m. The temperature had dropped to –7 degrees Celsius. Snow was whipping down off the trees, driven by a harsh, ice-cold wind doing some thirty knots and making the landscape sway and shake, but Andrea felt none of it, and she had no idea that a young woman of Chilean origin was approaching, hunched forward and suffering and moving much too slowly in the blizzard. It didn't feel as if she was going to make it or as if she would be able to help either.

Micaela herself still felt too unsteady and hunched over, and she felt terrible. She should never have left her hospital bed. She should have let someone else do the job, and she had no idea where she was supposed to be going anyway. All she had were a few words from a man walking a Labrador who had long since disappeared.

The man had said he'd seen a man and woman in early middle age walking in that direction not long ago, but nothing about them had seemed off. They'd been walking arm-in-arm, or at least close together, and had seemed like a proper couple more than anything, and whether they had continued toward the water or had followed the road up here he did not know. It was all pointless—hopeless. Micaela gazed toward the water and then up at the woods beyond the road. Could she hear something? More than the wind rustling through the trees? She didn't think so.

She put her hands on her thighs, struggling for breath, and felt a momentary impulse to lie down on the road to recuperate. But that would be madness—she'd freeze to death. She had to pull herself together, and it was then, still bent forward, that Micaela heard a sound. There was a movement up among the trees. It was most probably from an animal, but it gave her renewed strength anyway, and she stood up and shouted:

"Hello? Is anyone there?"

There was no answer, but she sensed an unexpected stillness up there, as if her words had caused the wind to rustle the branches a little less, and that was when she understood. There was something there in that sudden silence, and she set off in among the trees, still in a dire state, her whole body tensed, and she could still hear nothing. It was uncannily quiet, as if the woods were holding their breath.

Then she heard breathing, panting, and she stopped and yelled, "This is the police!" although it was possible she didn't manage to say the whole sentence. The branches in front of her gave way and rushing toward her came a man—a creature, it seemed—with black eyes and blood on his hands and trousers. The creature hurled itself at her and she toppled backward and hit her head on the ground. But if Micaela had been powerless before, she now had a rush of blood and began to fight tooth and nail and with her fists and to her own surprise she gained the upper hand and the man fell to the side, and she made it onto her knees. She was about to throw herself across him when he reached into his pocket and pulled out a knife—the same knife he'd been intending to mark Andrea Wrangel with, she assumed. Without hesitating, he launched toward her with it and stabbed her shoulder and neck, and Micaela staggered backward, blood pulsing out of her, and she just had time to look for something to grab hold of, a stone, a branch. Anything. But then the man was on her again, moving with lightning speed, wildly, like someone who had killed many times before. Micaela couldn't believe she'd been stupid enough to come alone, sick and exhausted after the end of a pregnancy she hadn't wanted.

SEVENTY-NINE

Per Morton's voicemail kicked in with the usual opening line in English inviting the caller to leave a message. But for once, Pontus Bremer said nothing, unless you counted gasping or swearing and slamming his fist onto the table. Per, of all people. He couldn't fathom it.

"Appalling," he muttered. "Appalling."

No-one called him Pompe any longer, but Pontus knew that it was his nickname as a young man, and he'd also known after speaking to Charlotte Wrangel that Dag and Per had driven down to Spain in a convertible BMW in the summer of 1988, and that Dag had returned home and fallen into a deep state of crisis that had, for a time, paralysed half his face. He'd written about it, Pontus recalled, and spoken about his Janus face as if it were cursed.

Then there was something else too: a memory that had always nagged at him and had now risen into his consciousness. It had been in the showers at the Frescati Sports Center after a game of badminton. Pontus had seen Per's feet and stared at them, mesmerized.

They were bloodied and covered in swollen wounds, and the explanation Per had given had not been credible, he remembered. Something or other about skin sensitivity and long mountain hikes in the wrong boots. Pontus hadn't really believed it, or perhaps he had at the time, but now it no longer seemed plausible, and he thought about Andrea Wrangel.

According to Dag's mother, Andrea had gone to see Per and hadn't come home yet. There had always been something odd about Per's interest in Andrea. Pontus didn't think they knew each other, and yet Per kept remarkably good tabs on her. It was as if he both admired and despised her.

"Dag doesn't deserve her," Per had once said. "She's way too much of a classy, intelligent bitch for that neurotic idiot. It almost makes you want to punish her for it," and perhaps that wasn't so unusual. People sometimes said things like that: *She's so pretty it makes you want to kill her. He writes so well you want to shoot him*, and that was why Pontus had liked Per. There was an energy to him.

But now, as Pontus sat at his desk staring vacantly at his manuscript, he thought he could recall the gleam in Per's eye as he'd said it. His gaze had been simultaneously dead and fired up.

Per seemed to hate Andrea without ever having met her, and if the game was already lost and Per really was a sadistic killer—well, what might he do out of pure desperation? And what would that mean for the film adaptation of Pontus's novel, and his career in general? Perhaps it wasn't the noblest question given the context, it occurred to him, but hang on, he was Pontus Bremer. He was a national treasure and he had to do something. He called out:

"Micki!"

She didn't reply, so he shouted louder.

"What is it?" she yelled back.

"Can you bring me a glass of Rioja?" he bellowed.

I need it stat, he thought. I've got to do something. But he couldn't think of anything better than calling Rekke. Calling that damn Professor to point out that he, Pontus Bremer, had set him on the right track from the very beginning.

The damn Professor heard the phone ringing and hoped it was Micaela. He had been searching for her frantically, but when he saw it was Bremer he sighed and continued along the Djurgården promenade, trying to think clearly: if you wanted to hurt someone, where would you go out here?

You'd head for cover. You'd head into the trees like a predator. But where? There were wooded areas everywhere, and it was impossible to hear anything. The snowstorm was roaring around him, and there was a helicopter too, and he couldn't see anyone or anything other than a hare dashing over the road and a badger disappearing into the undergrowth. The time was 5:44 p.m. He looked down at the road. It was icy and snow was falling. But the snow was being whipped away like grains of ice in the wind, and he could see no footprints. He had surprisingly little to go on, and he began to worry that he had run too far and turned back, his gaze roving, and soon he thought the road was easier to read after all, even if there weren't actually any clear tracks visible. He could at least see shifts in texture on the ground and right by the ditch an impression that had been partially left in the snow with a pattern he recognized. Fluted lines, and above them letters—an O and an inverse S. Micaela's Hugo Boss sneakers, size 38, the ones she'd bought in the sale at Åhléns earlier that autumn, and which she wore in all weathers. And once he'd understood that, it was easier to find the next impression and then the next, and he regained his laser focus and noticed that the strides had become shorter and the impact points deeper. She had slowed down, it seemed, and begun stumbling rather than walking. Leaving the hospital was madness, especially to chase a violent killer. But she was a sensible girl. She'd probably called for reinforcements—help wouldn't be far away. He glanced down along the road again and saw something that stood out: an impression that was clearer than the others, as if Micaela had stopped and pressed her foot down. When he took a closer look, he saw another print next to it, the centre of gravity in this one also toward the toes, which provided him with a clear picture. Micaela had been leaning forward, probably feeling nauseous, but the most remarkable thing was that the footprints then vanished. Well, they didn't vanish, he now saw. They had instead strayed from the road up into the woods, and in that moment his senses were sharpened. He could hear notes, or perhaps the woods were being presented to him as a series of notes ascending from the lowest intervals in the contrabass up to the highest in the thrice-accented octave. Muffled rustling, the whisper of the wind, the cries of birds, twigs bending and snapping, distant breathing, and suddenly panting and faltering steps. Rekke rushed in the direction of the footsteps and before long he saw her.

She was standing bent forward just as he had imagined her, holding her hand to her neck and was clearly about to fall, even though she was trying to make it look as if she might attack. She seemed to be fighting with the last of her strength, bleeding from the neck, and perhaps the shoulder too. Standing in front of her was a man, quite clearly Per Morton. Pompe. He seemed to be more alert and he was holding a pocket knife, the blade of which was bloody. Micaela's blood, Rekke assumed, and the man was about to attack her again. He quite clearly wanted to kill, to stab the neck again or the heart. That much was obvious from his body language, his dark gaze and his twisted expression. But now Pompe was distracted. He'd spotted Rekke and was waving the knife back and forth, and Rekke's entire world froze.

Every part of him was focused on the blade and on Per Morton's position, on his left leg, which was advanced—and on the right arm with the knife threateningly raised above his head. And the right foot that was angled back behind his torso, raised on the tips of its toes, a reminder perhaps of Morton's background as a dancer, while his hips were slightly twisted—promisingly so. It struck Rekke that one false move would leave Morton teetering on outright instability, which was a good thing—especially since those eyes were at once furious and crazed, with the vulnerability of the narcissist. Provoke him, Rekke thought. And go to the right.

He spoke calmly, or with the calm that came with absolute concentration and the sense of mortal danger, and perhaps also—not that he was aware of it—the determination that came from his love for Micaela.

"Here I am, Per. It's me you have to kill first," he said, lunging forward and to the right, and what he'd been hoping for did happen.

Pompe staggered, and Rekke rushed forward and kicked his left leg just below the knee, and although he didn't fall he lost his balance, and even then Rekke didn't hesitate. He struck a blow—which once, long ago, he'd spent countless hours practising so that he might master another enemy—and it was trained on the right wrist and the pronator quadratus, and it had the desired impact. The knife fell from Pompe's hand.

It fell toward the frozen ground and Pompe made as if to pick it up, and that was all it took. Rekke went for him again, and admittedly he had lost his precision and anatomical accuracy. But he compensated for that with a rapid series of blows, and he didn't stop. He was throwing more punches than he needed to.

Rekke succumbed to a vindictive rage and when he no longer needed to strike any more blows but was instead standing over Pompe breathing heavily, he thought of Sandra Ramirez and everything she might have done had her life not been extinguished in the way that rich lives of every era had been extinguished by petty, inferior men, and then he was tempted to start kicking Morton. *Oculus pro oculo*—an eye for an eye.

Fortunately, he was interrupted. Micaela staggered over and put a hand on his shoulder and pointed toward Andrea Wrangel, who was lying beaten and lifeless on the ground further into the woods, her lips blue. He rushed toward her and sank to his knees and performed CPR, while cursing heaven and earth for the time he'd wasted pursuing the wrong man.

EIGHTY

Señor Corales had brought his guitar with him and had played the solo from Pink Floyd's "Comfortably Numb," but he was now sitting on the green sofa in front of the piano and being far too long-winded and wearisome. Micaela felt obliged to listen nonetheless and offer affirmative comments, especially since Rekke didn't seem capable of sitting still but was dashing in and out of his study.

"Sit down, why don't you?" she said.

"Yes, yes," Rekke said, settling into the black armchair opposite the Spaniard, but apparently he couldn't help humming a snippet of music in a glissando loop—possibly the one that Corales had played—and Micaela became increasingly annoyed.

Surely he would soon calm down, but it was as if he'd sensed that something new was afoot. It was visible in his body language and his way of listening for sounds from the hall outside, although he was probably imagining them. He was always imagining things. Micaela ignored him and put a hand to her neck. She'd lost a lot of blood, but because her carotid artery hadn't been damaged and because Rekke had torn up his shirt in the cold and made a pad to press against it in the middle of everything else that he was doing before the police and paramedics arrived, she'd been just fine.

"Where was I?" said Corales.

"You were talking about the Dutch hippie," said Micaela.

"Ah yes," he said, squinting through the studio-loft window. The sun was already setting.

Señor Corales had pushed back his return journey by ten days to assist the Finnish, Danish and Swedish police, and he'd been able to supply an additional suspected victim to the list. One that had pertained to a Dutch man known as Kristian De Graaf, who was almost certainly the same man that Dag Wrangel had said in his statement had been following him, Per Morton and Sandra Ramirez up toward the old oak in Santander on the night of July twelfth, 1988.

De Graaf had been questioned early on in the murder investigation because he had prior convictions for fraud and sexual harassment, and he'd been seen outside the La Mar restaurant on the night of the murder. But presumably he hadn't dared to say a word at the time, afraid he'd wind up in trouble, and the police hadn't had much on him either. Afterward, he'd made a hasty exit from the city and had, as far as they knew, never returned to Spain. But he hadn't forgotten. He'd told friends that he'd seen something horrible. He'd even written a song about it, but he'd also become an increasingly untrustworthy witness. He'd descended back into his past addiction to heroin, and would presumably have vanished from the story had he not happened to see a photo of Per Morton in a German newspaper, where the Swede was being interviewed about the wave of Swedish crime fiction and string of movies that had hit the German market.

Afterward, De Graaf had headed for Stockholm and sought out Per Morton, presumably with the intention of blackmailing him, but nothing had worked out as he'd hoped. A few days later, De Graaf's body had washed up on the north shore of the capital's Södermalm neighbourhood. There had been heroin in De Graaf's system, and it had been late October and freezing cold. The incident had been written off as an accident, and it was only once Señor Corales had begun to dig into it that it had been possible to confirm that De Graaf and Morton really had met. It probably wouldn't amount to enough for a prosecution, and it wouldn't make a difference anyway, but it was obviously important to Corales.

"Only now is the course of events becoming clear to me," he said. "I'll be able to sleep at night again."

Micaela gave him a strained but benevolent smile.

"And there never were more than seven women?" said Corales.

"That's more than enough," Micaela said dryly. "Sandra in Santander, Anna in Krakow, Regina in Aarhus, Hafida in Tangier, Paula in Rio de Janeiro, Jodine in Cape Town and Jenni in Espoo. But yes, it seems he was lying with his numbering."

Corales fiddled restlessly with his guitar.

"Terrible. What do you think will happen to Dag Wrangel?"

Micaela looked at Rekke. This was his department; he was the one who'd spoken to Dag and got him to tell the full story. But Rekke didn't seem to have heard the question and she had to kick him gently on the leg.

"Hmm, well," Rekke said at last. "Dag is very likely to do time for harbouring a criminal, and failure to report a crime. But I mean to help him and testify on his behalf. His case fascinates me. He was subjected to absolutely diabolical brainwashing."

"He's a cowardly wretch," Corales said.

"I would be a little kinder, I think. His failure to report it cost lives, and he'll never be able to deny that. But it's psychologically interesting. While Morton has no conscience, Dag is the very opposite. He's always felt guilty, even for the sins of others, and I daresay it's helped him in his writing and given him an understanding of the finer details in life, but in this case it was a curse. Morton's torrent of words penetrated him like lethal poison, and it warped his whole world. We cannot underestimate the destructive forces that he was exposed to, and I'm pleased that his publishers have asked him to write about it. It will make for a most intriguing literary work."

"You're much too forgiving for my liking, Professor. But it's a relief that his wife pulled through," said Corales.

Rekke raised his gaze and took a deep breath.

"My goodness, yes," he said. "I thought I'd lost her. There were no signs of life—none at all—but then I remembered an old friend, a doctor, who said you just have to keep on going with CPR, no matter how futile it seems, and suddenly . . ." He leaned forward and seemed to remember it as a moment of delight. "Well, she vomited blood all over me. If it had gone differently, I don't think I could have lived with myself."

"I expect Dag isn't the only one who has a predisposition to guilt."

"That may be," said Rekke.

"And Popov?"

A wry smile played across Rekke's lips.

"Popov will be alright. With lawyers like his, he should be able to get through anything."

"But for goodness' sake—he gave Per Morton an alibi," said Corales.

"He claims that it wasn't deliberate. He says he thought Morton was at the party in Helsinki all night, and he's got the full backing of his employees and lawyers, so I guess he'll be able to continue hurting people. I'm glad I'm not part of the literary world. Now I must . . ." Rekke stood up.

"What?" said Micaela.

"I have a feeling I'm about to receive a new visitor," he said, and Micaela and Corales looked at each other as if to say, that's not the kind of thing you feel. But perhaps there were signs they had missed.

EIGHTY-ONE

"The darkness," said Pontus Bremer, wondering where he was going. "The darkness," he repeated, hoping his brilliant brain would think of a continuation. "The darkness has spread its wings in my breast," he said. Not bad, although he could do better. He gazed into the auditorium.

There were probably five hundred people in tonight, and they all looked spellbound, apart from a couple of the usual pissed-off feminists, and a few jealous colleagues who refused to indulge his refulgence. But he was above all that. He looked down at his black shoes. He was dressed in black from head to toe: black shirt, black suit, black signet ring, black necklace. He was like Johnny Cash—the man in black—and he'd said as much too. His grief and anger at the desecration and murder of the women were both as black as night. He'd been met with resounding applause. But he'd also devoted great energy to both apologising for and blustering about his efforts in the murder investigation. "Professor Rekke's contribution was a vital one, albeit modest," was how he tended to generously put it, and as he was the keynote speaker at the Stockholm Literature Festival he intended to keep going in this vein. He would show them all that he possessed both a bleeding heart and a brilliant mind. For a moment, he pondered whether to quote Conrad's Kurtz and say, "The horror! The horror!" No, that was too much of a cliché. He'd think of something brand-new: his own creation. So he solemnly said:

"I'm like an old oak; a split trunk where lightning has struck. Yet my branches reach upward as if in prayer to the sky."

He raised his hands toward the ceiling and thought, why should I hold back at all? After all, I'm Pontus Bremer, damn it.

"In the beginning was the Word," he said, quoting from the Gospel of John, which was surely a decent introduction to whatever dazzling display of intellect he was going to disgorge.

EIGHTY-TWO

Micaela said her goodbyes to Señor Corales and shortly afterward to Rekke, who said he needed to get out and think, and if she were honest so did she. It was over with Caspar—or more than over, actually. He really had been working for the Iranians, and that was way more than she could handle.

Nothing ever seemed to go right for her when it came to men. It never worked out; she always had high expectations at the start, but the one who was always left at the end was Rekke, who drove her insane. Especially now that he kept disappearing off and was impossible to talk to, and for want of anything else to do she went into his study.

She hadn't been in there since returning from the hospital, and neither, it seemed, had the cleaner. His desk was messier than usual. There were leather-bound volumes, notebooks it seemed, in stacks and scattered across the surface, and in one of them she saw the date April fourth, 1981. Beneath that, Rekke's sprawling handwriting swept across the page, at once beautiful, like flying birds, and also more or less illegible, even if she had learned to decipher it. *I can't stand Shostakovich*, she read at random from one of the notebooks. *He stirs up the dusts of hell inside me; I need clarity. I dreamed that the piano sank into the Hallstätter See like an ancient, primeval monster.*

They were obviously diaries, and she wondered whether to sit down and read through all of it, but she never made it past the piano sinking into the lake. She heard the door open and recognized the restless footsteps of Rekke and she tensed, unsure why. But perhaps it was to do with those lines she had just read, and the presence of his entire past in these notebooks. At any rate, she smoothed her hair and went to greet him, and at first he didn't seem to see her at all—he was as preoccupied by his thoughts as ever. But then he stopped and looked at her with his piercing blue eyes, as if he were seeing her anew. It was the same feverish look as when she had emerged from the bathroom a few weeks earlier, and she had taken a step toward him and her body had strained toward him and she'd thought kiss me then, you idiot, but of course nothing had come of it. She heard other steps on the landing outside, and so did he. For a second, he became anxious and then the spell was broken, and in the next moment the doorbell rang as it had done on so many occasions before, and they both went to open it.

"Is this what you've been waiting for?"

He nodded and pulled the door open, and what Micaela saw next made her gasp. The woman on the threshold smelling of exclusive perfume was the last person she'd wanted to meet when she'd almost gotten close to Rekke. The woman was not only unusually tall and beautiful—some two or three heads taller than herself—but she was also haughty and looked around with a gaze that seemed to see and judge everything at once. She was perhaps forty years of age, or older, and stylishly dressed in a grey cashmere coat over a green blazer and pressed trousers in a similar, but more sober colour. The woman contemplated

Micaela superciliously, as if she wanted to indicate from the beginning that she did not regard her as worthy of Rekke.

"Good afternoon," she said. "Am I interrupting?"

"Don't you always, Irene?" said Rekke. "As good fortune would have it, rumour of your arrival reached me. I had time to prepare somewhat."

"Very good, Hans. Although surely you're always prepared? Isn't that one of the gifts Gabor gave you?"

"You also helped me beautifully on that point." Rekke beamed. "And I am most excited to see what you're going to do next." He gestured toward Micaela. "By the way, this is my good friend and colleague Micaela Vargas, whom you evidently underestimate."

Irene—as the woman was apparently named—laughed lightly and said she didn't underestimate anyone close to him.

Then she nonchalantly handed her coat to Rekke, entered the living room and let out a girlish cry when she spotted the Steinway.

"Oh, how I've missed hearing you play. It was as if time itself stopped. I remember it like it was yesterday. But right now I'd like some wine. An exquisite and expensive red," Irene said, sitting down on the big green sofa, which flowed strangely well into her blazer, as if she'd dressed for that particular piece of furniture.

"I'll see what I can rustle up," said Rekke.

"Thank you Hans. I need it—you're not the only one who is nervous. I've been all over the place all day and I barely slept last night. Now run along, the pair of you, and pull yourselves together while I have a breather here."

Her smile was captivating—Micaela had to give her that, at least—and Rekke nodded at her and together they went to the kitchen and at first they said nothing. Instead, Rekke bent down quietly by the wine cooler, his hands trembling imperceptibly.

"Who is she?" said Micaela.

Rekke pulled out a vintage bottle of Burgundy red and fixed his gaze on Micaela.

"The most deceitful and cunning woman I've ever known. And the most intelligent. She's the only one to have outwitted me," he said, lost in his thoughts.

"Is that why you got out your old diaries?"

"I wanted help remembering."

"So you knew she was coming?"

He smiled, almost amused.

"I believe she wanted me to know. But I didn't think she'd come so soon. She only ever arrives when she's holding a trump card."

Micaela looked down at the bottle in his hand.

"Will that do?"

"I doubt it. Nothing is ever good enough for her," Rekke said, looking at her imploringly. "Don't believe a word of what she says," he added. "There's always a hidden agenda with her."

Micaela laughed, although she wasn't sure why, but there was something so dramatic about his choice of words and body language. They returned to the living room with the bottle and three glasses. Irene received them with a big, welcoming smile.

Rekke responded by looking just as amiable.

"Irene, I forgot to say that you're looking lovelier than ever. And a perfect match for the green," Rekke said. "But you've changed perfumes."

She made an elegant movement with her hand.

"I change everything all the time."

"Of course," said Rekke, settling down in an armchair opposite her. "You seek to surprise. Last time you brought promises of love and influence. What do you have to offer today?"

She straightened up.

"I come bearing news, and I fear it's not altogether good news."

"And here I was, expecting siren notes that would cause me to drift toward the rocks."

Irene smiled and sipped the wine, letting it wash over her palate, but didn't indicate whether it was up to her standards. Instead, she leaned forward, as if wanting to get straight to the point.

"Your sister is missing," she said, and silence followed.

This was the first Micaela had heard of a sister. There was a brother, Magnus, and that was quite enough.

"I don't have a sister," Rekke said with perfect calm, obviously wary.

"In that case I bring you two pieces of news," she said. "You have a sister, Hans. A most interesting sister and worthy of her brother—well, one of her brothers anyway. But now she is missing."

Rekke remained quiet while Irene told an astonishing story that could hardly have been true.

"I assume this is a trap you have set," he said. "But I suppose I might as well walk straight into it. Cast your die, dear Irene."

ACKNOWLEDGEMENTS

My heartfelt thanks to my brilliant and indefatigable copy editor Åsa Sandzén, my agent Jessica Bab, who always has my back, to Alfred Norberg, to my children and to my wise publisher Eva Gedin.

And as ever, thank you to my own Anne.

A NOTE ABOUT THE AUTHOR

DAVID LAGERCRANTZ had his breakthrough as a novelist with *Fall of Man in Wilmslow,* a novel about the British mathematician Alan Turing. The biography *I am Zlatan,* which he cowrote with international soccer star Zlatan Ibrahimović, was published in 2011, selling millions of copies worldwide. In 2013, Lagercrantz was asked to write a free-standing sequel to Stieg Larsson's Millennium Trilogy. *The Girl in the Spider's Web* (2015) became a global publishing phenomenon with simultaneous publication in twenty-seven countries, and was followed by *The Girl Who Takes an Eye for an Eye* (2017) and—Lagercrantz's final book in the Millennium series—*The Girl Who Lived Twice* (2019). Lagercrantz's next book was *Dark Music,* the first Rekke and Vargas investigation, an internationally bestselling series paying homage to Sir Arthur Conan Doyle's Sherlock Holmes stories.

A NOTE ABOUT THE TRANSLATOR

IAN GILES has a PhD in Scandinavian literature from the University of Edinburgh. Past translations include novels by Arne Dahl, Carin Gerhardsen, and Camilla Läckberg. His translation of Andreas Norman's *Into a Raging Blaze* was shortlisted for the 2015 CWA International Dagger. He is chair of the Swedish–English Literary Translators' Association and lives in Edinburgh.

A NOTE ON THE TYPE

This book was set in Minion, a typeface produced by the Adobe Corporation specifically for the Macintosh personal computer and released in 1990. Designed by Robert Slimbach, Minion combines the classic characteristics of old-style faces with the full complement of weights required for modern typesetting.

Typeset by Scribe, Philadelphia, Pennsylvania

Designed by M. Kristen Bearse